Dear Mystery Lover,

Now in its second DEAD LETTER printing, the first Nicholas Segalla mystery, *A Time for the Death of a King*, got critical raves: "A time-travel delight," said the *Anniston Star*. "In the company of Josephine Tey," said the Rockland *Courier Gazette*.

Luckily for fans of historical mysteries, the wonderfully original sleuth/time-traveller/scholar Segalla is back. This time he's thrust into late 18th-century France, where he must solve a mystery that has plagued scholars since the storming of the Bastille: What happened to the son of Marie Antoinette, the crown prince of France, in the wake of the revolution?

The next book in the series, *A Time of Murder at Mayerling*, will be published in hardcover by St. Martin's Press simultaneously with the DEAD LETTER edition of *The Prince Lost to Time*. Take a weekend away and read them both. You won't be disappointed.

Keep your eye out for DEAD LETTER—and build yourself a library of paperback mysteries to die for.

Yours in crime,

Shawn Coyne
Senior Editor
St. Martin's DEAD LETTER Paperback Mysteries

Other titles from St. Martin's
Dead Letter Mysteries

Also by Ann Dukthas

A TIME FOR THE DEATH OF A KING

THE PRINCE
LOST TO TIME

ANN DUKTHAS

St. Martin's Paperbacks

Library of Congress Catalog Card Number: 95-34742

ISBN: 0-312-95843-9

Printed in the United States of America

St. Martin's Press hardcover edition/November 1995
St. Martin's Paperbacks edition/November 1996

10 9 8 7 6 5 4 3 2 1

To Dr. Jim Grainger,

Education Officer, London Borough of Redbridge,

in memory of the times we have spent!

Historical Note

On 14 July 1789, the Bastille fortress in Paris was stormed and the French Revolution began. Within six years, King Louis XVI and his queen Marie-Antoinette, together with their surviving heir, the Dauphin Louis Charles, had been swept brutally from the political scene. France became a republic whilst Louis XVI's brothers, the Comte de Provence and the Comte d'Artois, could do nothing except fret in exile.

Nevertheless, those who start revolutions rarely finish them. The radicals, led by Robespierre, Danton and others, fought amongst themselves before falling from power. They were removed by the corrupt and mercenary Barras who, with four others, formed a new government called the Directory. They, in turn, relied too heavily upon the services of a young Corsican general, Bonaparte, who in 1799 swept them from power, becoming dictator and then Emperor of France. In 1814 Napoléon was forced to abdicate though he returned for one last, desperate throw which ended in failure at the Battle of Waterloo in June 1815.

The great powers assembled—Tsar Alexander of Russia; Lord Liverpool, Prime Minister of England—to decide on France's fate. The crown of Louis XVI was offered to his brother the Comte de Provence. Yet the allies also paid heed to the whispers, that the Dauphin, the son of Marie-Antoinette and Louis XVI, may not have died in the Temple on 8 June 1795. . . .

Prologue

Ann Dukthas sat outside the small café in the Rue de la Corbière; in the distance she could hear the noise and incessant car horns of the early Parisian traffic along the Champs Élysées. She sipped from her cup and congratulated herself on the previous week's holiday in the city; all expenses paid by the mysterious Segalla.

"I could grow accustomed to this," she murmured to herself.

She sat back in the chair, revelling in the rich smells of apple blossom, freshly brewed coffee and the smoke of Gauloise cigarettes. Next to her, a group of office workers just off the metro, were now breakfasting on large bowls of coffee, bread, butter and jam. She bit into the newly baked croissant she had bought and gazed down at the guidebook next to her plate. Ann had enjoyed the week, though now she felt lonely and rather homesick for Ireland.

As always, Dr. Segalla had been rather mysterious. She had flown from Dublin to Paris, stayed at a small hotel overlooking the Bois de Boulogne, and spent most of her time being taken round Paris by a tour company which specialised in the history of the city, particularly the era of the French Revolution. To begin with, Ann's knowledge of that period had been minimal. Indeed, most of it was gleaned from the novels of Baroness Orczy, but as the days passed, she had become more and more fascinated by those few violent years which had shattered the mould of European politics. Ann had visited Versailles where the women had marched to bring Louis XVI and his family back to Paris; the Place de la République where the guillotine had stood; the Conciergerie where the September massacres had taken place; and the ancient site of the Temple prison in which Louis XVI had spent his final days.

Ann sipped from her coffee, grimacing at its bitterness. She felt a tingle of excitement in her stomach. Such a trip could only mean that the enigmatic Segalla, the man who claimed he had been alive for centuries, was, once again, about to reveal his secret past.

Ann nodded at the waiter, who quickly refilled her cup. She sat playing with the spoon. "I can't tell anyone," she whispered. Ann glanced up as a rather noisy Citroën, packed with students, hurtled by. Who in Paris or London, she wondered, would believe that she had met a man who claimed to be alive when Harold was killed at Hastings? Who had witnessed the rise and fall of the great, the good and the bad? Who had involved himself in some of the bloody affrays of Western Europe? A man who, by his own confession, had met Mary Queen of Scots, Elizabeth of England, Catherine de Medici, Napoleon, Robespierre? She sipped at her coffee. Segalla had given her sufficient proof of his claims whilst she had done her own research. Time and again, the letters and diaries of different people, at varying times and places, all mentioned a man who slipped like a shadow across the stage of history. A man who could be traced in records separated by centuries. Hadn't Napoleon III set up a commission here in Paris during the 1860s to investigate such a person? Yet its records had all been destroyed in a mysterious fire. Whilst the American secret service, in the months preceding the outbreak of World War II, had organized a manhunt across the states for this enigmatic character? Ann had long accepted that Segalla was neither a fool nor a charlatan. Now, she wondered why he had brought her here to Paris.

"Bonjour, mademoiselle."

Ann, startled, stared over her shoulder.

"I am sorry," Segalla murmured, taking the chair next to her. "I did not mean to surprise you."

He snapped his fingers and called out for more coffee. The waiter asked if he wanted anything to eat. Segalla shook his head. "Too early." He smiled at Ann. "For, when in France, do what the French do. And they are, surely, people of the night?"

He extended his hand and Ann shook it. Segalla looked no different from the time they'd last met, some six months earlier in a London pub. He was dressed more simply yet just as elegantly in a dark blue jacket, trousers of the same colour and polished black shoes. His open-necked shirt was silk, a Celtic cross hung on a golden chain round his neck. Ann quickly guessed it must be of medieval origin and worth more than she earned in a year. In his turn Segalla stared, smiling at her, then he leaned forward.

"What are you thinking, Ann?" he teased. "Are you looking for some ancient spell or talisman?"

Ann blushed with embarrassment and looked away. Suddenly she felt rather plain in her simple, cotton dress and flat-heeled shoes. Did Segalla have girlfriends? she wondered. What did he do with his time?

"I have been abroad," he declared, taking the cup off the waiter and sipping it carefully. "Two months in Russia." He smiled over the rim of the cup. "We live in interesting times, Ann."

"And how long have you been in Paris?"

"Twenty-four hours. I followed you last night as you walked along the Quai d'Orsai." He held his hand up. "Ann, I'm sorry, but I have to be sure of you."

Ann pulled a face and drank from her own cup.

"You enjoyed your own trip?" he asked. "The hotel is comfortable? And the tour interesting?"

"Yes, yes," Ann replied quickly. "Though rather lonely. I am a little homesick for Ireland."

Segalla picked up the small briefcase he had been carrying. He unlocked the clasps and placed a manila folder into Ann's lap.

"This is the reason for your coming," he said quietly. He stared down the street. "It wasn't always like this," he murmured. "Paris in springtime. I was in this city long before Baron Housmann built his broad boulevards and tree-lined avenues." He sipped at his coffee. "I have been to the salons," he said softly, "to the opera house; I have danced to the tinkling tunes of Offenbach. I have also seen Paris barricaded, black smoke hanging like a coverlet above the city whilst the blood bubbled along the cobbles like wine from the press."

Ann lifted the folder. "And this?" she asked.

"A story of treachery, Ann. Of violent, bloody murders. Of innocence exploited and the doings of cruel men."

Segalla's face had paled and the anger blazed in his eyes.

"How can you feel," she asked, "so angry about events which happened so long ago?"

"The past is never behind us, Ann." Segalla leaned over and touched her gently on the forehead. "In the dark places in all our souls, the junkroom of our memories, evil is still evil whether it was perpetrated yesterday or a thousand years ago. Like the stars, the effect of explosions millions of years ago, evil can still make its presence felt across the centuries." He got to his feet. "But, come, let us walk the boulevards; then, this afternoon, go back to your hotel and read this part of my soul."

Chapter 1

A great, red fury descended upon the land. Some deadly mist which had sprung up in Paris and spread out across the kingdom. Men called it The Great Terror as the Four Horsemen of the Apocalypse made their presence felt. France had killed its own king, driven him in a carriage to the great square his own father had built. There, in the presence of the angry mob, they had dragged the descendant of Saint Louis, Christ's own anointed, onto the scaffold as the drumbeat of the National Guard rumbled like a clap of thunder. Executioner Samson had seized Louis, his former king, tied him to the plank then fastened the heavy, wooden collar round Louis's neck. The crowd had fallen silent. The drumbeat had increased, then Samson pulled the cord and the sharp, twinkling blade fell like the angel of death. Louis's neck was so fat that, instead of immediately slicing through it, the blade's penetration had been comparatively slow and the King's screams were heard even above the drumbeat. The anointed head tipped into the basket and a young guardsman seized it and went to the edge of the scaffold. He shook the bloody head but the crowd just gazed back in a terrible, awestruck silence. The young soldier remained unabashed, dangling the dripping head as he shouted, "Vive la République! Vive la République!"

At last the shout was taken up: Minute by minute the voices multiplied until the soldier's shout was repeated a thousand times as the hats of hundreds of spectators were thrown into the air in sheer exultation at the death of poor, fat, incompetent

Louis. Once the grisly spectacle was over, the King's corpse was taken to a city cemetery where it was placed in a wooden, battered casket—a pauper's coffin—the severed head jammed unceremoniously between the legs. Even in death the King was deprived of the usual courtesies: Abbe Edgeworth his confessor was forbidden to attend the royal interment. Instead, two state priests, who had taken a vow of loyalty to the state rather than to God, chanted the office of the dead. The lid was fixed and the coffin was lowered into a narrow, deep grave and covered with lime. Not for Louis XVI a ceremonial burial at Saint-Denis amongst his ancestors but, as Jacques La Rue, ex-priest and leader of the militant enrages had declared, Louis Capet, former King of France, had received no more than he deserved.

Nevertheless, many whispered that the King had been a good but weak man. Had he not been anointed with holy chrism? Was he not Christ's vicar on earth? And had he not suffered, albeit bravely, a horrid, unjust death? As if in response, these whisperings grew to a murmur and then, in the Catholic west of France, an enraged roar of outrage, the Four Horsemen of the Apocalypse arrived. Famine appeared; the weather turned foul; the rains fell and the corn turned to a rotten blackness as if the earth itself protested at Louis's death. The price of bread rose sharply. Flour became as rare as gold and the paper money of revolutionary France, the Assignat, was of so little value, the poor used it to paper the cracks and holes in their miserable hovels. The rulers of Europe also protested. England, Holland, Austria, Prussia and Russia mobilised their armies. In the Channel and the Bay of Biscay, English men-of-war prowled, snapping the chains of France's commerce and making the starvation in the cities worse. To the north and east, the rulers of Europe massed their troops and crossed France's border: They intended not only to crush the revolutionary movement in Paris but curb France's power once and for all. Those wild men who dominated the Convention and Commune of Paris, responded with a *levée en masse*, only to find their General Dumouriez defect to the enemy.

Meanwhile the revolutionaries' attack on the Catholic church finally provoked rebellion in the west. The radicals in Paris responded, sending agents to cities such as Lyons to collect priests "in baskets to shoot, hang or drown in the rivers." At the same time, in the Place de la République in Paris, Madame Guillotine became even busier. All those who were suspected of even thinking treason were sent in batches to be executed. Fouquier-Tinville, President of the Tribunal, sat throughout the night, listening to cases, his sallow, death-head features impassive under his broad-brimmed, black hat with its plume of pure jet. Fouquier-Tinville, a good family man, would listen attentively and then scratch in his ledger, *Mort sans phrase*—Death with no mitigation.

Across the city in his lodgings, Fouquier's master, Maximilien Robespierre, drew up lists and drafted instructions, increasing the severity of his drive to purify the body politic of any threat, either at home or abroad, to his Great Revolution. Those who opposed him could only watch and wait. When dusk fell, the Paris mob returned to its taverns and shops; the guillotine was no longer busy and royal sympathisers would slip along the Rue de Temple to stare up at the great, grim façade of the former head-quarters of the ancient order of the Templars. These sympathisers, fearful of the myriad of Robespierre's secret agents and spies, would shelter under the lime trees. They would either peer over the walls or through half-open gates, across the garden to where the donjon of the Templars stood. This donjon, more than fifty metres high, was crowned with battlements. On each corner the donjon was flanked by tall, rounded towers and, despite the gardens and greenery, looked a black, sinister building, harbouring secrets and mysteries of its own. At the time of Robespierre's rule, it was also the final shrine for royalist sympathisers. Louis XVI may be dead, but in the Temple were lodged his queen, the fair-haired Austrian Marie-Antoinette, her young daughter Marie-Thérèse and, more importantly, the dead King's only surviving son, the Dauphin Louis Charles. In secret houses throughout Paris, supporters of the royal family met and plotted on what they could do to free the Queen and liberate her children. A visit to the Temple soon dashed their hopes. The palace was secured, padlocked and guarded by the most fervent members of the National Guard.

In the west of France, the leaders of the royalist armies listened to these reports and despaired. If the King was dead and his son in prison, what hope for the future?

Robespierre, sitting in his stark, whitewashed chamber, heard of these royalist aspirations. He refused sleep, even food and drink, because of the dangers they posed. He sat up at night stroking the quill of his pen against his cheek as he looked for a way out of the impasse. The Dauphin and his sister, Robespierre concluded shrewdly, posed no real problem: children were mere pawns. But their mother, the Austrian woman? Robespierre's bleak face broke into a smile. She was another matter. By early autumn 1793, Robespierre reached his decision and petitions began to appear from the Paris Commune and the Convention that the Austrian woman be brought to trial to answer for her crimes against the people. Two of Robespierre's most insidious agents, Hébert and Chaumette, went to the Temple to begin their interrogation. Eventually the Queen, screaming and protesting at being removed from her children, was lodged in the Conciergerie and put on trial.

On 15 October 1793, Marie-Antoinette, "Capet's woman," was found guilty of treason and crimes against the people. Sentence followed swiftly. On the evening of 15 October, Marie-Antoinette was informed that she would die early the next day, so she prepared for her last evening on earth. Her cell in the Conciergerie was clean but bleak; a straw-filled mattress, a table, a chair and, more importantly, quills, ink and parchment to write her last letter. Marie-Antoinette, now a shadow of her former glory, sat at the table and prepared to write to her close friend and sister-in-law Marie-Élisabeth. She felt herself shiver and picked up the cracked mirror she had smuggled from the Temple.

"I have to be brave," she whispered to her reflection. "I was born a queen. I have lived as a queen and I will die one."

She studied her reflection and her courage faltered: Her once golden hair was now grey, unwashed and ungroomed. She stroked the mirror carefully. She had no need to worry about that; tomorrow her hair would be cut and what was left would be hidden under a cap, her neck unprotected, ready for the guillotine's kiss. She pinched her pallid cheeks; she wished she had eaten more so she could present a brave, full face to the mob, yet her poor body had betrayed her. Ever since she was a girl she had suffered severe menstrual pains. Now, in the Conciergerie, these pains had become so pronounced she had fainted twice in a single day, being forced to have recourse to a soothing potion containing lime flower water and Hoffman's drops.

Marie-Antoinette rubbed her hand across her stomach. She placed the mirror back on the table and listened intently to the sounds of the darkened gallery outside her cell. The guards had been changed at irregular intervals because of the many supposed plots to free her. Marie-Antoinette put her face in her hands. So many schemes, such subtle stratagems and cunning ploys, but they had all failed. All except one! Marie-Antoinette's head came back and, for a few seconds, her face was transformed by her old brilliant smile until she remembered the spy-holes in the walls and doors and schooled her features accordingly. She must act the part. She must never betray a hint of her plan; her life was over but her son's must go on. The Revolution would pass. Already it was beginning to destroy itself, Robespierre's party divided, becoming involved in a bitter civil war.

Marie-Antoinette dipped the quill into the ink and prepared

to write, then she paused, nervously stroking the side of her neck. Would she die bravely? Or would she weep? Marie-Antoinette shook her head.

"I have no tears left," she whispered to herself.

Would she scream abuse at the crowds? Marie-Antoinette recalled her once fiery temper and vowed to keep a still tongue in her head, even though her blood boiled at the accusations levelled against her. She put the pen down and began to restlessly pace up and down her cell, clenching and unclenching her fists. She had expected the allegations: conspiring with her relatives in Austria; waste of public money. But then Robespierre's creature Hébert had insinuated foul, devil-inspired crimes. How she had taught her own son to practise self-abuse. And how she and Madame Élisabeth had made the boy lie between them and taught him that sacred act which should only take place between man and wife. How the blood had beat in her head when she heard that, but she had kept to her vow and simply replied, "I have no knowledge of the incidents Hébert speaks of."

Marie-Antoinette stopped pacing up and down. She could feel her stomach churning and forced herself to take deep breaths to calm her beating heart and soothe the bubbling of her blood.

"For four years," she whispered to herself hoarsely. "For four years I have been in a nightmare."

She sat down, her mind going back to the Paris mobs swarming through the Tuileries, and that desperate ride to Varennes when she and her husband had so nearly escaped across the frontier. She picked up her pen. She was to die and she must prepare for that, but her line would continue. Surely they would not hurt her little girl? Perhaps royalist sympathisers amongst the exiles would bargain for her release? And her son? Marie-Antoinette lifted her head suddenly. The spy-hole in the door had been opened and, in the shadowy light of the candles, she glimpsed the eye watching her intently. Were they suspicious? she wondered. Did that creature Robespierre and those maggots from hell, Hébert and Chaumette, suspect? Marie-Antoinette put her head down recalling an age in another lifetime before these horrors began. How Louis had furnished a room, covering each wall with mirrors; she and her ladies-in-waiting had gone in, laughing and joking, dancing and spinning, becoming so dizzy it was difficult to distinguish between the reflection and the real person. If Robespierre ever searched for the truth, the same might happen to him. Marie-Antoinette stared down at the letter. Madame Élisabeth and the Englishwoman were the only living persons who knew the truth about her son. Would others find out what she had planned? She recalled Nicholas Segalla, that mysterious, enigmatic man who'd warned her about the coming Revolution.

"If only . . ." she whispered, then closed her eyes.

Somehow Segalla would return, the imminence of death informed her of that, but would he discover her secret?

"Oh," she prayed, "please God, let my son live, not reign or rule, but just live in peace!"

Marie-Antoinette heard a key turn in the lock and looked up, as composed and regally as she could. Fouquier-Tinville, a pale man with thick, black eyebrows, low forehead and jutting chin, came into the cell. He and Hébert, who followed, wore black from head to toe; their rounded hats, turned up at the front, were topped by tall black plumes held together by red, white and blue.

Marie-Antoinette gazed bleakly at them and, in a gesture of contempt started to drum her long fingers on the table as if she were back in the Tuileries playing the clavichord. "What do you want?" she snapped.

"Citizeness," Hébert replied, "in a few hours you die. Do you have any requests?"

"Yes, to be left alone."

"You accept the verdict of the court?" Fouquier-Tinville asked.

Marie-Antoinette stared at his death's-head face. "What verdict? What court?" she asked.

Fouquier's fingers clawed the air like some bird of ill omen. He gestured down at the table. "You are making a will?"

"I have no possessions," Marie-Antoinette replied.

"Then what are you writing?"

"A letter to my friend Madame Élisabeth." Marie-Antoinette's face softened. "You'll see it is delivered?"

"We are not your messenger boys, Citizeness."

"In God's eyes I am still your queen," Marie-Antoinette retorted.

Hébert smirked. "Then tomorrow you can converse with your God about that."

"No other letters?" Fouquier-Tinville asked.

Marie-Antoinette realised the trap, even as she stutteringly replied. "No, no, just this one, of your kindness."

The prosecutor took a step closer and, leaning on the desk, pushed his face only a few inches away from hers. Marie-Antoinette tried not to flinch at the sour smell of cheese and wine.

"Surely, Citizeness, not a letter to your son the Dauphin?" He spat the last word out.

"The boy is too young." Marie-Antoinette replied, holding his gaze. "Madame Élisabeth will give him my last message."

Hébert snapped his fingers and both men left the cell. Marie-Antoinette fought hard to keep back the tears. It was not their cruelty but their hatred which made her wonder what she had done to alienate such men. They not only plotted her death but levelled the most filthy allegations against her and openly exulted to see her brought low. She thought of her gardens at the Trianon with their beds of hyacinths, roses, tulips and irises. She had planted them in every variety of kind and colour: red, white, yellow and her favourite, blue. Or the orange trees which, in a good year, could yield up to a hundred pounds' weight of blossom. Marie-Antoinette closed her eyes and dreamed of her young son, the Dauphin, running amongst the trees.

"Maman! Maman!" he cried. "I have returned. Come, chase me!"

Marie-Antoinette opened her eyes. "I cannot chase you," she whispered into the darkness. "God knows what will become of me."

She felt the rough grained wood of the table and remembered the desk she had owned, her favourite one at the Trianon: a secretary of oak, veneered with purple wood and decorated with gilt, bronze and delicate flowers. It was there, around that desk, that she, Madame Élisabeth and others had planned the Dauphin's future safety.

"Citizeness!" a voice shouted outside the cell. "It is time those candles were doused. Tomorrow you have a long journey to make."

"Soon," Marie-Antoinette called back. "I shall be finished soon."

She picked up the pen and began to write to Madame Élisabeth. She recalled Hébert's hate-filled face and felt like asking her friend why such men hated her, but then she remembered her vow, and confined herself to her last farewells and good wishes. However, the image of her young son persisted, as well as those foul allegations concerning him which had been levelled against her. Marie-Antoinette paused, trying to control her anger. She would show them! She dipped her pen in the ink horn and reassured Madame Élisabeth about such accusations. *This child*, she wrote, *is still very young and does not know what he is saying*. Marie-Antoinette paused, letting a small blob of ink fall onto the coarse parchment. She felt calmer; the secret was implicit, but who would decode it? Her quill continued to write, skimming across the page. At last she was finished, extinguished the candle, and Marie-Antoinette, former Queen of France, lay down on her bed and began to prepare for death.

She was woken early the next morning as the first light of her last day came in slivers through the barred window. She rose quickly, changed her bloodstained linen, for, through the night, her body had betrayed her. She put on a white piquet dress, muslin shawl and plum-coloured high-heeled shoes. The gaoler came in, a burly, harsh-featured man with red tufts of hair peeping out from flared nostrils.

"Do you wish to eat?" he rasped.

Marie-Antoinette, determined to retain her dignity, smiled up. "A cup of chocolate, please."

"There's none here," the man retorted. He studied the pleading look in the Queen's eyes. "I'll send for one," he mumbled, and shuffled out.

An hour later a large cup of chocolate was served with a roll of freshly baked bread. Marie-Antoinette took small bites, chewing carefully. She drank the chocolate, savouring every drop, closing her mind to those lavish mornings of the Grande Levée at Versailles when chocolate was served by an army of liveried retainers carrying silver bowls and golden cups. As the bell of the Conciergerie clanged, the rattle of drums outside the prison began. Marie-Antoinette's blood froze and then, listening carefully, she heard the detachments of cavalry enter the courtyard outside, the shout of orders from officers and the trampling of excited horses. The cell door was thrown open and Henri Samson, son of the famous executioner, came into the cell, dressed in a black cowl and cloak. He did not bother to stop, bow or introduce himself, but seized the Queen, spun her round, expertly tying her hands behind her back. He then took a pair of sharp-pointed shears from his belt, grasped her hair and cut it just above the neck. He never made a sound or uttered a word. Marie-Antoinette felt herself going weak with fright and quietly prayed she would not faint or fall into a fit of hysteria. Samson seized her by the arm.

"Citizeness, we must go!"

He pushed her through the door—where officers of the National Guard watched her curiously—down a dank, mildewed corridor and out into the courtyard. Marie-Antoinette stared wildly around.

"Surely!" she exclaimed, staring in horror at the high-sided tumbril.

"You will travel in a cart," Samson rasped.

Marie-Antoinette closed her eyes as she began to tremble. She had not planned for this. Her husband Louis had been taken to the guillotine in an enclosed carriage accompanied by his confessor. As Samson thrust a white linen bonnet on her head, Marie-Antoinette moaned at the prospect of being taken through the streets of Paris, seated in the cart, her hands bound like some common whore. All her carefully composed dignity collapsed. For a few wild seconds she felt like screaming for mercy, for some shred of compassion, even offering to betray her great secret to them. She recalled the Dauphin's face and fought to control her own panic. She turned to Samson, tears in her eyes.

"Please," she whispered. "Undo my hands! Please!" She pleaded with his stony gaze. "I must relieve myself. I am sorry." She murmured, "I am not well."

Samson pulled out his shears and cut the cords. He and the other officers turned their backs as their former queen, the glory of Versailles, the exquisite sophisticate of the Trianon, squatted in the corner and relieved herself with all the dignity of some mad beggarwoman. Afterwards, Samson gripped her arms and retied the cords. She was pushed across the cobbles and made to sit in the great cart on a narrow bench with her back to the horses. The tumbril left the Conciergerie and entered the narrow, winding streets of north Paris. Once again panic engulfed the Queen at the streets packed with citizens carrying pikes and muskets, whilst on either side of the cart moved a corps of guardsmen five or six deep. At first the Queen was greeted by silence but then some fishwives, carrying branches wrenched from trees, trimmed with ribbons, others with flags, began to shout and scream abuse. Black, burnt loaves of bread stuck on sticks were thrust towards her, a sharp reminder of the favourite song of the Parisian poor about their royal family:

"Here comes the baker, the baker's wife and the baker's child!"

The shouting spread. Somewhere a musket was fired and the roar of the crowd grew like the growl in a huge animal's throat. Marie-Antoinette kept her poise, looking neither to the right nor to the left. She kept repeating to herself, "The baker's boy! The baker's boy!" These people with their dirty faces and snarling mouths, would never get their grimy hands on her beloved son.

Marie-Antoinette must have journeyed for just under an hour, listening to the screams and imprecations of the mob who packed the streets and narrow alleyways. Others climbed the roofs of houses or had paid good money for a vantage seat in some shop or garret window. As the cart, its driver wearing a red-fringed Phrygian hat with the Revolutionary cockade around it, rumbled into the square, Marie-Antoinette glanced up, a strangled sob in her throat. An eternity ago, when she had been a young bride, she had entered this very square beside her husband and the crowd had tossed their hats in the air, shouting their adulation. At the time someone had whispered in her ear, "Two hundred thousand people have fallen in love with you." The former queen dismissed the thought and glanced over her shoulder; the high, black-draped scaffold blocked her view and, on it, Madame Guillotine stood waiting. Two massive grooved posts soared twenty feet into the air; the two posts were joined at the top by a third from which hung a heavy steel blade, at least eighteen inches wide. One of the people in the crowd suddenly darted forward and grasped the end of the tumbril. The young man pulled himself up.

"Do not look, madame! Do not look!" he whispered hoarsely.

Marie-Antoinette obeyed. An eternity seemed to pass as the cart trundled across the square and that somber drumbeat began again. Then the cart abruptly stopped. Officers of the Revolutionary Guard dragged her from the cart and pushed her up onto the platform. Marie-Antoinette turned sideways. She glimpsed the sea of faces and heard, like a wave crashing onto a rocky shore, the shouts and curses of her former subjects. Marie-Antoinette staggered forward and stood on the toes of one of the executioner's assistants. The fellow yelped.

"I'm sorry!" she apologised. "Truly I am!"

Marie-Antoinette now looked squarely at Madame Guillotine, the lowered plank, the waiting basket, and she began to tremble and glanced in terror at Executioner Samson. His glance softened and, perhaps as a mercy, he quickly seized her and pushed her towards the blood-soaked plank. She was lashed to this, the wooden clasp secured around her neck. Marie-Antoinette began to murmur a prayer, trying to keep her voice steady. The drumroll began to rise as if the waves were now crashing all about her. She was no longer awaiting the blade but standing in the shadow of the orangery at the Tuileries. The gates were open, little Charles the Dauphin was running towards her.

"*Maman! Maman!*" he was shouting. "*I've come home! I've come home! And, look, the orange trees are in full bloom!*"

The crashing of the drums reached a crescendo. Samson let go of the rope and the silver blade swooped down even as Marie-Antoinette thought of her boy, her lovely son, near her now, almost touching—then the blade swept through her neck.

Normandy, 21 April 1796—the Château Vitry-sur-Seine

On that fine April morning, as the sunlight tried to break through the swirling mist which carpeted the fields and meadows of Normandy, Père Raoul Grossac, cure of the small village of Vitry-sur-Seine, walked up the path towards the great château. The priest always called there after the morning Mass for a cup of hot chocolate, some freshly baked bread, a little soft cheese and, if he was lucky, some sweetened jam. The old cure licked his dry lips and tried to brush the dust from the trackway off his black soutane. The cure stopped for a rest halfway up the hill and looked down the small valley; his village was not prosperous. He glimpsed his church tower with its broken window and the thatched-roof cottages of his parishioners.

"It truly is a poor place, Lord," he whispered. One meagre street, a poor brewery, a tannery which sometimes worked, an alehouse which smelt like a midden-heap. His parishioners' only comfort was to sit at their doors in the early-morning sunshine peeling onions or anything else they had been able to extract from the harsh soil of their little gardens. The priest, who had now caught his breath, walked on up the hill towards the château gates. He passed a small burial ground which housed the bodies of long-dead knights who now slept under the shadow of a massive wooden crucifix. Père Grossac stopped and knelt before this. He looked up at the tortured, carved figure hanging there. Even the Saviour's body looked poor, his dying face was thin, cheeks sunken, ribs clearly showing through the skin. Ah well, the cure thought, that was the scourge of France, war and poverty. Nevertheless, Père Grossac remembered hastily, at least the good Lord had delivered his parishioners from those insane atheistic revolutionaries in Paris. Under the new government of Monsieur Barras, religion had been restored, the churches reopened and the priests had now come out of hiding. Those minions of the devil Robespierre—Hébert, Chaumette and their terrible judge Fouquier-Tinville—had gone to the same guillotine to which they had sent so many. France, under its moderate rulers, had at last found a measure of calm.

Père Grossac looked farther up the hill towards the château. Did Monsieur Petitval, the rich banker who owned the château, have anything to do with this? After all, Petitval was a wealthy man. Had he not been entrusted by the martyr Louis XVI to look after his affairs? And had not Petitval, at the request of moderates like Barras, worked for peace between the republican generals and the royalist leaders in Brittany and Normandy? Père Grossac shook his head and fingered the rough-hewn wooden rosary he carried in his hand. He looked up at the face of the crucified Christ. "What will happen to poor France?" he whispered. The carved face of his Saviour looked as bleak as ever. "We are at war with the world," Grossac murmured. The young Corsican general Bonaparte may well be winning victories, but how would these improve the lot of his poor villagers? "The King should come back!" the cure exclaimed.

Yet even as he prayed, the old priest knew that was impossible. Louis and his Austrian queen had gone to the guillotine. Their young daughter Marie-Thérèse had eventually been released, but what about the poor Dauphin, the young boy Louis Charles? Grossac rose despondently to his feet. Some said the Dauphin had escaped from the Temple but his bishop had told him different.

"Oh no," he had whispered to Père Grossac when he had come to the village to give the sacrament of Confirmation. "Oh no, the young Dauphin died in the Temple, driven mad by the cruelty of his captors and now lies buried in some derelict cemetery."

The cure, now feeling the pangs of hunger more sharply, walked briskly towards the gates. Perhaps he would seek the advice of Monsieur Petitval, who always knew everything. He might even know why that troop of cowled horsemen had clattered through the village just before dawn.

The cure entered the large, paved courtyard and breathlessly climbed the stone staircase which swept up to the broad terrace before the principal door. Père Grossac stopped abruptly. Something was wrong. He leaned against the stone balustrade and looked at the carved urns and, at the top, the cleverly sculpted dolphins' heads which stared blindly out over the countryside. The eerie silence curled the hair on the nape of Père Grossac's neck. A sombre quietness which reminded him of the death-house in the graveyard. True, he could hear the barking of the dogs chained in their kennels and the liquid notes of some wood pigeon, but nothing else.

Père Grossac climbed more quickly and found the first corpse lying just outside the main door. Monsieur Petitval's *valet de chambre*, his face a ghastly white, eyes open, lay in a pool of his own blood which congealed round his head, matting his hair after it had poured from the great rent in his throat. Grossac's old heart began to beat faster. He pulled open the door and stepped into the château. He crossed the great hall with its old boar spears and knives hanging against the wall. In a corner lay the corpses of two women, their bodies cold, their heads slashed by deep sabre cuts. Grossac, gabbling prayers to himself, ran upstairs, throwing open the doors of bedchambers, only to find each contained a corpse. Madame de Chambeau, Petitval's mother-in-law, lay in her bed, her throat cut, the dark blood congealing thickly on the sheets. In the galleries sprawled other bodies, no sign of a struggle, as if some mysterious, insane swordsman had swept through the château like the Angel of Death. Grossac ran down a staircase and out towards the park. On the pathway, he glimpsed another corpse which he immediately recognised as Monsieur Petitval himself—only, the banker now lay dead, his head almost separated from his body by the deep cut through his neck. Such a look of horror twisted his face, the old cure could take no more, but fled, screaming blindly at the horrors he had just seen.

Chapter 2

France, 1815

Major Nicholas Segalla, special emissary of the English prime minister, Lord Liverpool, stepped out of the dingy, low-roofed tavern. He stared across the windswept quayside of the great French naval port of La Rochelle. Despite being the height of summer, a veil of rain-soaked mist hung over the iron-grey swell of the Atlantic and the treacherous sea roads which ran through the Bay of Biscay. Segalla pulled his greatcoat around him, clutching more tightly his thin leather case. He breathed in deeply, tasting the tangy, salt-edged sea air.

"God forgive me!" Segalla whispered to himself. "I hate the sea!" Even to look at the grey heaving swell clenched his stomach, never mind the prospect of a perilous journey across the water to His Majesty's man-of-war, the three-masted HMS *Bellerephon*, waiting at the mouth of the harbour.

Segalla sighed; there was nothing for it. The young officer had presented his compliments and told him the boat was waiting. Segalla hid his fears and walked across the quayside, past the barrels of tar, heaps of cordage and the nets drying in the sun. At the steps leading down to the waiting ship's boat, two red-jacketed marines snapped to attention. Segalla returned their salute and went carefully down the slippery steps where a grinning sailor carefully helped him into the waiting boat.

Orders rang out, the craft pushed away, oars were lowered and soon Segalla was being rowed across the choppy waters to the HMS *Bellerephon*, despatched from the Atlantic squadron to take General Napoléon Bonaparte, recently defeated at Waterloo, to his exile home in St. Helena. Segalla tried not to stare at the waves but kept his eyes fixed on the frigate. He recalled Liverpool's instructions: Bonaparte was not to be accorded any regal or civic dignity but simply addressed as "General."

"He's a bloody nuisance!" Liverpool had bellowed at the private supper to which Segalla had been invited. "Do you understand me, Nicholas? A tyrant and a warmonger! He may have escaped from Elba but it's a bloody long swim from St. Helena!"

Segalla sat impassively as the ship's boat rose and fell in a chorus of creaking oars and grunts and groans of the sailors who fought to keep their strokes in unison. In the poop, a young midshipman in full dress uniform stood clutching his sword and crying out orders. The sailor who'd helped Segalla into the boat caught the major's eye and whispered, "Believes he's Lord Horatio Nelson, God bless him!"

Segalla smiled back and the sailor returned to his rowing. As they neared the ship, its colours and trim more apparent, Segalla quietly hoped that Bonaparte would not recall an earlier meeting, some twenty-eight years previous. Segalla gripped his leather handcase even more tightly as the sailor who had just spoken, watched him curiously out of the corner of his eye. Ever since Napoléon's surrender, the *Bellerephon* had been in a high state of excitement, and, at the news of Segalla's approach, Captain Maitland had become even more tight-lipped. Naturally the sailor had heard the gossip.

"Segalla's an officer in His Majesty's Life Guards."—so a young lieutenant had told him. "But, really, he's a bloody spy or agent. Whatever, the captain's in a fair tizz at his approach, for he must see our prisoner before we sail for St. Helena."

What, the sailor wondered, did Major Segalla want of Napoléon? The Corsican's armies had been smashed and Waterloo had been Bonaparte's last desperate throw. The sailor scrutinised Segalla carefully. Of medium height, dark-featured, his black curly hair damp from the mist—Major Segalla looked, the sailor concluded, like a spy with his sharp nose, thin lips and close-set mouth. Yet it was the eyes which fascinated the sailor. They looked so old and held a world-weary gaze which seemed in sharp contrast to his rather youthful features. The sailor had seen that look before, in the eyes of men who had recently fought a long and bloody engagement at sea, as if their souls had taken all the horrors hell could throw at them.

The midshipman rapped out an order and the sailor decided to concentrate on his rowing as the boat came alongside, bumping and crashing into the now-awesome three-tiered man-of-war. A rope ladder was lowered and the sailor helped Segalla onto it; he glimpsed beneath the heavy coat, the tight-fitting buff jacket, starch-collared shirt and the dark blue breeches pushed into high leather riding boots. The sailor pointed to the latter.

"Take care as you climb," he murmured. "Make sure your heel doesn't get caught." Then he grinned. "And for God's sake, don't look down!"

Segalla smiled his thanks and carefully climbed the swaying ladder. Beneath him the boat pitched dangerously, waiting for him to finish his climb before the crew dipped oars and moved to the other side of the man-of-war. At last Segalla reached the top and, with as much dignity as he could muster, slid over the side even as the waiting marines presented arms and a bosun piped him aboard. For a few seconds Segalla leaned against the bulwark steadying himself, staring around at the assembled ship's officers. He walked slowly forward as Captain Frederick Maitland, resplendent in a blue dress-coat and snow-white breeches, shook his hand and quickly introduced him to his staff. Then, clutching Segalla by the elbow, Maitland led him to the great cabin in the stern.

"I find it difficult to keep my footing," Segalla murmured.

Maitland's harsh face broke into a smile. "I have seen worse," he replied. "Our last visitor positively fainted away." The smile faded. "Now, my instructions are quite clear, Major Segalla. You are to interview Bonaparte and, once you have left, we are to join the Atlantic squadron, pick up an escort of frigates and sail direct to St. Helena." He took Segalla down the steps to the cabin and pointed to the door. "He's in there, still bemoaning his defeat. He's had the courtesies of his rank but nothing else." The sea captain's blue eyes narrowed. "He didn't know you were coming until early this morning." Maitland opened the cabin door. "I wish you well."

Segalla entered the cabin; spacious but austere, its tables and chairs were all neatly screwed into the floor. A lantern had been lit and a tray bearing a jug of wine and some goblets stood on the table. Segalla glanced immediately at the small, thickset man who stood with his back to him, staring out of the stern-castle window.

For a while the man did not even flinch, never mind turn to greet Segalla. He stood, one arm behind his back, the other leaning against the timber, as if his attention were caught by some great drama beyond anyone else's ken. Segalla coughed but still the man didn't move. Segalla sat down, unlocked the clasps on his case and drew out a thin ledger which he placed on the table in front of him. The man turned and, without any introduction or by-your-leave, eased himself down into a chair opposite Segalla. He joined his hands together as if in prayer and stared coolly at his visitor.

"You have come from England?"

"Yes, General Bonaparte."

The round, olive-skinned face creased in a smile, though the dark eyes remained impassive.

"And your journey was pleasant?"

"General, no sea voyage is pleasant."

Napoléon grimaced. He undid the buttons of his greatcoat.

"I, too, hate the sea," he remarked. "No sea, no British navy. No British navy, then my conquests would have been complete." Napoléon leaned across the table. "I am the greatest general since Alexander." He continued in a flat voice. "I ruled an empire greater than Charlemagne and now I sit in a salt-soaked frigate talking to the emissary of my enemies. Why are you here, Major Segalla?"

"Sir." Segalla opened the ledger. "In the eyes of—"

"In the eyes of millions," Napoléon interrupted, "I am His Imperial Highness." Then he sighed, lacing his fingers together. "But your Lord Wellington put paid to that, as did my generals." Napoléon leaned back in the chair, his fist clenched against his stomach. "If Grouchy had turned up at Waterloo instead of eating bloody strawberries . . . !" Napoléon's sallow, olive-skinned face turned mottled with fury. For a short while he seemed to have forgotten Segalla, lost in his own memories.

"General," Segalla continued. "My instructions are quite clear. I am to discuss nothing with you except the matters in hand."

Napoléon made short, sharp gestures with his hands. " 'Nothing except the matters in hand,' " he mimicked. "Then tell me, Major Segalla, what are these 'matters in hand'?"

Segalla opened the ledger. "As you may know, sir, the Great Powers decreed that Louis, Comte de Provence, brother of the executed Louis XVI of France, be restored to the throne of France. In a secret protocol to their treaty of 1814, the Great Powers also decreed that Louis should hold the throne for at least two years, until they decide who is the rightful heir to Louis XVI."

"I am that rightful heir."

"The Great Powers," Segalla continued flatly, "are intent on restoring the Bourbons."

"Who have remembered nothing as they have forgotten nothing," Napoleon jibed, drumming his fingers on the table.

"True," Segalla replied. "But the question is, General, which Bourbon returns?" Segalla was pleased to see a calculating look in Napoléon's eyes. "Louis XVI," Segalla continued, "died on the guillotine; he left two brothers: the Comte de Provence, who now rules as Louis XVIII, and Charles, Comte D'Artois."

"Two cheeks of the same arse," Napoléon scoffed.

"That may be so, General, but Louis XVI also left a son and a daughter. The daughter is now safe and well and married to the Duke of Angoulême, but the fate of the Dauphin?" Segalla tapped the leather-bound ledger before him. "As you well know, his fate is a matter of mystery. His father died in January 1793, his mother Marie-Antoinette, nine months later. Now, during the Revolution or at least its early years, the King and Queen had been imprisoned in the old palace of the Temple. Their young son, the Dauphin, was with them.

"On 19 July 1793 the young Dauphin, then aged only eight years, was separated from his mother and put in the tutelage of one of Robespierre's friends, a cobbler named Simon. The latter, with his wife, became the sole guardians of the young prince. We do not know whether he was ill-treated or not, but he was kept isolated and never saw his mother again and, apart from one occasion, his eldest sister, Marie-Thérèse, now Duchess of Angoulême." Segalla raised his eyes and stared at Napoléon, who was watching him curiously. "In January 1794 the Dauphin's fate became a mystery. Monsieur Simon and his wife left the Temple and the Prince was virtually immured in a dark, fetid cell. He remained there, in total isolation, for the next six months. In July 1794 Robespierre was overthrown; he and his party, including Monsieur Simon, went to the guillotine."

Segalla paused. "General, you are aware of this?"

Napoléon, pinching his lips between his fingers, just nodded, his eyes intent on Segalla.

"Now, after the fall of Robespierre," Segalla declared, "a new government, the Directory, under Monsieur Barras, ruled France. Barras paid a personal visit to the Dauphin and found the child much changed: elongated limbs, tumours on his knees and other joints; his face and head were covered in sores. Apparently the young boy had been left in his own filth, meals being pushed through a grating as if he were a dog." Segalla turned a page of the ledger over. "Now, Monsieur Barras changed all that. A young Créole, Laurens, was put in charge of the Dauphin. He was later joined by a man called Gomin, then a third person, a former house painter, Lasne." Segalla tapped the pages. "Now these three—Laurens was later relieved of his command—tried to treat the boy well. He was given better food and quarters as well as suitable medical attention. However, on 8 June 1795, two years after his separation from his mother and sister, the young Dauphin died in his chamber at the Temple. The powers that be conducted a postmortem under a certain Dr. Pelletan. After this, the Dauphin's corpse was placed in a coffin and buried in the derelict cemetery of Ste.-Marguerite, a short walk from the Temple."

"So the Bourbon child died? In his grave for twenty years?" Napoléon sat sideways in the chair, pushing his hand under the white jacket beneath his greatcoat. "What is that to me, Monsieur Segalla? Many children die, including my own."

"His Majesty's government"—Segalla smoothed out the paper in front of him—"believe you are in a position to know a great deal, General. You ruled France for over fifteen years. Your spy master, Joseph Fouché, collected secrets and scandals like a magpie plucks up anything which glitters." Segalla paused to listen to the creaking sounds of the ship. Indeed, if it wasn't for the faint noises of the sailors and the occasional rise and fall of the ship at anchor, Segalla would have forgotten his surroundings as he waited to see which way Napoléon would jump.

"Now," Segalla leaned his elbows on the table, "General, we can sit here and play games until the heavens crack. You know a great deal about the whereabouts of the Dauphin. First, seven years ago, you tore down the Temple prison. Your edict said it was due to your building plans in the city." Segalla shook his head. "We doubt that. I believe you destroyed the Temple, taking it apart brick by brick, because you thought it contained some evidence regarding the Dauphin's whereabouts."

Napoléon glanced sideways at Segalla but then returned to gaze stonily at the cabin wall.

"Secondly," Segalla continued, "Barras was the leader of the

Directory. He was also a friend of your former wife, Empress Josephine."

A muscle high in Napoléon's cheek began to twitch. The general blinked furiously as if the mere mention of his first wife's name brought back a torrent of memories.

"Now," Segalla said softly, "the Empress Josephine died a year ago at Malmaison, shortly after a private and confidential interview with Tsar Alexander of Russia. Some people claim her death was due to influenza. However, malicious rumours claim that dark powers, fearful lest Josephine was telling the Tsar some secret about the Dauphin, poisoned your former wife."

Napoléon turned slowly in his chair. "You called her 'Empress'?" he remarked softly. "Yet I divorced her ten years ago."

Segalla smiled. "Crown or not, General, any man with a heart would have regarded Josephine as an empress."

Napoléon leaned abruptly across and touched Segalla's hand. The general's skin felt hot and dry.

"Major Segalla, I thank you for your courtesies." He looked away, tears brimming in his eyes. "I, too, have heard the rumours." He talked on, as if by himself. "Before I met Josephine Beauharnais, she was hailed as the most beautiful woman in Paris. Men would have fought and died even to kiss her hand." He sighed. "Anyway, when Robespierre and the other animals were destroyed, Barras and four others took over the government; they called themselves the Directory. Barras and Josephine became lovers."

Napoléon paused as if listening to a sailor far down the ship singing some song about a maid in an English port. "God knows, Major, but I tell you this—something happened in the Temple. Barras intimated as much to Josephine though he never gave any details. I thought little of it until many years later when a creature called Hergevault came forward claiming to be the lost Dauphin. He spun some story about escaping from the Temple and travelling the world until he returned to France. He was, in fact, the illegitimate son of a tailor from Saint-Lô."

Napoléon blew his cheeks out. "He also claimed to be Prince of Monaco. Fouché had him arrested and he spent some time in a French man-of-war before dying witless as a madcap in 1812."

"Is that why you had the Temple prison destroyed?" Segalla asked. "To look for evidence?"

Napoléon played with the gold button of the chasseur's uniform he wore under his greatcoat.

"Yes," he replied quietly. "The Bourbons in exile did not concern me." He glanced sharply at Segalla. "But Hergevault's claims did. Can you imagine, sir, what would happen if the real Dauphin . . ." Napoléon narrowed his eyes. "He was born in 1785, so he would now be what, thirty years of age?" He laughed abruptly. "Can you imagine, Major, what would happen if such a handsome Bourbon prince, who had mysteriously escaped from his captors, suddenly emerged as a figurehead for all opposition against myself?"

Napoléon picked up a jug and slopped wine into two of the cups. He pushed one into Segalla's hands then took his own and drank it quickly.

"There!" Napoléon exclaimed, slamming the goblet down on the table and slouching back in the chair. "You can tell your children, Major Segalla, that you were once served wine by the Emperor of France." He leaned across, his eyes bright and mocking, wagging a finger in Segalla's face. "But you won't have children, will you, Major or Monsieur Segalla?" He caught the look of surprise in Segalla's eyes. "I never forget a face, monsieur. Even when I inspected the Grande Armée I could tweak the ears of those soldiers who fought with me at Jena or Austerlitz. We met years ago, did we not, whilst I was in Corsica? I remember a man claiming to be a spy at the Vatican, only then he was a Jesuit priest, Father Nicholas Segalla." He lowered his voice. "Now, sir, I am much older." He passed his hand over the thinning, black hair. "My face is fatter, my hair not so thick and I have terrible pains in my gut. But, you, sir, have not aged a day."

29

Segalla fought to hide the churning in his stomach. Napoléon picked up Segalla's own wine goblet and slurped from it.

"I'll tell you more," he continued softly. "How my spies talked of a man who never dies: He has been seen in Constantinople, at the court of Catherine the Great, even in the steaming swamps of Louisiana. I wonder, monsieur, if that is the same person, also named Segalla, who now works for the British Secret Service?"

Segalla closed the ledger. "General, we were talking about the Dauphin and your late wife, the Empress Josephine."

Napoléon shrugged. "Ah well, I have nothing to lose. They say St. Helena is a barren island in the middle of nowhere." He tapped the side of his head. "And all I have are my memories." He leaned across the table. "Josephine, God bless her pretty backside, maintained that the young child who died in the Temple was not the real Dauphin. Moreover, the boy who died in June 1795—" Napoléon spread his hands. "Well, according to Josephine, he was quietly poisoned."

"And the real Dauphin?" Segalla asked.

"God knows, monsieur. There are many theories as there are hairs on a dog. Some say he was spirited away and a poor child from a Paris hospital took his place. The latter suffered from rickets and a terrible bone disease."

"But why was that poor replacement poisoned?" Segalla asked.

Napoléon beat his fingers on the table. "God knows, monsieur. However, I shall not play games," Napoléon continued briskly. "This conversation, monsieur, is beginning to bore me. Yes, I had the Temple prison taken to pieces stone by stone. What I was looking for was the corpse of the real Dauphin. I wondered if those wild creatures, Robespierre, Hébert or Simon, had murdered the child or so ill-treated him that he died of neglect."

"And what did you find?"

"Nothing," Napoléon snarled. "Not a shred of evidence. So

I comforted myself that the real Dauphin had died there and anyone who came forward was a dupe. More than that, I cannot tell you."

Segalla continued to gaze at him.

"You think I am lying, don't you?" Napoléon taunted.

"General, I think you know more."

"And why should I tell you, the agent of those who have defeated me? who have destroyed my dreams, my soul, my country, my empire!" Napoléon's dark face became mottled as he fought to control his temper. "Let the Bourbons," he snarled, "suffer the same nightmares as I did." He paused to clear his throat. "Fat Louis at the Tuileries, like your Macbeth, has every reason to suffer nightmares."

"What makes you say that?" Segalla asked.

"You were a priest, Monsieur Segalla. Why not ask to hear his confession?"

Segalla sighed and closed his leather journal.

"Life could be made sweeter for you on St. Helena," he murmured.

Napoléon started to chuckle; throwing his head back, he laughed until the tears rolled down his cheeks. He placatingly held a hand out at Segalla.

"Your English masters have trained you well. Here I am, Napoléon Bonaparte, once Emperor of France and master of the world! What do you think I want?—sweetmeats, some of your roast beef?" He paused as Segalla pushed the chair back and made to rise. "Don't go yet, Segalla. Josephine believed the Dauphin escaped. Something mysterious happened in those dark chambers of the Temple. But, if you wish to know the truth, then let's exchange secrets."

Segalla, his hand already on the latch of the door, recalled Lord Liverpool's words: *"Use anything you can, Segalla."*

He turned and, going back, leaned over the table.

Outside the cabin Captain Maitland glimpsed, through the window, Lord Liverpool's mysterious emissary whispering in

Napoléon's ear. Never once, Captain Maitland did later report, had he seen a man's face change so quickly as the former emperor's. Napoléon's jaw dropped, his eyes looked dazed as if he had been struck a blow. Captain Maitland, wary of appearing too inquisitive, walked away though he would have given his ship to know what Napoléon had just learnt.

Inside the cabin the ex-emperor of the French, his face now pallid, a light sheen of sweat on his brow, continued to gaze openmouthed at Segalla.

"Why have you told me this?" he asked throatily.

"Because you are Napoléon Bonaparte, once Emperor of the French, soon to be a lonely recluse on the island of St. Helena. So, who will believe you?" Segalla eased the belt round his waist. "Now you know where I come from. I am Segalla who has never tasted death, not because of some reward but because I broke faith. My punishment is mine. Indeed, many years ago I knelt in the palace of the Louvre and swore allegiance to the first Capet; twenty-eight years ago I made a similar vow to Marie-Antoinette. When I discharge that duty, my debt will be finished. So, General"—he continued briskly—"what do you know about the death of the Dauphin, or his disappearance?"

Napoléon, still slightly dazed by what Segalla had told him, shook his head. "It's a maze," he answered slowly. "You take one path and find it blocked off. You take another and you're back where you started from. Fouché turned over every stone, interrogated anyone he could. At the end he presented me with three conclusions, each based on a veritable mound of evidence. First—" Napoléon stretched out a stubby thumb. "The Dauphin Louis Charles, son and heir of Louis XVI, mysteriously disappeared in January 1794. Secondly, that the Dauphin may have been mysteriously abducted later in the same year some time in the autumn of 1794 but how and why he could not discover. Thirdly," Napoleon shrugged, "that the Dauphin was not abducted but died either from natural causes or by poisoning on 8 June 1795." Napoléon leaned back in the chair, lacing his fingers across his stomach, pressing hard as if he was in pain. "When you go to Paris, Monsieur Segalla, seek out Joseph Fouché and ask him. . . . Oh, he'll lie and pretend he knows nothing." Napoléon smiled cynically. "By now he will have destroyed all his papers, but one thing I do know. In 1812, after the death of the pretender Hergevault, whilst I was busy in Russia, Fouché launched another investigation. He never completed it; other matters interfered. However, Fouché wondered about two things. First, something the Dauphin's father Louis XVI said whilst he was imprisoned in the tower."

"What was it, General?"

"Fouché never told me. He just shook his head and wondered if the King had lost his wits before he lost his head."

"And, secondly?"

"Fouché was more forthcoming on this," Napoléon replied. "He believed the Dauphin's abduction and disappearance was connected to a violent and bloody murder which took place at the Château Vitry-sur-Seine in April of 1796. The château was owned by Petitval, a banker and fervent monarchist. He definitely supplied money to Barras and others to overthrow Robespierre. Now there are rumours, though very little evidence, that Petitval offered huge sums of money for the life of the little Dauphin."

Napoléon refilled his wine goblet. "Well, in the spring of 1796 Normandy, indeed the whole of France, was beset by a civil war, gangs of bandits who roamed where they liked and did as they wished. However, to cut a long story short, Major Segalla, one fine morning in April 1796, Petitval and all his household were found murdered: They had their throats cut or their heads staved in. The purpose of the attack remains a mystery because the château was not plundered or pillaged."

"Surely there was an investigation?"

"No, monsieur, there was none. No papers, no interrogations, no court of enquiry. Indeed, that is what intrigued my dear little spider Fouché." Napoléon fell silent, staring into the wine which he swilled round the goblet. He looked up sharply. "Monsieur, can I ask you about your secret?"

Segalla shook his head. "A bargain is a bargain, General. I told you I would speak once and I have done so." Segalla now pushed back his chair.

"One further thing," Napoléon murmured, staring up at this mysterious stranger as if memorising every detail of his face. "Sweet Josephine would be disappointed with me," Napoléon continued, "if I didn't tell you the full truth of her conclusions. Do you realise, monsieur, that the Dauphin, who was a prisoner for almost six years and had suffered more depredations than any other child, died at a most fortuitous occasion?"

Segalla looked at him askance.

"A few days before he died," Napoléon explained, "the Revolutionary government had actually reached a rapprochement with the rebels in the west to usher in a lasting peace. One of the terms of that peace was that the young Dauphin would be released. A similar clause was negotiated with the court of Spain where King Charles had offered to hand over certain Spanish towns and provinces, provided the Dauphin and his sister were released into safe hands."

Napoléon put his goblet down on the table. "Josephine always believed, and perhaps she learnt it from Barras, that the young boy in the Temple was poisoned because the government in Paris did not want him moved."

"Because he was an impostor?" Segalla intervened.

"Perhaps. Or because he showed signs of such neglect he would have roused the anger of all of Europe. Now, monsieur, I have told you everything I know." Napoléon held out a podgy hand which Segalla grasped. "We shall not meet again, Segalla. At least, not this side of Heaven."

Segalla drew himself up and saluted. "No, Your Imperial Highness, we will not."

As Segalla left HMS *Bellerephon*, eager to return to the Duke of Wellington's headquarters, the news of his planned investigation had already seeped into Paris, awakening the fears and recalling the nightmares of many people.

Grave-digger Betrancourt was a hapless victim of these but, as he fled, gasping and spluttering, the old corpse-collector desperately wished he had kept his mouth shut. Why, he wondered despondently, did he have to babble about his own claim to fame? He was only a poor peasant who, twenty years earlier, had been ordered to dig a hole in the common grave in the derelict cemetery of Ste.-Marguerite for the corpse of the young Dauphin. Betrancourt had, for many a year, dined out on that day's work, embellishing and embroidering his yarn as he sat in the corner of his local tavern slurping his wine and puffing on his dirty clay pipe. Now it was all over. The Bourbons were back, eager to pick over the bones of what had happened during the Revolution. Scores had been settled, bodies found bobbing in the Seine, their throats slashed from ear to ear. Those old revolutionaries, once heroes of the Paris mob, were now shunned as if they were lepers. Betrancourt's past had come to judge him.

The old grave-digger stopped outside a house, his breath coming in tight wheezes as he hammered on the door.

"*Aidez-moi! Aidez-moi!*" he shrieked, but the door remained shut.

Somewhere high above the overhanging house, a shutter was opened and faces, ghoulish in the candlelight, peered down at him. Betrancourt repeated his shrieks for help. The shutters closed quickly and the grave-digger, leaning against the wall, stared blindly around. He could glimpse no flicker of light; nothing but the pale moonlight shining in the scum and filth of the overbrimming sewer. Behind him he heard the patter of feet, slithering like rats across the greasy cobbles. Betrancourt ran on, gasping and sobbing. Somewhere in the darkness a dog howled. Betrancourt remembered how, years earlier, a soothsayer had told him that would be the last sound he would ever hear on Earth. Why did it happen? he thought. The men who had followed him from the tavern had, before old Betrancourt broke free and fled, mentioned Monsieur de Paris. If Monsieur de Paris wanted him, then sentence of death had already been passed.

Betrancourt stumbled on, straight into the masked figures waiting for him. The old grave-digger fell to his knees and stared up into the darkness.

"Mercy, please!" he whispered. "I know nothing, nothing at all! What I said were just stories!"

"Tell me," a voice asked silkily. "Only you, Monsieur Betrancourt, know where the Dauphin is buried?"

"Yes, yes," the old grave-digger whispered. "In the common grave."

"Only you," the voice repeated.

Somewhere in the darkness a dog howled and Betrancourt, the old grave-digger, realised that he had dug the very pit he was falling into.

"Aye!" he gasped.

The masked figure in the centre raised his musket and pressed it against Betrancourt's head. The sound of the musket rang like a clap of thunder through the alleyway as the back of Betrancourt's head exploded in a mass of brains and blood.

Chapter 3

Two months later, as a cold grey autumn swept in over Paris, Major Segalla finally reached the trackway which would lead him to the main thoroughfare to one of the northern gates of the city. All around him the trees were shedding leaves, brown and gold, which fell fast and furiously in a thick and soggy carpet which covered the forest floor. Segalla reined in. He stared through the trees at the tendrils of mist curling amongst the branches like some mysterious ghost intent on smothering him. For a while Segalla sat listening to the silence. Above him, ravens and crows cawed noisily. Somewhere deep in the forest, another bird chattered whilst, in the undergrowth on either side of the trackway, came cracks and scuffles.

Segalla listened but ignored these, trying to distinguish between his own loneliness and a growing sense of unease. He had left the main roads, packed with the troops of the Great Powers: cossacks in their furred caps mounted on small shaggy ponies, the brilliant colours of the Belgian and Dutch infantry—their black uniforms with skulls and crossbones on their helmets; the Prussian grenadiers in scarlet-and-green jackets; and the black shalakos of Wellington's crack corps. All marched amidst the crash of cart and the rumble of cannon as the allies, in accordance with agreements between them, withdrew their troops beyond France's frontiers.

Segalla became used to the silence; gently stroking his horse's neck, he concentrated on the cloud of breath from its flared nostrils. Then he heard it. The crack and rustle which betrayed a much more dangerous predator than some fox or badger. Segalla gripped the heavy horse pistol in his saddle holster. Another crack. The rustling grew closer. Segalla let out a yell and drew the pistol, even as he dug spurs into his horse. The two men who jumped out of the carefully concealed ambush were caught by surprise. One stared, his mouth a round O; Segalla loosed the horse pistol straight at him, tearing a bloody wrench in his chest; whilst the second was hit by the charging horse and sent spinning like a top back into the bushes. Segalla relied on the iron discipline of a mounted dragoon as other figures appeared. He pushed his horse pistol back into its holster and drew his sword, spinning it round like a scythe. Then he was through his attackers, pounding along the forest track whilst behind him, the perpetrators of the ambuscade ruefully attended their wounds.

For a while Segalla gave his horse its head, only slowing down to a canter when a tavern sign came into sight. Segalla reined in and studied his fob watch. He repocketed it, wiped the sweat from his face, dismounted and led his sweaty animal into the stableyard. Segalla took his saddlebags off and tossed a coin to one of the grooms to carry the saddle into the tavern. Inside it was dark and musty, but fragrant with the smell of cooking.

"I want the horse well looked after," Segalla instructed the landlord, "towelled, fed and watered when it's cooled."

The landlord, bright-eyed at the prospect of profit, nodded his head vigorously.

"Some wine," Segalla continued, "and whatever smells so nice in your kitchen."

"Rabbit cooked in mushroom sauce," the fellow replied.

Segalla went into a corner near the window, ignoring the curious looks of the few peasant farmers. They soon became bored. After all, in the early autumn of 1815, English "milords," soldiers and courtiers had become a common sight on the roads to and from Paris.

For a while Segalla sat with his back to the wall, staring out of the window overlooking the small garden at the back of the tavern. He eased his boots off, still wondering whether the ambush he had just escaped was some common bandit attack or a planned sortie by those who did not wish him to reach Paris. Segalla loosened the high collar of his shirt, doffed his riding cloak and carefully ate the meal the landlord pushed in front of him.

"Where have you travelled from?" the landlord asked.

"Wellington's headquarters," Segalla replied.

The man pulled his face in admiration. "The great English milord?"

Segalla just smiled, unwilling to continue the conversation. You wouldn't think that if you met him, Segalla thought, watching the landlord's retreating back. The "great English milord" had been in a foul temper after Segalla had informed him about his meeting with Napoléon. Naturally, Segalla had been selective in what he revealed but in the main, his report was truthful: Napoléon had admitted there was a mystery over the Dauphin's fate though he could provide very little detail.

"Then you are off to Paris!" Wellington had barked, scratching his hooked nose. The duke played with a small rock on his polished desk, a memento from the La Haye Sainte farmhouse which his troops had so valiantly defended during the battle of Waterloo. He picked up some documents and a money belt and tossed them towards Segalla. "These are your warrants and money for expenses!" he declared.

"You mean bribes, my lord?"

Wellington glared at Segalla. "Aye, if you want to put it that way, bribes." He tapped the rock noisily on the desk. "You have spoken to Liverpool and, for once, I agree with the politicians back in London. I fought Napoléon at Waterloo. Believe me, Segalla, it was a near damn run thing. We lost good men. In some places . . ." Wellington's face softened. "In some places," he repeated, "my boys lay like a scarlet carpet. We want no more trouble with France. No more stupid escapades to plunge Europe into war. We are not really bothered about the past.

Louis XVI and Marie-Antoinette are dead, God bless them! The crown of France will go to Louis XVIII and, if he dies without an heir, then to his brother, Charles d'Artois. If Charles can't beget a son—and I doubt if he can—" Wellington added forcefully, "then the crown goes to the Prince, who is married to Marie-Thérèse, Louis XVI's only surviving child."

"Then the Bourbons' future is safe?" Segalla observed.

"If Liverpool had not told me about you, Segalla, I'd have thought you were secretly smirking. Louis XVIII is fat, lazy and has one sole ambition—to survive. According to him, only one fly in the ointment exists. What happens if, by some miracle of God, Louis XVI's son, this mysterious Dauphin, suddenly reappeared and claimed the throne of his father? So, His Majesty's government, not to mention myself, wants you in Paris. Your orders are quite simple." Wellington held up his hand. "First—" His bony index finger came only a few inches from Segalla's face. "Did the Dauphin die in the Temple? If he did, God rest the lad, then your task is finished. However, if he escaped, where is he now?"

"And if I find him, my lord?"

Wellington lost some of his certainty; his hand fell away.

"He'll be killed, won't he?" Segalla said quietly. "He'll be taken for a ride in a carriage, shot, and his corpse disposed of."

Wellington looked up. "Neither I nor Lord Liverpool would be party to murder," the English commander in chief replied brusquely. "But I cannot speak for everybody who has assembled to watch this drama unfold." He put his face in his hands and rubbed his eyes. "I don't know what will happen, Segalla," he declared softly. "I really don't know. But, if you find the Dauphin, don't take him to London; you'll never reach the coast alive. Find shelter amongst the first group of English soldiers you meet. There are enough of my bastards hanging around the suburbs of Paris to keep you company."

"So, there is danger?" Segalla asked.

Wellington threw his head back and laughed. "Danger?" He

looked at Segalla sardonically. "England and France are supposed to be allies now." His face became grave. "This is how dangerous it is, Major Segalla. It's rather like Daniel entering the lion's den. Only this time he is blindfolded, gagged, bound hand-and-foot, and the good Lord is busy elsewhere. You are to go to Lion d'Or tavern in the Île de France; stay there and Liverpool's agents will contact you. Tell the landlord you are looking for number 105 North Tower."

Wellington made Segalla repeat it. "Shortly afterwards our agents will contact you and," Wellington smirked, "you may well be in for a surprise. Now"—Wellington placed the rock back on the table—"until these agents contact you, be most careful. Try and enter Paris by night. Tell no one, I repeat, no one, why you are there or what you are looking for. If anyone calling himself Monsieur de Paris makes an attempt to contact you, you are to leave the Lion d'Or immediately and seek refuge in the English embassy. So," Wellington pushed his chair back and rose. "Take your money and your letters. You are to be on the road in the hour."

"My lord—my lord? You want more food?"

Segalla opened his eyes and shook himself as he stared at the anxious face of the landlord.

"My lord is tired. Do you wish to sleep?"

"How far is it to Paris?" Segalla asked.

"Another ten kilometres."

Segalla picked up his goblet. "Till my horse is rested," he declared. "I'll stay a little longer."

Segalla waited, noticing how it grew colder as daylight began to fade over the tavern garden. He felt rested, a little sleepy but determined to press on. He collected his horse from the stable and rejoined the trackway. By the time darkness had fallen he had reached the main thoroughfare which took him to Paris's northern gate, closely guarded by Bourbon troops in their white uniforms under the command of allied officers. Segalla showed his papers, and went through and into Le Marais. This was the most wretched quarter of Paris: Tawdry, blackened houses lined the streets which were thronged by crowds of beggars, harlots, sellers of nostrums and old hats. Segalla was forced to dismount and hire a *fallot*, a night watchman, to lead him through this mean, squalid quarter where a change of ruler meant no difference to its inhabitants.

At last the derelict tenements gave way to broader roads and avenues and the towers of Notre Dame and the Louvre palace came into view. The lantern man took him across the Pont Neuf, past the huge statue of Henri IV and, after a few more winding alleyways, into the lighted courtyard of the Lion d'Or. It was a spacious, elegant building with its own courtyards and gardens. Inside, the drinking-rooms were full of officers wearing the uniforms of various nationalities. Segalla stayed in the doorway, warily watching his horse, held by a heavy-eyed ostler. The landlord approached, a rather dandified man dressed in a velvet waistcoat, silk shirt and nankeen breeches all covered in white snuff powder.

"Good evening, monsieur—and your business?"

"I need a chamber."

The landlord spread his hands. "Monsieur, I am Henri Mallon and my word is my bond. We are full. Look." He gestured round, peering through the fug of pipe and tobacco smoke at the officers squatting on stools or lounging in chairs.

"Sir, we are full. I could not even put my own mother up."

"In which case," Segalla replied, "could you please advise me where I can find 105 North Tower?"

Mallon's jaw fell. "Oh, monsieur." He smacked the palm of his hand against his forehead. "I forget. You are . . . ?"

"Major Nicholas Segalla."

The landlord waved him in, took him upstairs to the first floor and ushered Segalla into an elegant chamber. The ceiling was painted a light pink, the walls were wainscoted with polished oak; thick, woollen carpets covered most of the floor, the windows were large with thick paned glass which mirrored the lights from the courtyard below. In one corner stood a huge bowl of crushed rosemary which filled the chamber with the sweet fragrance of summer. On the wall hung a large, oak-framed picture of Louis XVI, fat-faced and pop-eyed, as if staring into the terrors which would later engulf him. A white wreath of flowers now circled the picture. Segalla smiled. The landlord saw this.

"Aye, Major, times change." And then softly closed the door behind him.

"They certainly do," Segalla murmured to himself. "And the more they change, the more they stay the same."

He went over to the casement window, checked each catch and lock and stared down at the alleyway alongside the tavern. He then unlocked the clasps of his leather saddlebags; he took out the muskets, making sure they were primed, putting one in the drawer of the desk and the other under the bed, whilst he kept a small handgun near him.

After a quick wash in the bowl of rose water on the lavarium, Segalla ordered some bread and wine. Once this had come he locked the door, took out a battered missal for, unknown even to his masters in London, Segalla was a Catholic priest and intended to celebrate the Mass of the day. After this was finished, he pulled off his boots and lay on the bed staring up at the quilted tester, studying its intricate design, whilst his body relaxed and his mind drifted over the purpose of his visit to Paris.

For a while he let the images and pictures flare like stabs of lights in his mind: the huge donjon of the Temple, the baby-faced Dauphin's elfin features framed in a halo of candlelight whilst around him dark shadows circled. Segalla smiled at his own fanciful imagination. He recalled the Temple as he had seen it, some six hundred years previous when its Grand Master, Jacques de Molay, had been burnt on the Île de France before Notre Dame. Segalla had stood in the crowd and watched the flames hungrily lick the old soldier's body. Before he died, de Molay had thrown his head back and screamed, cursing the

Capets until the thirteenth generation. Segalla wondered, If a man could live so long, why not a curse? The thirteenth generation had been Louis XVI and his wife Marie-Antoinette. Were their deaths the result of this ancient curse?

Segalla rubbed his eyes. Wellington had mentioned Monsieur de Paris, the official title, bestowed in the Middle Ages, on the Executioner of Paris. The current title was held by the leader of the secret Templars, an organisation which dated back to the fourteenth century. On the dissolution of that great military order, many of its members had died violent deaths on the rack and at the gibbet or stake. Others had fled, whilst a few had formed an underground secret society constantly plotting against the Capetian monarchy, which had destroyed its order. The Temple palace in Paris had once been the headquarters of the Templars and Segalla wondered at the irony of the last King of France, his wife and his son spending their last days there. Why, Segalla wondered, some twenty years after the Dauphin's supposed death, were the secret Templars so interested in the truth about his fate?

Despite the warmth in the room, Segalla shivered. Down the long, dusty corridors of the years, he had often crossed swords with such secret societies. Did Wellington know the true identity of Monsieur de Paris? Or did he just see him as another leader of the many sinister organisations which now flourished in Paris as thickly as weeds on a dunghill: revolutionary covens, gangs who fiercely resented the restoration of the Bourbons; societies devoted to the memory of Napoléon; members of the ultra-right, powerful noblemen who wished to wreak vengeance on anyone who had had dealings with the Revolution in the terrible days of the Terror.

"They will all be interested in the Dauphin," Segalla murmured to himself. "Adherence to the Bourbons would be divided: some will see him as a nuisance, others will regard him as their rightful king. The Bonapartists will view him as a potential rival to Napoléon's heir in Austria. The revolutionaries and radicals will regard the Dauphin as a leftover from a bygone age whilst the Templars will merely regard him as unfinished business, that part of de Molay's curse not yet fulfilled.''

Segalla wondered about how successful he would be in this maze of mysteries. His eyes grew heavy and he drifted into sleep, plagued by nightmares from the past as well as fears of things yet to come.

In the old faubourg of St.-Antoine, Harmand of Meuse was an agitated old man. Those who had known him in his youth would have been shocked by the change in his appearance. At the height of the Revolution, in the great days of Robespierre, Harmand had been an important commissioner with his colourful sash, velvet hat with the tricolour cockade, exquisite clothes and high-heeled leather boots. Harmand had swaggered through the corridors of power and people had shrunk from his very shadow. Harmand had been a revolutionary amongst revolutionaries. His frown could mean death. His written command bore the force of law. He had been the personification of the Revolution itself, but that was twenty years ago and Harmand, like Lucifer, had fallen from his glory, never to rise again. He had grown old, bent and arthritic. His wealth had disappeared and now he was forced to live in a small, thatched cottage on the edge of a common in one of the poorest districts of Paris. Its alleyways were full of thieves, pickpockets, petty assassins and men who constantly hid from the light of day. Harmand had grown used to it. His hair was now long and greasy, his face yellow and seamed, but at least he had a table, a fire and a bed to sleep in at night and, of course, the glories of all his yesterdays.

Harmand would squat in front of the fire and dream about the banquets he had attended, the fine wines he had drunk, and the pretty young aristos who had shared his bed, using all their exquisite, sensuous skill so as to please him and avoid the dungeons of the Conciergerie.

"You either ride me and do it well," Harmand would threaten, "or you ride Madame Guillotine's plank and you lose your head!"

The threat had never failed but now all that was past. Harmand thought he had been forgotten until whispers came fluttering down the dark alleyways and fetid runnels. Monsieur de Paris wished to have words with him. Harmand had grown most fearful. At night he would lock his door. He'd bought a musket and adopted one of the hungry mastiffs which hunted amongst the midden-heaps of St.-Antoine. He never went out. An old woman brought him his food and wine.

Now, as Segalla drifted into sleep at the Lion d'Or, Harmand knew Monsieur de Paris was coming. He sat by his fire, musket in hand, dozing then abruptly waking. The noise of the faubourg fell silent, only the occasional shout or cry faint on the evening breeze. Harmand started; the mastiff chained to a post outside was barking furiously. Then it whined and fell silent. Harmand sprang to his feet, cocking the old musket.

"Who is it?" he cried, trying to make his voice sound steady.

A loud knock on his door.

"Open up!" a voice shouted.

Harmand stood, rooted to the spot.

"Open up!" the voice repeated, "or we'll burn the place above your head!"

Bewildered, almost fainting with fright, Harmand unlocked the door and stared into the cold blackness of the night.

"Throw down your weapon!"

Harmand let the musket fall and the men appeared as if out of the ground, filling the room. From under their cloaks Harmand glimpsed the butts of pistols and dagger handles. Most of the men were masked. Others had large stripes of black paint across their faces. The old revolutionary's wrists were seized and bound by tight cords and he was pushed back on his stool in front of the fire. Gibbering with fright he crouched there. The gang of assailants had parted and a tall, strongly-built man strode into the room. His face was masked by a piece of red velvet. On the cheeks and forehead of this mask were three large white crosses. He wore a large tricorne hat edged with black feathers, a blue soldier's coat, trousers with a blood-red sash around his waist, high boots over his knees; in each hand were pistols, whilst a long dagger and a large sabre were pushed into the sash. He stood over Harmand. The old revolutionary glimpsed soft, merry eyes through the eyelets of the mask.

"You are Harmand of Meuse?"

"Yes sir."

"Do you know who I am?"

"No sir," Harmand lied.

"Where is it?" the masked figure asked.

"Sir," Harmand whined, "where is *what*?"

The masked figure sighed like a father disappointed with a favourite son. "The report you drew up when you were a commissioner. You remember, on 19 December 1794 you and two others, who are now far beyond my reach . . ." Beneath the mask Harmand saw the man smile as if savouring some secret joke. "You visited the Temple and drew up a report of your visit with the Dauphin. Now we have searched high and low but your report eludes us." One gloved finger stroked the side of Harmand's unshaven face. "Now, you must have kept a copy."

The old revolutionary slumped to his knees and lifted his bound hands in supplication.

"Sir, believe me, I have no report. No copy was kept."

"But you saw the Dauphin?"

Harmand nodded vigorously.

"And what was he like?"

Harmand closed his eyes and tried to remember. "He never spoke or showed any surprise."

"And his description?"

47

Harmand shrugged and stared round at the silent, shadowy figures now filling his meagre room.

"A typical Capet, blond-haired and blue-eyed."

Again his face was stroked by the leather-gloved finger.

"What a pity," the masked man murmured. "What a great pity." He shook his head. "But I don't believe you." The leader looked over his shoulder. "Bring some wood."

Immediately members of the gang began to smash up the shabby, rickety furniture and piled it in the hearth. A large fire was lit. Harmand's tattered boots were removed, his feet bare to the flames, then both he and the stool were lifted onto the hearth. Harmand screamed as his feet entered the flames, the muscles shrivelled and his ankles began to roast. Every so often he would be pulled back and the soft questioning would begin again. Harmand could only groan and shake his head as he tried to recall his visit to the Dauphin in those far-off days of glory.

"Tell me what you want to know," he shrieked, "and I'll reply."

Slowly but surely, under the influence of the terrible pain, Harmand's memory was shaken and he stuttered out a description.

"The boy was tall," he gasped. "Too tall, sores on his joints, shoulders bowed. He had blond hair and was dressed in a sailor jacket but never spoke to us. He was silent as a mute."

At last his torturers were satisfied. Monsieur de Paris quietly ushered his band of assassins out of the cottage. Inside, Harmand lay on the floor where he had been tossed. He could only watch, bound hand-and-foot, as the burning brand his assailants had left lying on the straw began to turn the room into a raging conflagration.

Segalla woke early the next morning. He groaned as he realised he had not undressed. Outside, the sun was beginning to rise, burning off the heavy mist which had rolled in from the Seine. Segalla went out and ordered water to be brought up from the well; when this arrived, he quickly stripped, washed, shaved and swiftly donned fresh linen, a high-necked shirt above his dark blue velvet breeches and over this a blue serge jacket. Segalla then went downstairs and broke his fast on a large bowl of café au lait, bread, cheese and a dish of diced fruit which tasted rather acrid and must have seen better days.

Segalla was halfway through his meal when a dandy, hips swaying, tottered into the tavern. He was dressed like one of the Macaronis in London, a powdered silken wig on his head, his thin, effeminate face rouged with a beauty spot on each cheek. He stood dressed in a tight-fitting, frogged jacket, silken stockings, exquisite maroon breeches and a pale cream shirt so covered in lace it reminded Segalla of the hem of a lady's petticoat. He stood leaning on his cane, carmine lips pursed as he stared languidly round the tavern. Some of the other guests started to laugh but they hid their faces behind their hands. They were soldiers and, like Segalla, recognised something dangerous about this fop. The rapier on his side hung as effortlessly as a piece of jewellery. There was also something about the way the fop's long fingers kept drumming a beat on the hilt which gave the impression of a fighting man, one of those professional duellists who lived for the cut and the thrust over some insult, be it real or pretended. Segalla returned to his food.

"I am looking," the dandy declared languidly, "for the way to 105 North Tower." His English was as exquisite as his dress.

Segalla rose and the fellow tottered across, his polished black high-heeled shoes tapping like a dancer's on the wooden boards. He stopped, turned sideways and looked Segalla up and down.

"So, you can help me, sir?"

"In fact I know where it is," Segalla replied, biting his lip to stop himself laughing. He caught the amusement in the fop's eyes and realised he was only acting a part. One small, soft hand came forward.

"The name's Jacques de Coeur." Then he shrugged and giggled behind his hand. "Well, that's what my friends call me and you, sir, can be my friend. What is your name?"

The introductions were carried on in hushed tones. Segalla felt as if he was playing some part in a drawing-room drama.

"I'll collect my coat," he declared abruptly, and hurried upstairs

He donned his sword-belt, took his cloak, made sure his possessions were secure and went downstairs where de Coeur was waiting for him in the courtyard. The fop sidled up to him, simpering like some lady of the town.

"We won't talk," he said in a half-giggle, "but just walk. You never know who is watching you. *Là*, sir, Paris is full of strange creatures. The other night a cossack officer tried to kiss me."

Segalla could contain himself no further and started to laugh. His companion threw him a look of mock anger and, still walking ridiculously, led him out into the street towards the Pont Neuf.

In the full light of day, Segalla was surprised by the changes on the bridge. The shops, stores and small houses had been removed, and the bridge was more like a broad avenue dominated by the life-size figure of Henri IV on his mounted charger. They passed La Samaritaine, a fountain flanked by statues of Christ and the Samaritan woman offering him a cup of water. Above the fountain a clock, in a small gilt tower, chimed on the hour and half hour. De Coeur stopped before it and crossed himself quickly.

"I love this statue," he simpered. "It always reminds me of Maman's stories."

He led Segalla on, adroitly avoiding the women in their high-heeled clogs, carrying huge paniers on their heads. Fine gentlemen, swords at their sides, hats under their arms, swaggered alongside long-haired, black-garbed lawyers, or priests in their dusty soutanes. Every so often de Coeur would stop as if he were some city guide to point out some famous sight.

"Monsieur," Segalla interrupted him, "I have been to Paris before."

De Coeur turned. "*Là*, sir, but this might be the first time you have been followed by one of Monsieur de Paris's agents!"

Chapter 4

Once across the Pont Neuf, de Coeur led Segalla through a maze of streets and across broad avenues. Segalla had not been in Paris for years and was surprised at the renovations of Napoléon's engineers. Streets had been broadened, boulevards laid out and, on a number of occasions, Segalla found it difficult to find his bearings and would have become lost if it had not been for de Coeur. Time and again the fop turned but failed to see any pursuer and mumbled an apology that perhaps he had been mistaken. At last they reached the Rue de la Forge, a broad clean street with a brown-gold carpet of leaves in front of the high railings of the stately mansions built there. De Coeur led Segalla up the broad white, freshly scrubbed steps of one of these. He raised the gold-coloured clapper on the polished black door and tapped gently. A small grille, just above the lock, flew open.

"What is it?" a voice asked.

"Open the door, Canary!" de Coeur hissed. "And don't play your games!"

The door swung back soundlessly on its hinges. A dwarf of a man stood in the entrance, a shabby wig on his head, the rest of his miniature body being covered by a bright yellow coat above black, shabby boots. His face was brown and wizened as a walnut. He looked at Segalla with bright, malicious eyes.

"Madame Roquet," he intoned in a surprisingly deep voice, "is awaiting you."

They went along a passageway. Segalla marvelled at the splendour of the house. The walls were covered in a fine pink paper, decorated with scarlet roses and lilies of the valley. The floor-boards were polished but thick, woollen carpets deadened all sound. A broad, sweeping staircase dominated the hallway, its newel and banisters polished to a gleaming brown. Large canvas paintings, all framed in gold and coloured wood, hung on the walls. Delicate furniture stood about whilst a delicious fragrance, redolent of costly creams and expensive perfumes, teased Segalla's nostrils.

At the back of the house was a lavish parlour where Madame Roquet was waiting. She was Junoesque—a strong, pallid face with a prominent chin and nose; her auburn hair, piled high on her head, was held in place by gold and silver pins. Her eyes were remarkable, wide-spread and a chilling blue. She was dressed exquisitely in a high-necked, tight-fitting gown; her shoulders were covered by a muslin shawl, poppy-red and fringed with lace tassels. Segalla bowed and kissed her proffered hand, which held a fan.

"You are Major Segalla?" Roquet's voice was soft and low.

"Madame, I am. I was brought here looking for 105 North Tower."

Madame Roquet's hand fell away. She chuckled then spread the fan, tapping it flirtatiously against her lips.

"Rest yourself, Monsieur Segalla, or is it Nicholas? No cere-mony here. My name is Françoise."

Segalla sat down in an oval-shaped chair whilst Madame Ro-quet sat opposite, her every movement delicate and flirtatious.

"You have met my companions? Jacques de Coeur, my man-ager, and Raoul Fettyon, whom we call the Canary because he wears, whatever the season, that damned yellow coat." She glanced up at de Coeur. "You can leave us now. And take the Canary with you."

Both her retainers bowed. Segalla glimpsed the annoyance in the Canary's face as he backed out of the room, slamming the door behind him.

Madame Roquet then lifted the bell on the small, ivory-topped table next to her and rang it gently. A servant came in, a young girl, pretty as a picture in a long white, flowing dress with a red sash round her waist. She served them both chocolate and biscuits. Roquet sipped from a china cup, watching Segalla intently.

"It's the best chocolate," she remarked. "You won't taste finer in Paris." She put the cup down and leaned across. "Major Segalla, I'll be honest: I am no more French than General Wellington. My real name is Grace Atkins. I was born in Horsham, Sussex, and, for a few years, I was in Paradise. My husband Robert was an officer in the Royal Engineers." She paused and moved the cup a little farther away from her. "I want you to know because what you might see in this house will make you wonder."

Segalla stared impassively back but, thinking she might consider him rude, glanced quickly around the parlour.

"It is beautiful, isn't it?" the woman murmured. "The cornices are gilt-edged. The paintings are originals. The carpets are hand-woven and some of the furniture once stood in the palace of the Tuileries." She paused and played with the tassel on her shawl. "In London you'd call this a molly house, a brothel. This is the only room in the entire mansion which does not have squint-holes or peep-gaps in the walls and paintings. I am its madam, its owner. Jacques de Coeur is my manager, or bully-boy. The Canary—" She shrugged. "Where de Coeur goes so does he. Twenty years ago," she continued, "my husband and I became involved in a scheme to smuggle Catholic priests and nuns out of France during the Reign of Terror. Robert resigned his commission to do this. He was a Catholic. We were caught and transported to the prison at Arras and, believe me, monsieur, we entered a hell I thought never existed this side of death. We were captured by an agent, a Terrorist called Jacques Le Bon. You have heard of him?"

Segalla nodded. "Vaguely, madame. A man who loved killing more than life itself."

"A devil in human flesh," Madame Roquet replied. "He came to Arras to purge the town of all counterrevolutionaries; but, if he was a devil, his wife Mimi was even worse—she loved executions. This precious pair set up a guillotine in the centre of the town and used to stand on a balcony of a nearby house to watch the executions. Because we were English, technically prisoners of war, they could not touch us. They carried no warrants for that but they made us watch what Madame Mimi Le Bon called 'the apricot's fall,' the decapitation of their victims. It became a circus: refreshments were served at the foot of the guillotine and, when the day's business was over, Monsieur Le Bon and his bailiffs would sometimes arrange the nude and decapitated bodies in obscene or ridiculous attitudes. They also organised a choir of children who, in the evening, would stand round the blood-drenched scaffold and sing songs before being entertained by a puppet show."

Roquet paused, swallowing hard. "After two weeks of this, my husband became ill. Gaol fever or the cruelty of his captors, I don't know. One night he just slipped away, murmuring he had seen enough evil for one lifetime. Le Bon then left, and my gaoler had compassion on me. After I had shared his bed with him for a month he threw me out onto the highway and I made my way to Paris. The Sisters of Charity took me in and, when I was feeling better in body if not in mind, I began to plot." She shrugged and ran her fingers along the arm of the chair. "I became a madam, the owner of this house, financed by the British government. I entertained the officers of the Revolution as well as those of Napoléon. I learnt their secrets, tittle-tattle, scraps of gossip, juicy morsels of scandal and all went back to London."

"Why do you tell me this?" Segalla asked. "We have hardly met and I have your life story."

"I sought vengeance against the Revolution," Roquet replied. Now her eyes gleamed with feverish excitement. "I danced and sang; I organised the most lavish soirées as each wolf pack fell from power and were devoured by the very terror they had begun. I also became interested in the fate of the Dauphin imprisoned in the Temple. I schemed and I plotted but there was little I could do." She pulled a face. "I had to pretend because anyone who showed undue interest in the Temple or its prisoners fell under suspicion. However, I did hear stories that the Dauphin may have escaped. I passed this information on, not only to His Majesty's government in London, but to the Bourbons in exile." She laced her fingers together. "Monsieur Élie Decazes, Louis XVIII's Minister of Police, became a firm friend and patron of this establishment." She leaned back in the chair, laughing softly and Segalla wondered if the terrors at Arras had scarred her soul and mind in a way which could never be healed.

Madame Roquet rose to her feet and walked over to the window. "Now both the allies and the French government," she continued, "are determined to resolve this matter one way or the other. I asked Liverpool to send his best agent." She smiled coquettishly over her shoulder at him. "And that is why they sent you. My lord Liverpool did not furnish you with every detail?"

Segalla shook his head. "He said there was a mystery," he replied. "A possibility that the Dauphin may have escaped."

"It's more than a possibility," Roquet retorted fiercely.

"You have proof?" Segalla asked.

"No," she replied, returning to her seat. "Just a feeling!"

"And do you have any dealings with Fouché?" Segalla asked.

Roquet's eyes narrowed. "That fox," she whispered. "I have never made up my mind whether Monsieur Fouché is a monarchist, a Bonapartist or a revolutionary. In the end I think Fouché believes in no one but Monsieur Fouché."

"Do you think he might help us?"

"If he does, it will be the first time that man of mystery steps out of the shadows. . . . I doubt it," she added, tossing her head like a schoolgirl.

"And Monsieur Barras?"

Roquet glanced slyly at him from under her brows. "Everyone would like to speak to Monsieur Barras but he is hiding in exile. Monsieur Barras is a man best left alone; he knows too many secrets."

"He was leader of France when the Dauphin died."

"And, if you found his hiding place, he would only declare that, to the best of his knowledge, the Dauphin was well looked after, given food and physic but unfortunately died." Roquet clenched her hands firmly in her lap. "That is the great barrier across this mystery, monsieur. According to all the facts the Dauphin died. People witnessed his death—doctors, officials. He was actually given a burial."

"But you believe different?"

"Sometimes you can peep over the barrier, monsieur. This pool of mystery is already being stirred. Your arrival in Paris is well known. Is it a coincidence that the man who buried the Dauphin—Betrancourt—had the top of his head blown off a few weeks ago? Whilst Harmand of Meuse, the old revolutionary who once visited the Dauphin after Robespierre's fall, died mysteriously in a fire in his hovel in the St.-Antoine?"

"They were both murdered?" Segalla asked.

"By Monsieur de Paris," Roquet replied.

She daintily picked up her cup and saucer and sipped delicately. Segalla watched, fascinated by her constant changes of mood. Now she looked like some vicar's serene wife, taking tea on a Sunday afternoon.

"Now you've arrived," she murmured. "Everything is in hand. As soon as we learnt of your coming, preparations were begun." Madame Roquet licked her lips. "You must not waste any more time, Major. You are to be given a room at the Tuileries and all the documentation you need to study has been extracted from the archives."

Roquet looked over her shoulder at the door as if she feared an eavesdropper; she then leaned so close Segalla caught her spicy perfume and saw the blood-red flecks in the woman's large eyes.

"A secret court will sit," she whispered. "La Chambre Sécrète. It will be chaired by Monsieur Decazes, Louis XVIII's principal favourite. No records will be kept. You will be allowed to interrogate certain people."

"What about Fouché?" Segalla insisted.

Roquet straightened up, her lips curling in a sneer. "Fouché," she murmured, "must consider himself the most fortunate man on God's earth. He served Robespierre, Barras, Napoléon, and now Louis XVIII. He has the devil's own luck in surviving. He's a closed book, Major. If he agrees to talk to you, consider it a miracle." She smiled and rose, smoothing the front of her dress. "I'll return soon," she murmured. "You wish something more to eat or drink?"

Segalla shook his head and watched as Roquet walked daintily out of the room, smiling over her shoulder conspiratorially at him.

She's insane, Segalla thought; cunning but consumed by a desire for vengeance. He got to his feet to ease the cramp in his limbs and walked across to the paintings on the wall. The first was of the Dauphin, or so the little plaque attached to the open frame declared, an impression by the artist Moitet. Segalla studied the round, babyish face, the girlish cast to the lips, chubby cheeks, large eyes and fair hair which fell to the child's shoulders. The picture was a stylised portrait and could represent the features of any well-fed child in some wealthy Parisian mansion twenty years ago. The portrait beside it, however, was more interesting: Marie-Antoinette as a young archduchess, by some unknown Austrian painter. Segalla studied it and smiled sadly to himself: It was a true likeness of the woman who had risen to become Queen of France and whose fall had been so swift and tragic. He gazed into those lustrous eyes, noticing the strong cast to her mouth, determined chin and that beautiful hair piled high and kept in place by a bejewelled gauze net. Marie-Antoinette, sitting at her spinet, stared back at him. All around her, on the walls hung the lavish tapestries of some Austrian palace.

"If you had only known," Segalla murmured; the woman's face smiled serenely back. He half closed his eyes. If he concentrated he could almost hear the liquid notes of the spinet: Marie-Antoinette's white fingers touching the keys whilst, now and again, she would stop and laugh whenever she struck a wrong note.

"I can't help it!" she'd cry. "My mind is so full, I can't concentrate." Then she'd grin impishly before returning, even more determined, to master that particular piece.

"Where was it?" Segalla murmured to himself. Ah yes! He had met Marie-Antoinette only a week before she had left for her triumphal journey to Paris: full of life, flirtatious, strong-willed, determined to be a good queen. "So, what went wrong?" Segalla whispered at the portrait; the alabaster face just stared back.

"I want to be loved, Monsieur Segalla," Marie-Antoinette had laughed at him. "Beside a great King I can be one of France's great queens."

"Be careful!" Segalla had warned her. "France is like a seething cauldron. Remember, when water boils, the scum rises to the top and tipples over."

Marie-Antoinette just looked at him strangely. Then, clutching at her skirts, she had spun on her heel, walking away, back rigid, head erect, apparently furious that anyone could dare advise her to be cautious.

Segalla returned to his chair. Marie-Antoinette had traveled to France and married fat, genial Louis, good-natured but incompetent. She had become spoilt, unable to be accepted by the court or the people, resented by her husband's brothers who now held power. Gradually, the Queen had lost herself in an orgy of pleasure and frippery. Segalla had met her, one last time, as he passed through Versailles, two years before the Revolution broke out. Marie-Antoinette had received him warmly enough at her little home in Versailles where she and her ladies played at being milkmaids.

"We must play the cards! We must play the cards!" the Queen had exclaimed. One of her ladies brought a pack of tarot cards which Marie-Antoinette pressed into Segalla's hands. "Turn them out! Turn them out!" Marie-Antoinette ordered.

Segalla had done so. Later, he always wished he hadn't. Time and again, despite his desperate shuffling, the French queen had drawn the figure of Death, a huge skeleton dressed in black armour riding a dark warhorse, carrying a purple standard with a white rose on it. Marie-Antoinette had accused him of cheating. Segalla had protested, desperately reshuffling the cards, but the result was always the same. At last the Queen had sprung to her feet, dismissing her ladies; beneath the costly makeup, her face had gone a deathly pale and tears brimmed in her eyes.

"I don't think this is amusing, monsieur!" she had cried.

Segalla just spread his hands in despair. "Your Majesty," he had whispered when the other ladies had withdrawn. "I do not play games. I cannot see the future, yet this could be a warning."

"You warned me once before." Marie-Antoinette pushed her face only a few inches away from Segalla's. "I am always being warned." A note of desperation entered her voice. "But what can I do? Those who ride a bucking horse must either master it or be thrown."

"Your new son?" Segalla had asked, hoping to ease the tension.

"Perfect," the Queen replied. "He has a mole above his left breast, a scar on his foot, but he is well." She'd smiled tearfully. "He cried when he was inoculated; the physician left a dreadful mark on his right shoulder but he prospers." She'd flailed her hands. "Yet what about the future? Will he prosper? Will he even live? Whatever happens, I pray he will have a happier life than I!"

Segalla had now risen, gone on one knee. He grasped the Queen's cold fingers but she turned away; thinking he had been dismissed, he was walking through the orangery when a page came running and breathlessly asked him to wait. Marie-Antoinette followed behind, her beautiful court dress now hidden under a great cloak, for it was a cold autumn and a stiff breeze was whipping up the falling leaves. This time Marie-Antoinette was different. Gone was the imperial hauteur—just a frightened woman, clutching at straws. She had stared up at the dark clouds. "If the storm comes, monsieur, I will have few friends." She looked directly at him. "I know you, Segalla. You move like a shadow through the courts of Europe. If the storm comes," she repeated, "I will have few friends: Will you be one of them? Will you protect me, my sons?"

"Yes, Your Majesty," Segalla had replied. "But whether I will be able to help is another matter."

"But if you are asked?" Marie-Antoinette insisted.

"Then, Your Majesty, you will not have to ask a second time. You have my solemn vow."

Marie-Antoinette pushed a locket into his hand. "Keep this," she begged. "It is the truth!"

He tried to ask her what she meant but she'd kissed him lightly on the cheek and hurried away.

Marie-Antoinette had returned to her pleasures and Segalla had left for England where he had been despatched to Washington as Prime Minister Pitt's secret emissary. By the time he'd returned to Europe, the Revolution had broken out and both Louis XVI and his queen Marie-Antoinette were prisoners of the Terror.

Segalla opened the locket Marie-Antoinette had given him and stared at the cherub-faced, dark-haired Louis Charles, then at the stylised picture on the wall. They were alike yet different. He turned suddenly as the door opened. Madame Roquet came

61

in, dressed in the height of fashion, a small, bejewelled turban on her head and a dark blue, gold-edged hooded cloak draped exquisitely around her.

"Are you dreaming, Major?"

Segalla shrugged. "Paris brings back memories, madame."

"Of what?" Roquet's eyes had a hard, searching look.

"I have been here before," Segalla continued deferentially.

Roquet smiled but this was merely a twitch of her lips. Segalla wondered how much she knew about him.

"What time are we expected at the Tuileries?" he asked.

"Whatever time we arrive, Major!"

Segalla walked towards the door, conscious of Madame Roquet's irritation. At first he decided to ignore it but then, with his hand on the latch, he pushed the door closed.

"Madame," he said softly. "What I am, or who I am, or where I come from does, with all due respect, not concern you."

"What you are, monsieur," she replied tartly, "is your own concern, but the mood in Paris is now rather eerie, like a stage still darkened and full of ghosts. People from the past, Major Segalla, men and women with secrets to hide. Are you one of them?"

Segalla just shrugged. "I am an English officer, madame, sent here with a specific task. When it is done then I shall leave."

Madame Roquet pulled a face. "I wonder, monsieur. You see, there are many men in England who have knowledge of Paris, so why did Lord Liverpool send you?"

Segalla opened the door. "In that case, madame, you should really ask him, not me."

Madame Roquet flounced out. Segalla sighed and followed her along the elegant gallery into the hallway and out to where a dark mullion-covered cabriolet was waiting. It was pulled by two black horses, their coats gleaming like satin, their harness embossed and decorated. De Coeur and the Canary glowered down at him from the postilion seat. Segalla ignored them as he opened the door, its windows covered by white muslin, and helped Madame Roquet in. He had hardly taken his own seat opposite her when, with the crack of a whip, the carriage lurched forward. Madame Roquet sat back, her eyes closed, humming a tune. She was sulking, pretending to ignore him, so Segalla leaned in the corner and listened to the sound of the city. After a while the trundle of the wheels and the jogging motion lulled his mind and, pulling back the blind, he stared at the different scenes they passed. Traders, well-dressed citizens, a wig-maker hurrying along, covered in powder from top to toe, a pair of curling-tongs in one hand, a wig in the other. Behind him tottered two boys in linen jackets, bearing café au lait for the wig-maker's customer.

"Please close the blind!" Roquet snapped.

Segalla pulled a face but let it go and sat in a half-doze as the cabriolet thumped and rattled across the cobbles. They sped along the boulevards and the journey became easier. Segalla gauged that they had now entered the Tuileries, going along the pebble-smooth paths which surrounded the palace. At last he heard a loud shout. The carriage came to a halt, followed by voices as an officer asked de Coeur to identify himself. The fellow replied and there was a rap on the door. Segalla opened it, an officer of the royal guards stood there, elegantly dressed in a black tricorne hat, impeccable blue-and-white uniform, silver epaulets and a gold sash across his chest. Once the officer glimpsed Madame Roquet, he doffed his hat in a most courtly bow, pushing his hat under his arm as he carefully read the small note she handed to him. He handed this back and bowed once again.

The door closed and the carriage continued on its way. They entered the Cour du Carousel. Here bewigged footmen and flunkeys opened the door, bringing a small set of steps, helping both Segalla and Madame Roquet out. A chamberlain dressed in a black frogged coat, and a collar starched so stiffly it was a miracle he could even move his head, led them up a sweeping, stone staircase and into the Tuileries palace. They passed through elegant halls and opulent salons, richly decorated and furnished with Gobelin tapestries, Savonnerie carpets, Sèvres vases, Thonire brasses and elegantly carved furniture by the master craftsman Jacob de Desmaltz. In many rooms workmen were busy, high on scaffolds or ladders, removing all trace of Napoléon's sixteen-year stay at the Tuileries. They briskly knocked out the silver carved Ns of Bonaparte's insignia as well as the small gold-carved bees and eagles.

They climbed the sweeping staircase. Segalla felt he was almost climbing on air, for each step was thickly carpeted, drowning all sounds. Along a gallery, where the floorboards gleamed and the walls were studded by large oil canvas paintings; then into a surprisingly dark chamber. At the far end was a great buffet or cabinet carved out of black oak. Paintings hung on the wall above a large, marble fireplace. Around this, seated in huge chairs with padded backs and sides, were three men. The chamberlain coughed, indicating with his hand for Segalla and Madame Roquet to stay near the door. He went across and, going on one knee before the central chair, he whispered hoarsely, bowed his head as he listened to the reply then, rising, the chamberlain beckoned them forward.

"Welcome to Paris," the corpulent man in the central chair murmured. His rubicund face, sheeny with fat, was wet with beads of sweat which rolled from under the white, powdered wig. He was dressed in a salmon-pink jacket and knee breeches, silk stockings and black, low-heeled shoes. His huge belly strained under a silk shirt. Across his chest was a gold sash with silver fringes held in place by the brilliant cross of Saint Louis. Segalla went on one knee and kissed the puffy, bejewelled fingers of Louis XVIII whilst, beside him, Madame Roquet performed the most elegant of curtsies. Segalla stayed on one knee, even as the chamberlain brought across other chairs and the King's two companions moved theirs to accommodate this.

"You are most welcome," the King muttered.

Segalla looked up and gazed into the King's chilling green eyes.

"You may sit down," Louis ordered.

Segalla obeyed. The King snapped his fingers and a servant stepped out of the shadows, dressed in gorgeous livery, and placed small cups of iced wine on a small oval table. Segalla looked out of the corner of his eye where Madame Roquet sat like some mannequin. The King seemed now to have forgotten them and sat overflowing his chair of state. At first glance he looked like some genial uncle but those obsidian, unblinking eyes showed the true nature of his soul. During Louis XVI's reign the Comte de Provence, as he was then known, had acquired a reputation for cold ruthlessness, a deep dislike of his own brother the King and a murderous hatred for Marie-Antoinette.

The two men who sat on either side of him were equally cold and distant. Fouché, his thinning hair swept forward over a narrow brow, reminded Segalla of a brooding falcon with his sharp nose, sallow cheeks and bloodless lips. He was dressed soberly in a frock coat and tight-fitting breeches, silk cream stockings and black pumps; his shirt collar stood upright, his neckcloth, in the form of a cravat of pure white silk only emphasized Fouché's cadaverous appearance. On the King's left, Élie Decazes, however, had the face and features of some classical statue. Olive-skinned, his black, silky hair carefully coiffed, Decazes was the epitome of fashion in his double-breasted, square-cut coat; the sleeves close-fitting, slightly puffed at the shoulder; his tight-fitting, murrey-coloured nankeen breeches eased into polished riding boots. Decazes sat languidly, apparently more interested in Madame Roquet than Segalla. At last the King finished his wine and, wheezing and puffing, stretched forward.

"Welcome to Paris, Major Segalla," he gasped, dabbing at his face with a lace handkerchief. "Madame Roquet, you are always welcome."

Segalla caught the implied snub. The King smiled falsely

across at Segalla, then he grasped his cane and eased his ponderous bulk out of the chair. He came and towered over his visitor, leaning down, the effort turning his fat face puce, his mouth only a few inches away from Segalla's. The King licked his lips, a gesture which reminded Segalla of a striking viper.

"I shall leave you to my good friends, Messieurs Fouché and Decazes," he murmured. "You can tell your masters in London, Major Segalla, that my poor nephew the Dauphin was murdered by Robespierre and his Terrorists. I was born to be King of France and I will die the same."

And, without further ado, the King, his cane tapping on the marble floor, stalked out of the chamber, slamming the door behind him.

Chapter 5

Once the King was gone the atmosphere lightened. Both Fouché and Decazes stirred in their chairs. Decazes beamed benevolently and spread his hands.

"Major, the King is out of sorts. You must appreciate that he is most grateful to his ally England but, these are French matters and should not really concern you."

Fouché nodded solemnly in agreement.

"I am here," Segalla replied, "because His Majesty's government in London want me to be here." He paused to choose his words carefully. "They welcome the restoration of France's rightful ruler but the mystery surrounding the Dauphin, or should I say the boy king Louis XVII, could pose problems both now or in the future."

"How could a child, a dead child," Fouché stated, not bothering to turn his head, "threaten the French monarchy? The Dauphin died twenty years ago, Major. His poor little corpse lies buried in the graveyard of Ste.-Marguerite."

"Is that the truth, monsieur?" Segalla said softly. "You have held power in Paris for some twenty years. Now you tell me, the English Crown's representative in Paris, that the Dauphin is dead."

"Gentlemen." Madame Roquet broke in, staring pleadingly at Segalla and then Decazes. "We are not here to quarrel."

"No, we are not." Decazes got to his feet.

Segalla noticed he never bothered to look at Fouché, and spoke as if his former enemy did not even exist.

"His Majesty the King has provided fresh quarters for you, Major Segalla, here at the Tuileries, a small bedchamber. Our police in Paris have seized all the archives for the period during which the Dauphin was in prison. They are in a separate room. You will have the services of a trained archivist, Raoul Tallien. Are there any questions?"

Segalla bit his tongue; he was tempted to ask, If the Dauphin was dead why had the grave-digger Betrancourt and the old revolutionary Harmand been murdered? Instead he smiled his thanks even as Decazes walked across and pulled the bell-rope. A footman, silent as a ghost, came into the chamber.

"Take Major Segalla to his quarters," Decazes declared. He beamed brilliantly at the Englishman. "I will have your bags brought from the Lion d'Or whilst Madame Roquet will always be welcome to see if you need"—Decazes raised one eyebrow—"any other diversion."

Decazes extended one hand which Segalla grasped. He then followed the footman from the room, conscious that he was being dismissed like some errant schoolboy.

"Keep your temper," Liverpool had warned him in London. "The French will, and must, cooperate with you but don't expect them to like it."

"Oh, Major." Decazes stood by the fireplace and held up his hand. "You will have access to these documents for two days. On the third, you and I will chair a secret tribunal. Every living person who had access to the Dauphin will appear before that tribunal and answer our questions on oath." He dropped his hand. "I will keep you informed."

Segalla nodded and followed the footman out along the galleries and up a flight of stairs to a small, richly furnished bedchamber. There were carpets on the floor, pictures on the painted walls, a writing desk, chairs, cupboards for his clothes and a comfortable four-poster bed screened by gold curtains with silver tassels. Segalla took off his jacket and his sword-belt, loosened his cravat and lay down on the bed. He heard a sound outside and, going to the door, opened it; two soldiers of the royal guard had now taken up position, bayonets fixed, outside his chamber.

"We are here for your own protection, Major," one of them announced in good English.

Segalla looked at the man's epaulets.

"Thank you, Corporal."

"If you need anything, sir, just ask."

Segalla smiled his thanks then closed the door, fully aware that he was, until this matter was finished, a prisoner in the Tuileries. Segalla went back to the bed and slept for a while.

When he awoke he felt hungry and decided that, as he was the King's guest, he was free to wander the palace. He left his room, and, with the guards shadowing him, found his way to the kitchen. A red-faced cook served him some food, bread dipped in honey, a huge bowl of sweetened black coffee and a cup of red wine. The kitchen was a hive of activity; cooks, scullions and maids scurried about amidst a mixture of steam and smoke as well as the savoury odours of freshly baked bread, roast chicken and other meats.

Segalla looked up at the huge clock but its glass case was deeply misted over. The corporal lounging behind him shouted, "It's three o'clock in the afternoon, Major."

Segalla finished his meal and wandered back to the entrance vestibule where Madame Roquet had taken him. Now it was thronged by courtiers hurrying to some engagement or hoping for an invitation to the King's evening repast.

"Major Segalla! Major Segalla!"

He turned. A small, mousy-haired man dressed in a plain grey suit with matching hose stood in front of him; he stared up shortsightedly, his little nose furrowed, mouth half-open.

"I've been looking for you everywhere," the little man gasped.

"And why is that?" Segalla asked, amused at the little man's intense air. He noticed how his lace-edged shirt and polished, high-heeled, buckled shoes were covered in fine grains of snuff.

"I am Tallien," the little fellow replied, extending his hand which Segalla shook. "I am your archivist and everything is ready for you." The man's hand flew to his mouth. "I didn't mean to be insolent but we have only two days."

Segalla's heart warmed to this little intense official, totally wrapped up in his important duties.

"You'd best come with me. You'd best come with me."

"If it is that important, Monsieur Tallien," Segalla replied drily, "then we shouldn't waste another second."

The little man saw the humour in Segalla's eyes and relaxed. Once again his hand flew to his mouth as if he kept forgetting his manners.

"My first name is Raoul."

"And I am Nicholas," Segalla replied.

He looked over his shoulder at the corporal who was now grinning at him. Tallien followed his gaze.

"They are there for your own protection," he whispered. "But, come, you had best accompany me."

And, without further ado, Tallien took him up flights of stairs through halls and chambers and into a spacious library. The floor was of polished cedarwood, French windows at the far end, whilst every inch of wall was covered with shelves and shelves of books all bound in different types of leather. Once they were inside, Tallien locked the door and lit the lamps along the long, polished table. Tallien then pushed a lever behind a stack of books and a section of the wall shelves swung slightly open on greased hinges. The room inside was like a prison cell: small, barred windows high in the whitewashed walls, a table, two chairs and, at one end, a huge chest with three padlocks. Tallien deftly undid these and took out and placed on the table stacks of neatly piled documents. Segalla watched him curiously.

"These are all documents," Tallien announced portentously, "concerning the royal family's activities either here at the Tuileries or in the Temple. They are arranged in years. You will notice how, as the years proceed, the stacks of documents get smaller. This"—he hit one sheaf and a small puff of dust arose—"is 1790." Tallien walked round the table to a fairly thin stack. "This is 1795, the year our Dauphin died."

"Why?" Segalla asked abruptly.

"Why? Because he was ill-treated."

Segalla shook his head. "No, why did they put you in charge?"

The little man blinked. "All I know, monsieur," he replied, "is the world of books and manuscripts. During the Terror, as a young man, I hid in the Hôtel de Ville. Afterwards I entered the household of Madame Josephine."

"Napoléon's wife, the Empress?"

Tallien smiled, blinking shortsightedly. "Yes, yes. She was a great lover of books and built up an extensive library at Malmaison." Tallien's eyes misted over. "A lovely, gentle woman."

"They say she was murdered," Segalla declared.

The transformation in Tallien was wonderful to behold. He suddenly became very agitated and began arranging papers on the table, not daring to raise his eyes.

"Well, is it true?" Segalla asked.

"I don't know," Tallien mumbled, and glanced fearfully round.

Segalla picked up a pen lying on an inkstand. He seized a scrap of paper and wrote, *Are we being watched?*

Tallien glanced up; he shook his head but then tapped his ear. Segalla smiled. He knew of such chambers, impossible to contain a peep-hole but a gulley built in the wall could create an echo and allow people elsewhere to hear what was going on. Segalla pushed the scrap of parchment into his pocket. Tallien took a deep breath.

"Of all these documents, monsieur, the most important are those between July 1793 and June 1795. You know their significance?"

"Yes, 1793 was when the Dauphin was taken away from his

71

mother and given his own quarters under the care of the cobbler Simon. Of course the last date is when he died. Have you," Segalla asked, "studied these yet?"

"Oh no." Tallien's eyes became rounded. "That is not my task."

"But you are sure that every document is here?"

"Oh yes, Major, even Louis XVI's secret papers, those he kept in an iron box hidden in a wall in the Tuileries. They were later found by a servant. Robespierre used them in condemning the King to death. They are letters, memoranda, kitchen accounts, doctors' bills, receipts for items purchased. They'll tell a dreadful story." Tallien fished in his pocket and put on a pair of thin, wire-rimmed glasses. "So, Major, we should begin."

Segalla agreed. Through the half-open door of the secret chamber he heard a clock chiming the fourth hour as he and Tallien began to sift through a veritable sea of paper.

Segalla, who had his own information, began with those documents of July 1793 after the Dauphin had been taken away from his mother. At first, he studied them lacklustrely but then became more engrossed. In London he had been advised that the cobbler Simon and his wife had ill-treated the little prince, but these documents proved the opposite. They were medical bills: three doctors, at least, visited the royal child. They prescribed a water-bath with an infusion of veal, the juice of bats, frogs and other herbal potions when the young boy contracted a skin condition. A billiard table, thermometers for baths and changes of laundry, illustrated a comfortable lifestyle. There were food bills as well as receipts for nankeen breeches, velvet jackets, linen shirts, stockings and shoes.

"He seems to have been well looked after," Tallien murmured. "Look." He tossed a piece of paper over. "They even bought him a cage with mechanical singing birds."

"How was he guarded?" Segalla asked.

"There were sentries in the grounds and in the Temple itself whilst, every day, commissioners from each faubourg served a tour of duty which lasted a day."

They worked on, sifting through the mound of papers but, as they did and as the shadows lengthened, Segalla shivered; although the Dauphin was gone and the Temple was long destroyed, he felt as if he were imprisoned with that young prince who had been so cruelly snatched away from his mother. Glancing up at Tallien, he saw the little archivist was also disturbed by what he read.

"Never once," the archivist murmured, "did they allow him to see his sister?"

"Yes they did." Segalla picked up a grease-covered piece of paper. "This is a memorandum drawn up on 6 October 1794. I think you had best study it yourself."

Tallien did so: even in the poor light, Segalla saw his face pale.

"Mon dieu!" he breathed. "Major Segalla, what is this?"

"Just before they executed Marie-Antoinette," Segalla explained, "two of Robespierre's agents visited the Dauphin in the Temple. They were looking for evidence against the Queen and closely interrogated the boy in the presence of his sister. They made him say things against his mother, how she had initiated him into sexual practices and shared her bed with him."

Tallien threw the piece of paper down on the table.

"And the Dauphin agreed to that?"

"His signature is on that document," Segalla replied. "They made him confess that his mother was some corrupting Agrippina or Mesalina."

Tallien studied the documents again. "But the Dauphin's signature is shaky, irregular." His fingers flew to his lips. He picked up a leather-bound exercise book and placed it beside the document.

Segalla compared the two: the signature was not like the neat, regular handwriting of the Prince when he wrote his exercises for his father during the early days of their captivity.

"They probably forced him to sign," Tallien murmured.

Segalla returned to his search and, despite the apparent comfort and luxury in which the young prince lived, the ordeal definitely coarsened the boy. There was a report from a municipal officer that, when he visited the Temple, the Dauphin was playing with his gaoler Simon; on hearing a noise in the room overhead where his sister and aunt were imprisoned, the Dauphin exclaimed, "Aren't those damned bitches guillotined yet?" On another occasion, one of the doctors who visited the Dauphin found Simon trying to teach the young boy some indecent verses; when the little boy refused, Simon grabbed him by the hair and shouted: "You wretched viper! I would like to smash you against the wall!"

Segalla passed these across to Tallien who brushed away the tears brimming in his eyes.

"It's so cruel," the archivist whispered. "They killed his father and mother and, after 7 October 1794, never once did he see his sister."

He crossed to a table in the corner, filled two goblets with wine and handed one to Segalla.

"There's nothing," Segalla murmured, sipping at the cup. "After 19 January 1794 all the bills and receipts cease. Now, why is that, eh?"

Tallien couldn't answer so Segalla went back to the notes he'd made.

"Ah!" he exclaimed. "On that day, 19 January 1794, Citizen Simon gave up his custody of the Dauphin. A new law had been passed that no one could serve as an elected representative and be a public official at the same time."

Tallien nodded. "Yes. Look!" He threw a piece of paper across the table. "Simon's release from office."

Segalla studied the document which stated,

At 9 o'clock in the evening of 19 January 1794, Citizen Simon and his wife gave up their prisoner and left the Temple. The prisoner Capet was in good health.

"After that," Segalla explained, "every type of guardian and all kind of attention was, of course, withdrawn from the Dauphin and his sister. They were left alone, each in their room. No one had access, not even to make up their bed or remove or sweep up the dirt. Food was passed to them through a sort of revolving box which had been built in the doors of their chambers." He glanced up. "Some sort of wicket with a ledge. Food would be placed in it, then it would be revolved for the prisoners to take."

They returned to their researches but could find little new until 28 July 1794, some six months later, when, after the fall of Robespierre, Barras visited the prisoners.

"Here!" Segalla exclaimed. "This is the description left by Barras himself." Segalla paused to clear his throat: " 'I found the Prince in his cradle bed in the middle of the room. It was indescribably filthy, the windows shuttered up. He was drowsy and woke up with difficulty. He was dressed in breeches and a vest of grey cloth. Asked him how he was and why he didn't lie down on the big bed. The Dauphin indicated by signs how his swollen knees made him suffer when he stood so the little cradle suited him better. I then examined the Dauphin's knees. They were swollen as well as his ankles and hands; his face was also puffy and pale.' "

Segalla leaned back in the chair and whistled under his breath. "What monsters," he murmured. "So, we have the young Dauphin taken from his family and left under the custody of Simon from October 1793 to January 1794. Physically, he is well looked after though there is evidence that he was brutalised and kept separate from his sister. On 19 January 1794, Simon and his wife leave. The boy is left in a sealed room amidst terrible squalor with his food being pushed through a wicket gate. These conditions lasted for six months and, when Barras visited him in the summer of 1794, he finds a tall, sick, mute boy.''

"Perhaps," Tallien shrugged, "the Dauphin gave up the will to live so his body began to manifest clear signs of degradation.''

Segalla pushed the papers away. "I don't know about you, monsieur, but I can stomach little more.''

The little man rose and closed the door of the library.

"I would like to continue," he declared. "At least until . . .''

"Until what?" Segalla asked.

"Well, Robespierre's dead; Barras is in hiding. Simon went to the guillotine when Robespierre fell, his wife has died. Now, in two days' time, the secret court sits. Let's at least reach that point in time where we do have living witnesses who guarded the Dauphin.''

Segalla scratched his head. He was about to refuse but he felt a kinship for this eager, studious little man so he agreed. They worked on, building up a picture of the Dauphin's fate after Barras' visit.

"It would seem," Segalla muttered, "that Barras appointed a Créole from Martinique to look after the young boy.''

"I know of him," Tallien exclaimed.

"Of course." Segalla stretched, easing the cramp in his limbs. "You worked as a librarian at Malmaison for Josephine. She, too, was a Créole, a friend of Barras'.''

Tallien nodded.

"Tell me," Segalla asked. "Did you ever question your mistress about the Dauphin's imprisonment?''

Tallien put a finger to his lips, shook his head and went back to his work. A few minutes later he pushed a scrap of parchment across.

Not here, the note read. *But, later on, I have much to tell you.*

Segalla smiled his agreement. They continued and within the hour had produced a draft which showed that, once Laurens was appointed, the Dauphin's condition improved. He was moved temporarily into what had been his father's bedroom on the second floor of the Temple. A doctor attended to him, his sores were bathed and dressed. He was bought new clothes; his hair was cut and he was regularly bathed in herbal water. His room was scrubbed and cleaned, the door replaced and the windows thrown open.

"He was apparently bought toys, pencils and paper, even playing cards," Tallien declared.

"But the rooms must have been in a terrible condition," Segalla observed. "Laurens had to buy arsenic to kill the rats which disturbed the Prince's sleep at night. Nor is there any proof that the young Dauphin ever met his sister again."

"What's this?" Tallien exclaimed.

He pushed a warrant across the table, still bearing a red wax seal. Segalla studied it carefully. It was dated 1 August 1794, shortly after Barras's arrival, a short, terse note by Laurens demanding that

all papers, documents, manuscripts of the executed revolutionary and follower of Robespierre, the cobbler Simon, be seized.

Tallien waved his hand. "But I have never seen those papers. They are not here."

"Perhaps they were destroyed?"

Tallien winked at Segalla and tapped the side of his nose.

"Major, I am hungry: It is time we ate."

They cleared away the documents, secured the secret door, left the library and went down the stairs to the kitchens. They passed officials, arrogant in their own importance, gaggles of courtiers who brushed superciliously by them, their silk clothes drenched with perfume, their hair pomaded a silver-white.

They looked Segalla and his companion up and down and hurried by giggling, holding their scented pomanders to their noses as if Segalla and Tallien were some animals who had wandered in from the alleyways. Segalla would have loved to confront them but Tallien tugged at his sleeve and led him belowstairs. They went along galleries thronged with servitors and servants, each carrying trays of food: ham stuffed with cloves, seasoned with cinnamon and sprinkled with sugar; fillet of venison with truffles; partridge; beef flavoured with marjoram and surrounded with slices of pheasant sprinkled with tarragon and violets; chickens and capons specially cooked and stuffed with fresh oysters. Segalla's mouth watered. Tallien, however, led him past the kitchen and, taking a key out of his belt, stopped before a door, unlocked it and ushered his companion into the musty darkness.

Candles and lanterns were lit. Segalla stood by the door and watched the room being transformed by light. It was really no more than a cell, a deserted, whitewashed chamber with a table and two high-backed chairs at either end.

"It's my little hideaway," Tallien confessed. Then he clasped Segalla's hand. "I'm glad I'm working with you, Major. Even though you are English. They said you were strange but . . ."

"Who?" Segalla asked curiously.

Tallien dropped his hands. "Well, you know the gossips. But . . . never mind! Never mind!"

Like some flunkey in a restaurant, he ushered Segalla to one of the chairs. "Now, just stay there and I'll see what I can get."

Segalla sat down and Tallien hurried from the room, locking the door behind him.

Some time later, just as Segalla became a little uneasy, the door was unlocked and Tallien reentered. He was beaming from ear to ear, carrying a tray stacked with food: freshly baked bread, slices of ham, beef, capon legs, a dish of herbal sausages, two bowls of vegetables, knives and forks and two deep-bowled goblets. Tallien courteously served Segalla then held his finger up.

"Wait, there's more!"

He hastened away and reappeared with another tray, bearing two jugs of wine, one red, one white, and a dish of pudding coated with chocolate sauce. Tallien filled Segalla's goblet, locked the door and hurried back to take his own seat.

"I understand you English always like pudding after you have eaten. I ordered this specially."

Segalla sat back in his chair. "You are very kind."

His companion lifted his goblet and toasted him.

"Major, *santé*, let us eat and then we can talk."

Both men were hungry and the only conversation was murmurs of approval at the skill of the royal cooks. At last Segalla sat back, dabbing at his mouth with a napkin.

"You always dine here?" he joked.

"It's the one room in the palace," the archivist replied, putting his dishes away, "where I know you cannot be overheard. These walls are part of the foundations, the door is pure oak."

"There's only one problem," Segalla murmured, placing his cup down. "How can I trust you? And, more importantly, what makes you think you can trust me?"

In the candlelight he saw the hurt in the little man's eyes.

"I have lived through the Terror," Tallien murmured. "I survived one purge after another. You become like an animal, Major Segalla. You instinctively know when danger threatens. You are an English officer. You have no knife to . . ." He paused.

"To grind?" Segalla added.

"Exactly." Tallien refilled his own cup. "As for me, I am bound by a great oath to a beautiful lady."

"The ex-empress Josephine?"

"Yes. She was kind. She protected me. She let me live in a wonderful world of books."

"And did she ever talk about the Dauphin?"

"Only on her deathbed. You see, Major Segalla, after Napoléon's defeat in 1814, and the allied armies swept into Paris, Josephine was visited by the Emperor Alexander of Russia and other allied leaders at Malmaison. Now, up to that time, she had said nothing about the Dauphin but, with the allies determined to establish who should be the ruler of France, well, perhaps she became imprudent"—he lowered his voice—"and paid for it with her life!"

Chapter 6

The tears welled in Tallien's eyes. He looked nervously towards the door and blinked like an owl.

"Josephine," he continued in a whisper, "was a friend of Barras', who introduced her to the young Napoléon." Tallien spread his hands. "As you know, Napoléon overthrew Barras and sent him into exile." Tallien took a deep breath. "According to Madame Josephine, when he was in Brussels, Barras fell into conversation with one of her friends. He had been drinking heavily and exclaimed: 'I would like to live to see Bonaparte, that Corsican rascal, hang because of his ingratitude to me. I made him what he is and, in return, he condemned me to exile. However, his ambitious plans will all come to nothing: the son of Louis XVI is still alive.' " Tallien drank noisily from his goblet.

"Why are you telling me all this?" Segalla asked.

"Because I trust you. Because of my oath to Madame Josephine. You see, Major Segalla, when Alexander visited Josephine at Malmaison, she must have told the Tsar that the Dauphin had escaped. A few days later she fell ill. Some say it was a chill, others that she was poisoned. What I do know, monsieur, is that Josephine was watched by Decazes' spies and afterwards her papers were confiscated."

"But what proof," Segalla interjected, "is there for this? When did the Prince escape?"

"I don't know but, on her deathbed, Madame Josephine called me to her." Tallien pulled from the inside of his coat a gold-lined prayerbook. He rose and handed this to Segalla. "Josephine whispered," he continued, "that she was dying because of the Dauphin. I asked her what she meant but she just shook her head because there were others in the room. She pressed that prayerbook into my hands, smiled at me and bade me good-bye. I withdrew. A few hours later she died."

Segalla, curious, leafed through the prayerbook. However, set in elegant print with a few holy pictures, it was nothing more than a simple book of devotions. He handed it back.

"Aren't you frightened?" he asked. "The authorities would like to know what you do, not to mention the mysterious Monsieur de Paris."

"I have heard of him," Tallien remarked. He smiled faintly. "But who would suspect someone as insignificant as myself?"

"And you see no coincidence in your appointment?"

"I am a trained archivist, Major Segalla. Whilst I was at Malmaison my skill was brought to the attention of many great men. I am patronised. No one sees any danger in poor little Tallien."

Segalla rose and refilled their cups and then patted Tallien on the shoulder.

"I trust you, sir. So I shall tell you the little I know. The Dauphin apparently had a birthmark on his breast just above the left nipple so it looked as if he had two rather than one nipple. He also had a scar on his foot and a large inoculation mark high on his right shoulder. Did you know this?"

Tallien shook his head.

"One further thing," Segalla continued. "A year ago, a French officer, a Comte d'Andigne, was in London; he had dinner with the Foreign Secretary. Now, d'Andigne had been a prisoner in the Temple in 1802. One day, whilst digging in the grounds, he came across a skeleton of a child which had been buried in quick lime without a coffin. D'Andigne turned to an officer called Fauconnier and asked, 'Who is this?' Fauconnier replied, 'I am not sure but I think it's the Dauphin.' "

The excitement faded from Tallien's face.

"Don't you see?" Segalla explained, rising to his feet. "We know the Dauphin was separated from his mother in October 1793. From then until 19 January 1794, he was in the custody of Simon. But, from January of that year until the following July, he was kept in total isolation—that is, until Barras' visit. Now, a number of hypotheses are possible: First, that during Simon's custody the young Dauphin escaped and was replaced with a poor, sickly boy from some hospital. This was the creature whom Barras found: taller, covered with ulcers and scabs on his head."

"So, you agree?" Tallien cried, his fingers flying to his lips as if he regretted shouting. "The Dauphin may have escaped?" he whispered hoarsely.

Segalla shook his head. "Remember the papers we have read tonight, monsieur. Apparently Simon could be violent to the child. What happens if, in a fit of rage, he killed him? Buried the boy in the grounds of the Temple prison and replaced him with someone else? Was it his skeleton d'Andigne found?"

Tallien put his face in his hands.

"It's possible," Segalla continued remorselessly, "that Robespierre and his ilk would not want to publicise the fact that the young Dauphin had been brutally and mysteriously killed whilst in their care." Segalla sat down and drummed his fingers against the tabletop. "We did hear a rumour in London," he remarked quietly, "of a report by a member of the Revolutionary Tribunal, a man called Harmand of Meuse. He and others visited the young Dauphin on 19 December 1794; many years later Harmand drew up a report but no one can find it. I was given instructions in London to seek Harmand out but, apparently, others were more interested in him: A few weeks ago he was brutally murdered."

Segalla ran his finger round the rim of his goblet. "Well, I have no proof that he was murdered, but he did die mysteriously in a fire at his little hovel."

Tallien, who had his head bowed, looked up and grinned

slyly. "I, too, have heard of this," he remarked.

Then he got to his feet, took off his jacket and, with a small knife, began to unpluck the lining of its satin backing. He brought out a thin roll of parchment which he handed to Segalla.

"Read this, monsieur. But come," he added briskly. "Our meal is over. Read Harmand of Meuse' report at your leisure and then destroy it. It's only a copy of what he wrote in 1813."

"Where did you get it from?" Segalla asked.

Tallien blushed. "I stole it," he stammered. "I found it amongst Josephine's papers just after she had met Alexander of Russia. I was intrigued so I made copies. I never saw it again and, as I have said, when my mistress died, her papers were seized."

"How do we know other reports haven't been suppressed such as this or the papers of Simon the cobbler?" Segalla asked. "My masters in London were given a solemn promise that I would be allowed access to all materials."

"Do you really believe that?"

Segalla could not answer.

"In which case," he shook Tallien's hand, "I thank you for your company, your kindness and your hospitality."

Segalla left and, having asked directions from a servant, found his own way back to his chamber. He grinned at the guards lounging there.

"You were supposed to wait for us," the corporal grumbled. "I have been searching the palace for you."

"I didn't know you cared," Segalla retorted, and, before the soldier could think of a suitable reply, he opened the door and entered his room. He had brought his personal valise from the Lion d'Or and now his other baggage was piled neatly at the foot of the bed. Segalla checked this and locked the door. He then lit the lamps and sat at the table to study Monsieur Harmand's report.

We came to the door, Harmand declared, *behind the terrifying lock of which the sole innocent son of our King was confined, himself our King.*

Segalla smiled: Harmand must have written this when Robespierre and his gang had been removed. He read on.

The Prince sat beside a small four-cornered table on which were scattered a number of playing cards; some of these were folded so as to make little boxes or pockets; others were built up in the form of a castle. He was busy with these cards when we came in, and did not stop his game. He was wearing a sailor-suit made of a slate-coloured material; his head was bare; the room was clean and well-lighted. His bed consisted of a little framework of wood; the mattress and linen seemed quite good.

I approached the Prince. Our movements seemed to make no impression on him. I told him that the Government had been too late informed of the sad state of his health as well as of his refusal to take any exercise or to answer either the questions which were put to him or the proposals that he should take certain medicines and be examined by a doctor; that we had now been sent to him to obtain confirmation of these facts, and to repeat these proposals to him in the Government's name; that we hoped that he would assent to them, but that we took the liberty of advising him, even of warning him, against keeping silence longer and taking no exercise; that we were empowered to give him the opportunity of extending his walks and of offering him whatsoever he might wish to distract him and help him to regain his health; and that I begged him to give me his answer, if he so pleased. While I was in the course of making this little speech to him he gazed blankly at me without changing position. He was openly listening to me with great attention, but he gave no answer.

I therefore repeated my suggestions as though I thought he had not understood me aright, and explained them to him somewhat as follows: "*It may be that I have expressed myself badly, or that you, sire, have not understood my meaning, but I have the honour to ask you whether you would maybe desire a horse or a dog, a bird, or a toy of any sort, or one or two companions of your own age, whom we would present to you before they took up their abode here. Would you care now to go down into the garden or up the tower? Would you like sweetmeats, cake or anything of the sort?*"

I endeavoured in vain to suggest to him all the things which a boy of his age might covet, but I got not a single word or answer from him, not so much as a sign or movement, although he had his head turned towards me and gazed at me with a most astonishing fixedness, which seemed to express complete indifference.

I therefore allowed myself to take a more emphatic tone, and ventured to say to him: "*Sire, so much obstinacy at your age is an unpardonable fault; it is all the more astonishing since our visit, as you see, has the purpose of making your residence more agreeable, and of providing care for the improvement of your health. If you continue to give no answer, and do not say what you desire, how can we attain our end? Is there any other means of making these suggestions to you? Be so good as to tell us and we will arrange ourselves accordingly.*"

Always the same fixed gaze and the same attentiveness, but not a single word.

I began again: "*If, sire, your refusal to speak only touched yourself, we would wait not without concern but with resignation until it pleased you to break silence, since we must draw the conclusion that your situation displeases you less than we supposed, as you do not wish to leave the Temple. But you have no right over yourself. All those who surround you are responsible for your person and condition. Do you wish to compromise them? Do you wish to compromise ourselves? For what answer can we give the Government, whose agents we are? Have the kindness to answer me, I beseech you, or we shall be compelled to order you.*"

Not a word. Always the same immobility. I was on the verge of desperation, and my companion also. That look in particular had an extraordinary expression of resignation and indifference, as though it seemed to say: "What does it matter? Leave your victim in peace."

I repeat, I could not go on; I was near to breaking out in tears of the bitterest sorrow, but I took one or two paces up and down the room, recovered my calm, and felt myself impelled to see what effect a command might have. I made the attempt, set myself quite close beside him on his right hand and said to him: "Be so good, sire, as to give me your hand." He gave it to me and I felt it up to the armpit. I found a kind of knotted swelling on the wrist and another at the elbow. These swellings apparently gave him no pain, since the Prince seemed to feel nothing. "The other hand, sire." He gave me that too, but there was nothing there. "Allow me, sire, to examine your legs and knees as well." He got up. I found similar swellings on both knees and in the hollows behind the knees.

In this condition the Prince showed symptoms of rachitis and deformation. His thighs and legs were long and thin, and the arms also. The upper part of the body was very short, the breastbone very high, the shoulders high and narrow; his eyes were blue, the head was very handsome in all its details, the hair long and fine, well-kept and very light in colour.

"Now, sire, have the goodness to walk a little." He complied at once; walked to the door which lay between the two beds, came back again at once and sat down. "Do you consider, sire, that that is exercise? Do not you rather see that this apathy is the cause of your sickness and of the ills which threaten you? Be good enough to believe in our experience and our zeal. You cannot hope to restore your health if you do not follow our wishes and advice. We shall send you a doctor, and we hope that you will answer his questions. Give us at least a sign to show that you consent." Not a sign, not a word.

"Be so kind, sire, as to walk about once again, and for a little longer." Silence and immobility. He remained sitting on his chair

87

with his elbows propped on the table; the expression on his face did not alter for an instant. There was not the slightest movement to be seen in him, not the slightest surprise in his eyes, just as if we had not been there and I had not spoken.

My companion had kept silence; we were looking at one another in astonishment and were just about to exchange our opinions when his dinner was brought in. Another pitiful scene followed; one must have seen him to have an idea of it. We gave orders in the anteroom that the disgusting diet should be altered in the future, and that from that day some dainties, such as fruit, should be added to his meals. I wished that he should be given some grapes, as they were rare at that season. As soon as the order had been given we returned. The Prince had eaten up everything. I asked him whether he were pleased with his dinner. No reply. Whether he liked fruit. No reply. Did he like grapes? No reply. A moment later the grapes were brought and set on the table before him. He ate them without saying a word. "Do you wish, sire, that we should go away?" No answer. After this last question we went out.

Segalla pulled the candle closer and reread the document carefully, then sat back in despair. What have we here, he thought— a poor boy neglected, suffering sores—but what was so important about Harmand's report? The boy is taller but elongation of the limbs was one of the symptoms of rheumatoid arthritis. He would only move with great difficulty but there again, Segalla reasoned, if the boy suffered from some form of rheumatism or arthritis in the joints, the cramped conditions of his cell in the Temple would only have exacerbated such a malady. Segalla tapped the report with his fingers. Harmand of Meuse, he reasoned, had been an important revolutionary commissioner in 1794 but, if Tallien could be believed, this report had been drawn up in 1813, some nineteen years later.

"Now why should he do that?" Segalla murmured, staring into the candle-flame. For a while he tried to put himself in the place of the murdered revolutionary and went back to the beginning of the report, studying the sentences carefully. It's all a lie, Segalla reflected. I doubt if a man like Harmand of Meuse would turn up offering this and that, even promising to provide companions for the young Dauphin to play with. And why did Harmand keep emphasising the boy's silence? Harmand had written his report as if the boy had deliberately stayed quiet, totally obdurate in his refusal to answer the commissioners' questions. It's a pack of lies, Segalla decided; the whole report is a fiction.

He threw it down on the table. Harmand wrote it to defend himself, Segalla concluded; those who had accompanied him on his visit to the Temple were now dead so Harmand wished to present himself as a loving, caring man. Someone who tried to do his best for the Dauphin but was unable to, because the Dauphin himself refused to cooperate. Segalla smiled grimly. In 1813 Harmand must have read the signs of change: Napoléon's invasion of Russia had failed and the allied armies were threatening France itself. Harmand must have written his report in preparation for the Bourbons' return. Segalla sighed; yet, if it was a pack of lies, why was it so important Harmand had to be killed?

Segalla rubbed his eyes then returned to the report. Harmand claimed that he was unable to do anything because the boy could not speak. But that could be the result of intense fear. Segalla rolled the report up and hid it in the secret pocket of his cloak. He walked over to the elegant escritoire and sat down, pulling across parchments, inkpots and pens. He used his own leather folder to rest on: he was sure that everything on the desk would be studied when he left. He stared round the chamber, wondering if there were peepholes in the walls. If there were, he reasoned, the desk and chair, not to mention his bed, would be positioned to the invisible watcher. He got up and moved both the table and chair to a far corner so it was level with the wall which divided the room from the gallery outside.

After his meal and long day, Segalla felt sleepy, but he was determined to marshal his thoughts before he retired for the night. He picked up the pen and listed the principal dates and events of the Dauphin's life.

1785: Louis Charles born.

1789: Bastille stormed.

1790: Louis and Marie-Antoinette's attempted flight to Varennes.

1791: The attack on the Tuileries by the Paris mob.

1792: Royal family imprisoned in the Temple.

1793 (January): Louis XVI executed.

1793 (October): Dauphin separated from his mother and sister and put in care of Simon the cobbler.

1793 (6 October): Marie-Thérèse, the Dauphin's sister, sees her brother for the last time.

1793 (October): Marie-Antoinette guillotined.

1794 (19 January): Simon the cobbler relieved of his duties as guardian of the Dauphin.

Segalla leaned back in his chair and nibbled the tip of the quill. For the next six months, he thought, the Dauphin was isolated, kept like an animal in a single room. Segalla continued his list of dates:

1794 (17 June): After Barras's visit, the Créole Laurens is appointed.

1794 (8 November): Gomin is appointed to assist Laurens.

1794 (December): Harmand's visit.

1795 (April): Étienne Lasne appointed.

1795 (June): The Dauphin dies.

Segalla put the pen down and considered his conclusions.

"First," he murmured to himself, "the poor lad may have died; all these changes to his size and appearance could be due to the effects of imprisonment." Segalla wrote this down. "Secondly—" Segalla paused for a while, then his pen began to race across the parchment, writing in a secret cipher known only to himself:

> *The Dauphin was killed, or died of natural causes, and was buried*
> *secretly in the Temple. Thirdly, he escaped. . . .*

Segalla threw his pen down and walked over to the window and stared out into the darkness. A full moon had risen and, between the space in the buildings, Segalla could see the faint outline of trees. An owl hooted and, as if in answer, a dog in the royal kennels began to howl against the night. If the Dauphin escaped, Segalla reflected, then he felt it must have been just before or just after Simon was relieved of his command. He clenched his fingers: Yet Simon was dead, gone to the guillotine with his master Robespierre, and any secrets with him. There is no doubt, Segalla reasoned, that something in Harmand's report was significant. But what? He drew it out of his pocket, read it again, then, in frustration, refolded it and lay down on the bed considering the possibilities. His eyes grew heavy and he drifted into a deep sleep.

The next morning Segalla was woken early by sounds in the palace. He felt slightly thick-headed, rather hot, as he had slept in his clothes. From the courtyard below a trumpet blew as the royal guard were called to arms and the tolling of the bell from the parish church of the Tuileries echoed through the Palace. There was a knock on the door and a train of servants entered: a barber carrying a jug of water and a bowl; another servant bringing clean linen; another, fresh candles; and the fourth a tray of fragrant-smelling coffee, soft baked bread, a bowl of butter and a small tub of strawberry jam. Segalla protested but the servants were insistent. Segalla removed his shirt and allowed the barber to shave him, half listening to the man's chatter about the weather and who was visiting Versailles and how glad he was that the King had come back into his own. Every so often he would pause so Segalla could drink his coffee and nibble at the bread and jam the other servant had brought. At last he was finished. Another flunkey brought up jugs of hot water then they all retired, bowing and scraping, "to allow monsieur to finish his toilette." Segalla did, smiling to himself.

"Such luxury," he murmured, "is tantalizingly attractive."

He changed his clothes, dressing more soberly: his shirt with its high-necked collar, clean breeches, a waistcoat and knee-length jacket of dark blue which the servants had laid out on the bed and brushed before hanging in a cupboard with the rest of his clothes.

Segalla was about to leave, his valise under his arm, when he heard a commotion in the gallery outside; the guards snapping to attention, followed by a knock on his door which was then thrown back. A dark-haired woman, her dress covered by a bottle-green cloak, the deep hood drawn back to form a sort of halo around her head, swept regally into the room. Another woman would have followed but the lady turned and clicked her fingers.

"Non! Non!" she hissed imperiously. *"Toute seule! Toute seule!"*

The guard closed the door.

Segalla drew himself up and bowed. "Madame."

He stared at his visitor's pale face, her high brow, large eyes, imperious nose and the firm set of her thin lips and chin.

"You know who I am, monsieur?"

One hand came languidly forward, Segalla grasped and brushed it with his lips.

"Madame, you have me at a disadvantage."

"In which case," the woman replied, "That will be the first time in my life."

Segalla half guessed who she was but remained silent.

"I am Marie-Thérèse, Duchess of Angoulême, daughter of the martyred Louis XVI and Marie-Antoinette." Her voice was brittle, hard, as if concealing a maelstrom of emotion.

Segalla clicked his heels together and bowed from the waist.

"Your Highness, this is a great honour."

"No it isn't!" she replied, going over and sitting at the desk. "Oh, for God's sake!" she declared over her shoulder. "Come and sit by me! The palace is full of flunkeys all bowing and curt-seying whenever I appear!'

Segalla moved the chair to sit opposite, and stared at this re-markable woman. Marie-Antoinette's only surviving child, who had seen all horrors of the Revolution: the sacking of this palace in which she now moved like a queen, the Red Terror of Robespierre and the lonely imprisonment with her brother in the Temple.

"Highness, your English is very good."

"So is Her Highness's German," the Duchess replied with a half-laugh. "I have had plenty of time to learn, monsieur. Yes, yes." She continued without waiting for an answer. "Five years in imprisonment, sixteen years in exile." She played with a pen on the desk. "I am a relic," she remarked. "A leftover of a by-gone age." She looked up sharply. "I can see it in all their faces: 'Why didn't you die? Why come back and remind us about the Terrors?' "

Segalla sat quiet, recalling the advice he had been given in London. *"The Duchess walks on thin ice,"* Liverpool had re-marked. *"Some say she is only a short distance away from madness, haunted by nightmares of what happened to her brother and her parents. Be wary of her! Sometimes she will chatter about the past. At others she will become hysterical at even the slightest reference to it."*

The Duchess turned abruptly in the chair.

"You are wondering why I am here, Major Segalla?" She smiled conspiratorially but her light blue eyes remained icy dead, devoid of any emotion. "Don't worry," she whispered. "So far Monsieur Decazes has not reached this part of the palace. I doubt if there are any gaps between the walls." She leaned over and grasped the lapel to Segalla's coat, staring at him curiously like a child. "Did you know Maman?" she asked.

"On one occasion I had the honour, Your Highness."

"Yes, I remember that." She forced a laugh. "You age slowly, monsieur. You must tell me your secret. Maman never forgot her last meeting with you in the orangery."

Segalla went cold.

"Oh, don't worry," she whispered. "When you have been through what I have, monsieur, or is it now Major Segalla? Everything seems strange." Her voice rose. "Here am I in the Tuileries, first lady of the kingdom. Yet I remember when the mob swept in." She half cocked her head. "The baying of the Paris *sans-culottes* still echoes through the palace. They killed my dog," she continued slowly. "A little spaniel. Picked it up and smashed it against the wall! And there was a Hungarian, one of our footmen, he used to ride behind me. Tall as an oak, he was." The Duchess narrowed her eyes. "Resplendent in a blue-and-white uniform with gold facing. They caught him down near one of the lakes and cut his throat. They stripped his corpse and allowed some old women to play with him before they hung him upside down like a pig on one of the staircases." She shivered and blinked slowly like an owl, then rubbed her face. "I am sorry, Major." She sat upright, hands in her lap, brushing aside the folds of her cloak and revealing the purple silk gown beneath. She sat for a while, head erect, as if listening for someone. "They've sent you," she declared, "to look for my brother, haven't they?"

"Highness, your brother is dead."

"Is he?" She giggled, her fingers flying to her lips. "Oh, of course, he is. He is buried in quicklime in the common grave of Ste.-Marguerite."

"Highness, have you been there?"

The Duchess shook her head. "I can't understand that," she murmured. "Uncle has been back in Paris for some time." She stared curiously at Segalla. "He removed Papa's and Maman's bodies from the Madeleine and had them taken to St.-Denis where the other kings are buried. But nothing of poor Charles? Don't you think that's strange?"

Segalla watched as this young woman, probably in her mid-thirties, tried to make sense of the terrible past; her mind drifting in and out of the nightmare she had suffered.

"Your Highness—" He leaned over and touched her hand. It was like brushing ice. "Your Highness, why have you come here?"

The Duchess grimaced, running her lips between her teeth as if trying to remember herself. "I want you to find out," she declared. "I want you to find out what happened to poor Louis Charles. Did he die or did he escape? I know nothing." She clutched her throat. "I saw him in October of 1793 before Maman died. I remember quite clearly the night Simon and his wife left. I heard them moving boxes and trunks down the stairs but I never saw Louis again. I did not know he was ill or that he had died."

"Never once, Your Highness?"

"Never once were we allowed to meet, or walk, or play together. However, once he was dead, things changed. The guards were reduced. I was given a lady-in-waiting to attend me." She smiled. "A few months later I was provided with an escort to the frontier." She laughed abruptly. "I was handed back to what remained of my family."

"Your Highness," Segalla persisted, "what happened when your brother died?"

"I have already told you," she snapped. "Everything became more relaxed. I was given fresh clothes, toys, new servants. Those nice men, Gomin and Lasne, the last to look after my poor brother, they allowed me to see the records of his last few days."

"How old were you then, Your Highness?"

"I was fifteen. Yes, I think I was fifteen."

"Did you ever ask yourself why they did not allow you to visit your brother, even when he was dying?"

The Duchess, a dreamy look on her face, just shook her head. "Even before the Revolution," she whispered, "I hardly saw my brother. Maman kept him separate in her own household. He was my baby brother yet I hardly knew him. Perhaps that is why they never let me see him, even for the last time."

"But they broke their own law," Segalla insisted. "According to a regulation passed by the Revolutionary Tribunal in September 1792, a corpse had to be identified by the deceased's nearest living relative."

"Well, they didn't," the Duchess declared, flailing her hands like some young girl on the edge of a tantrum. She stared at Segalla then closed her eyes and stood, swaying for a while. "I shouldn't have come! I shouldn't have come!" she repeated. "I don't want to hear anything about this again!" She swept out of the room, slamming the door behind her.

For a while Segalla sat, trying to make sense of what the Duchess had said. He concluded she had come to plead for his assistance but couldn't abide the memories of the past. There was a knock on the door and Tallien entered. He looked as if he, too, had slept in his clothes, though he was shaved and cheery-eyed.

"You had a visitor?" the archivist remarked. "The Duchess of Angoulême?" He came over and sat down. "You found her?"

"Strange," Segalla answered. "A woman torn between desire to find out what happened in the past and a determination to utterly forget it." Segalla picked up his leather valise. "What I find strange," he continued, "is that here are a brother and sister locked in the same prison but they are never allowed to meet or even catch sight of each other. The brother dies, yet never once do his gaolers show the slightest compassion in allowing him a visit from his sister. Even when he is dying, she cannot make her last farewells. However, once he's dead—" Segalla got to his feet and stared down at the archivist. "Once he's dead, she's given her liberty, shown every courtesy, given every comfort." He bent down, his face only a few inches from Tallien's. "Do you know what I think, Monsieur Tallien? Indeed, believe? That the young man buried in the cemetery of Ste.-Marguerite is not the Dauphin. However"—he straightened up—"just what happened to the real Louis Charles Bourbon, Duke of Normandy, is a complete and utter mystery."

"And when do you think he escaped?"

"If he did escape," Segalla retorted, "then I suspect . . ." He paused and recollected the Duchess' words about Simon leaving the prison, the noise of their trunks and boxes being loaded on the carts. "I think he may have left the very night the Simons did because, for six months after that, nothing is heard of him."

Tallien smiled and looked over his shoulder at the door.

"And Harmand's report?"

"I couldn't see anything amiss," Segalla recalled.

"What's amiss," Tallien retorted, "is contained in a picture on the walls outside."

Chapter 7

They walked out into the gallery, Tallien warning Segalla to keep any comments to himself. In the small hallway at the top of the flight of stairs, Tallien stopped. He pointed to a portrait on the wall.

"This is a picture of the Dauphin," he murmured. "Doesn't he have beautiful dark hair?" And then, taking Segalla by the arm, they continued downstairs.

Segalla had to school his features as he suddenly realised the importance of Harmand's report, which had declared the Dauphin was fair-haired.

"When was that portrait painted?" he asked.

"In about 1790," Tallien replied, "when the young prince was at Versailles."

Instead of making their way to the library, they walked out into a small garden laid out in one of the great courtyards, squares of grass still white from the morning's hoarfrost. Around these were paths of crazed paving, leading to flower beds where the last straggling remains of summer slowly died in the cold morning mist.

"Keep walking," Tallien urged.

At last they reached the centre of the garden and stopped before a small fountain, a bowl on a plinth, with a statue of a rather battered Cupid in the centre. The stone was crumbling and covered in green lichen moss.

"Well." Tallien blew his breath out. "Now you can see why Monsieur Harmand was murdered."

"But you did say his report was drawn up in 1813?" Segalla pointed out. "He may have made a mistake."

"I doubt it. Look." Tallien drew out of his pocket a small leather pouch. "This is a lock of the Dauphin's hair, cut off by Dumont, one of the guards, when the doctors were making their postmortem." He cradled it in the cup of his hand.

Segalla's heart skipped a beat: The hair was fair.

"You are sure?" he asked.

Tallien nodded. "Now, monsieur, I have heard of children with fair hair turning dark but never dark hair becoming fairer. I have heard of the effects of the tuberculosis, rheumatism and arthritis, but the boy described by Harmand seems much older and taller. Now," he put the lock of hair away, "we are in agreement, eh? The boy Harmand visited was not the Dauphin."

The archivist whirled round as the two guards followed them into the garden.

"Wait inside!" he ordered.

"That would explain," Segalla declared, once the guards had left, "why I was attacked on the way to Paris. Someone in authority does not want this investigation to take place. It also explains the murders of Harmand and the grave-digger Betrancourt."

"Who?" Tallien asked.

"The man who dug the Dauphin's grave in Ste.-Marguerite cemetery. He was recently murdered."

"But what would a grave-digger know?"

"Where the body lies buried," Segalla retorted.

"And you think Monsieur de Paris, the leader of the secret Templars, is behind these murders? But why should he want to kill a grave-digger and an old revolutionary?"

They turned, walking back up the pavement towards the palace.

"If we could prove that Louis XVI's heir is still alive," Segalla replied, "if we can even hint at his whereabouts, then the Templar curse is not fulfilled."

"Even though Louis XVI's brother is now on the throne."

"For how long?" Segalla murmured, pausing before the door where the guards were standing.

Tallien shook his head. "Agreed, but we are investigating more than that: a real attempt to hide the true fate of the Dauphin."

He turned round and walked back along the path; although Segalla was now beginning to feel the cold, he followed him.

"Before I came here this morning," Tallien continued, "I made enquiries about what happened to Simon's papers which Laurens ordered to be seized." He raised his eyebrows. "There's no trace of them but I did discover two curious facts. First, Simon was forced to give up his custody of the Dauphin in the Temple because of a new regulation which debarred anyone elected to a committee from holding public office. Well, it would appear that, although Citizen Simon gave up his post as gaoler, he was immediately appointed as Inspector of Carriages."

"In other words," Segalla concluded, "he deliberately gave up his post and took up a new one which would allow him to transport anything he wanted in or out of Paris."

"Precisely."

"And the second thing?"

"Simon appears to have been a very strange character. He was a member of Robespierre's Jacobins, his hand turned against the King, the state and, above all, the Catholic religion. However, during the Terror, Simon would often go to hear Mass in one of the secret chapels around Paris. In other words, Simon may not have been the revolutionary he appeared to be. And one final thing, Major Segalla, it may not be important, but Simon owned two properties. He took lodgings very near the stables in the Temple grounds but he also had a house, even grander lodgings, at the old Franciscan convent in the Rue de Marat."

Segalla crossed his arms and looked across the gardens.

"Nothing is what it appears to be," he remarked. "Simon the revolutionary really is a secret Catholic and a property owner. It does make you wonder where he got the money to finance two homes. His stipend from the revolutionary committee would have been minimal and Robespierre's new currency, the Assignat, was not worth the paper it was printed on. Finally," he glanced at Tallien, "Simon leaves the Temple but buys lodgings nearby as if he wanted to eavesdrop on what was going on there. Now, two conclusions spring to mind. First, was Simon really a secret Royalist in receipt of bribes, who spirited the Prince away and then stayed nearby to see what would happen? Or, secondly, did he kill the young Dauphin, or allow the Prince to die, and stay near the Temple to make sure that the substitute child posed no problems?"

Tallien glanced quickly over his shoulder at the guards who were staring curiously through the French windows at them. "We cannot stay too long here," he murmured. "But one further problem remains. Let us say the Dauphin escaped—why didn't the Revolutionary authorities raise the alarm? Why substitute a child when they knew that, in a matter of months, perhaps even weeks, the real Dauphin might appear in England, or elsewhere, to be proclaimed as Louis XVI's rightful successor?"

"That, Monsieur Archivist," Segalla replied, "is the great mystery."

"Nor is it all," Tallien replied dolefully. He shivered and beckoned Segalla to walk back to the door. "What happens if the French authorities, men like Robespierre and the other revolutionaries, knew that the Dauphin was dead, murdered or died because of illness? They would not want the rest of Europe to know that a child left in their care had perished so miserably. We must never forget, the substitute child could have been a cover for all this."

Segalla closed his eyes, images floated through his mind.

"Did not a similar thing," Tallien continued, "happen in

your English history, Major Segalla? The two sons of Edward IV, the princes who disappeared in the Tower of London whilst under the care of their uncle Richard?"

Segalla frowned as he remembered Richard of Gloucester's white, pinched face; the secret passages, galleries and cells of the Tower and the dreadful secrets they contained.

"Major Segalla?" Tallien was staring up at him curiously.

"Why is your English so good?" Segalla asked abruptly.

Tallien blinked furiously and shuffled his feet. "Many years ago, just as the Revolution broke out, I married an English-woman, Priscilla Johnson." He sighed. "If you want to learn anyone's tongue, Major Segalla, live with someone you love who knows that language. Come, we should go!" He turned away. "We have only one day left and there is still a great deal of work to be done."

They reentered the palace and made their way back to the library, the two soldiers taking up guard on either side of the door. Inside, a servant had left a tray bearing a jug of hot coffee, a bowl of cream and some thin, baked pastries covered with marzipan. After their cold walk, they stood for a while clasping the steaming cups in their hands. Tallien then opened the secret door and they returned to their work of the previous day. Segalla realised that the reference to Priscilla Johnson had deeply upset his companion. For most of the morning he left Tallien alone as they sheafed through the papers regarding the Dau-phin's imprisonment.

Slowly but surely they drew up a picture of the last few months of the Dauphin's life. On 21 March 1795 the Créole, Laurens, had resigned his position, giving up his post to his as-sistant Jean Baptiste Gomin, aged thirty-eight years, son of a Parisian upholsterer, a member of the Revolutionary Guard. He was joined on 1 April by another keeper, Étienne Lasne, an ex-house painter who had also served on the Revolutionary Guard. Like Gomin, he too had seen the young Dauphin at the Tuiler-ies palace before he and the rest of his family had been imprisoned in the Temple. Segalla's heart sank when he read this. If these men had seen the Prince some three years earlier, surely they would have noticed that the real Dauphin had escaped and another substituted? Or were they, too, part of the great conspiracy to hide the true facts? Whatever, Gomin and Lasne had taken their duties seriously and did their best to ensure the Dauphin was well looked after. There were bills and receipts for jam and a pound of chocolate, asparagus and fish, linen ribbons, stockings and a new billiard table, toys and paper.

Segalla threw his pen down, leaned back in his chair and stared farther down the table where Tallien was busily writing. They were now working smoothly but silently together. Segalla would gather the different entries, bills of receipt, and pass them down to Tallien, who would arrange them into some sort of chronological order. In the last month of the Dauphin's life, as the boy's health began to deteriorate, the evidence began to accumulate. On 3 June 1791 a physician, Pelletan, a lecturer on anatomy at the School of Health, was called in to attend the Dauphin. There had been an earlier reference to this physician but now, in the first week of June, his visits became more frequent. Diets were recommended: meat; soup; boiled, roasted or grilled meat; and dishes of vegetables such as asparagus and spinach. Segalla sighed and continued; at last he reached 8 June 1795, the day the Dauphin died. A pathetic bundle of documents containing the death certificate and sworn declarations by several witnesses that the corpse was truly the Dauphin's. Segalla pushed them away.

"Monsieur Tallien!" he called out.

The archivist raised his head.

"To feed the body," Segalla remarked, "is to feed the mind. Shall we not stop and take some refreshment, perhaps a walk?"

"I am sorry I have been quiet," Tallien replied. "Priscilla was killed by a mob during the Terror." He shook his head. "No, don't apologise." He smiled weakly. "At least you know why my English is so good." He sighed and began to collect his papers. "But you are right, we are nearly finished. Tomorrow the secret court sits. Many of those who attended the Dauphin during his last few days will appear before it."

"And will you be there?" Segalla asked.

"I am its clerk."

"How long do you think it will last?"

Tallien lifted a finger. "One day. It will be presided over by Monsieur Decazes, ably assisted by Monsieur Fouché."

The mention of Napoléon's ex–Chief of Police recalled Bonaparte's reference to the murder at the château of Vitry-sur-Seine. Segalla waited until they had put their papers away and were walking down to the kitchens.

"I have something to ask."

"Then not here, monsieur," Tallien replied. "And let's not go to the room we visited last night."

Instead, Tallien collected some food: bread, cheese, a small tray bearing goblets and a jug of wine; and led Segalla back into the little garden where they had walked a few hours earlier. The guards, now bored by this routine, stayed inside whilst Tallien and Segalla went out to enjoy the weak sunlight. They sat on a stone bench near the fountain. Tallien poured the wine whilst Segalla shared out the bread and cheese. He nodded back towards the palace.

"It's very quiet. Apart from ourselves and the servants, everyone seems asleep."

"That's because they are." Tallien grinned. "Life is now one long round of pleasure, Major. But, by two o'clock this afternoon, the ovens in the kitchens will be fired. The flunkeys will appear, the courtiers will rise for their hot chocolate and sweetmeats, then eagerly prepare for tonight's banquet. I understand the King is hosting a banquet in honour of his generals. But, before you continue, Major Segalla, we are being watched. Don't look now but, when you have a moment, stare out at the window on your right, the second floor, the one at the far end. You will see a curtain move."

"Will they not interrogate you about what we talk about?"

Tallien bit the bread and chewed it carefully. "I am a small, fussy man, Major Segalla, who has spent most of his life fiddling with pieces of paper in dusty rooms and quiet libraries. They regard me as ordinary to the point of boredom. So, when they ask me, I will reply: 'Major Segalla is impatient with the task and wishes to return to England. We both believe that Louis Charles, Duke of Normandy and Dauphin of France, died in the Temple on 8 June 1795.' Now, Major," Tallien gestured with his cup, "what is your question?"

"Before I came here," Segalla replied, "I had a short but memorable interview with France's beloved ex-emperor Napoléon Bonaparte. I was ordered to interrogate him about the Dauphin's death. He told me very little but he did refer to a murder at the Château Vitry-sur-Seine which occurred about a year after the Dauphin's death. He intimated that Joseph Fouché knew something about it and that it might be connected with the matter in hand."

Tallien stared into his wine cup.

"I know nothing about such a murder though I will see what I can find out. The name does sound familiar. Madame Josephine mentioned it once. But what was it?"

For a while the archivist just sat.

"Ah!" he exclaimed. "That's right. Every 2 November, on the Feast of All Souls, Josephine asked for Masses to be sung. I'd draw up her list for the priest, there was always a reference to a Monsieur Petitval and his family and household at the Château Vitry-sur-Seine. Now, if I remember rightly, Petitval was a very, very wealthy banker. When Louis XVI was imprisoned, Petitval was one of those entrusted to look after the King's affairs."

"You mean his attorney?"

"Yes. Now, when the King died, Petitval left Paris for his château. Madame Josephine once told me that Petitval provided Barras with huge sums of money to assist him in his coup against

Robespierre." Tallien paused. "That's all I know but I'll do my own researches." He drained his cup and got to his feet. "It's time we returned."

They went back to the library and drew their researches to an end, studying carefully the events from 8 to 10 June 1795, when the Dauphin was buried.

"We'll be meeting all these," Tallien declared, running his fingers down a list of names, "at the secret tribunal. All those who were in attendance to the Dauphin."

"It would appear," Segalla remarked, "that the Dauphin died on the afternoon of 8 June but, for reasons of security, the National Assembly did not proclaim it until the ninth. Nevertheless, the Assembly acted quickly, for a postmortem was carried out by Pelletan, the latter's assistant Dumangis and two other doctors, Lassus and Geanroy. Listen, this is a report of their identification of the child." Segalla cleared his throat. " 'We arrived, all four of us, at eleven in the forenoon at the outer doors of the Temple, where we were received by the commissioners who led us into the Tower. In a room on the second floor we were shown the dead body of a boy who appeared to us to be about ten years old. We were told by the commissioners . . .' " Segalla looked up. "Those were the guards on duty at the time?"

Tallien nodded.

" 'We were told,' " Segalla continued, " 'by the commissioners that this was the son of the late Louis Capet. Two of us, i.e. Pelletan and Dumangis, recognised the child as the one to whom we had given our attention during the previous three days. The child's death must be ascribed to a scrofula of long standing.' " Segalla tapped the document. "This is not the original but only a copy of a report?"

"No, no, it is," Tallien interrupted. "Though you will find the death certificate is a facsimile.'

"What is interesting," Segalla commented, pointing to one of the phrases, "are the words 'Two of us recognised the child.' It seems to indicate that the other two were not sure or"—he tossed the document back on the table—"just didn't know. Finally," he picked up another piece of paper, "this is the Dauphin's death certificate." He read it out. " 'On the twenty-fourth of Prairial of the Year III of the Republic (12 June 1795). Certificate of the decease of Louis Charles Capet; age ten years, two months; born in Versailles, Department of Seine-et-Oise; resident at Paris in the tower of the Temple. Son of Louis Capet, last King of France, and of Marie-Antoinette of Austria.' " Segalla handed it to Tallien. "So it goes on; I wonder what happened to the original?"

"I think it was genuinely lost," Tallien replied. "Decazes said it was a copy made by some petty official and it's the best we have."

The afternoon drew on but, eventually, Segalla declared he could go on no further. "We are finished here," he declared. "Let us hope the secret tribunal is a little more forthcoming."

"It should be!"

Segalla spun round. Decazes, dressed in the most elegant of suits, stood leaning languidly against the door-post. Segalla quietly cursed; they had not shut the door and he wondered how long Louis XVIII's silent-footed minister had been standing there. Decazes walked into the room and sat down, pulling the tails of his coat over his lap. He raised the lorgnette which hung from his neck on a silver chain: he stared at Segalla then at the documents on the table.

"Did they tell you much?" He directed the question at Segalla; Tallien he totally ignored as if beneath his notice.

Segalla pushed the documents away.

"They tell us that the Dauphin was imprisoned in the Temple for almost three years. What he ate, how he was dressed, what medicines were given to him."

"And was it the Dauphin?" Decazes asked.

"There is nothing to the contrary," Segalla replied.

"And will you tell His Britannic Majesty's government that you were given every cooperation and shown every document?"

"What else can I say, monsieur? His Majesty's government," Segalla declared drily, "would be very angry if their envoy was not shown all the relevant documents and memoranda."

Decazes let the lorgnette fall and leaned his elbow on the table. "I know what you are thinking, Major Segalla, not to mention your masters in London. So, let me be frank. You must remember the Dauphin died twenty years ago." He smiled falsely. "Or at least we think he did. There have been successive changes of government in Paris and people become frightened. If," he emphasized, "there are gaps in the documentation, or biased reports . . ." His eyes slid towards Tallien and Segalla wondered if the minister knew about Harmand's report. "If such a situation existed"—Decazes' voice rose—"it's because there are many men in Paris, Major, who have a great deal to hide."

Decazes got to his feet and pulled a gold fob watch out of the pocket of his salmon-pink waistcoat. "If you are finished, then, Major Segalla . . . And you, Monsieur Tallien, must rest from your labours. Tonight His Majesty the King is hosting a banquet. Your presence is required. Now—" He clasped his hands together. "I really must go." And, with a sketchy bow, he walked as quietly from the room as he had entered.

Tallien waited until he heard the door of the library close.

"I suspect he is telling the truth," Tallien murmured. "And, Major Segalla, you must remember that tomorrow when the secret tribunal begins and those who attended the Dauphin are interrogated, they have a great deal to hide and may all sing the same song." Tallien gathered up his writing materials and smiled apologetically at Segalla. "I must go," he exclaimed, "but I shall speak to you tonight." He put the records back into their sealed trunks and coffers and scurried from the library.

Segalla followed him at a more leisurely pace. His escort were still waiting for him, lounging against the wall. The corporal looked bored to the point of distraction and stood cradling his musket, stroking his long, drooping moustaches. By the way he walked, Segalla guessed he was a veteran and must have served under Napoléon.

"Where to now?" the corporal snapped.

Segalla put his hand in his pocket and thrust a silver piece into each of the soldiers' hands. Their mood changed radically: smiles from ear to ear, muttered thanks and shuffling of feet. They readily replied to Segalla's questions.

"Yes," the corporal said, "we served with Napoléon." His face couldn't conceal the look of adoration. Then the soldier remembered where he was and coughed self-consciously. "We are happy enough now," he added. "Isn't that right, Gervase?"

His companion nodded.

"So, why are you here?" Segalla asked. "Why are you guarding me?"

"We are not guarding you, Major." The corporal replied so hastily Segalla knew he had been primed. "We were told to look after you, just in case."

"Just in case what?"

"I don't know, monsieur. I am a soldier, I carry out orders. Our officers told us that you were important and were not to be troubled. Those are our orders, so that's what we do."

Segalla, his happy escort trailing behind him, returned to his chamber. Even though he now had the key to the room, Segalla knew, by the way he had left it, that he'd had visitors during his absence. A chair slightly moved; the blotting pad on the desk had apparently been examined; even the bed had been shifted to see if there was anything underneath. He threw his leather valise onto a chair then over and looked out the window. He had been so enclosed at the Tuileries that the outside world seemed as far away as the other side of the moon. He noticed how the weather had changed: the sun was brighter yet, looking down into the courtyards, he could see the pile of golden-brown leaves accumulating as the autumn winds reaped their harvest.

Segalla recalled Marie-Antoinette and knew that, as matters stood, there was little he could do to discover the truth about the true fate of her son. There were hints, possible suspicions, but nothing definite. All those involved in the last year of the Dauphin's captivity did sing the same song: He suspected the same would happen when the secret court met the following day. "Something did happen," he whispered, watching a bird wheel and dive across the courtyard below. But what? Harmand's report was the only inconsistency yet that could easily be rejected. Harmand was dead and the report had been drawn up years later, so it could easily be dismissed or put down to a failure of memory. Segalla went and sat on the edge of his bed. Is that why, he wondered, neither he nor Tallien had faced any danger in their investigation? They were now following the party line. The Dauphin had been imprisoned in the Temple, he had died there and been buried in Ste.-Marguerite's cemetery. . . . Segalla scratched his chin.

But what would happen if the apple cart was upset? Would Louis XVIII and Decazes object or even obstruct his report? Or would Monsieur de Paris and the secret Templars show their hand? What difference would it make if they found out that the Dauphin had escaped? The Bourbons were back in France. Was it something else they wished to hide? Segalla recalled Napoléon's words about the murder at the Château Vitry-sur-Seine and a faint suspicion began to form in his mind. If Petitval, the wealthy banker, could provide Barras with the funds to overthrow Robespierre, was it possible that he bribed that corrupt politician to free the Dauphin? In which case, was the Dauphin quietly released and that sickly child put in the Temple in his stead, left in the care of men like Laurens, Gomin and Lasne?

Segalla got to his feet and began to pace up and down, forming the argument in his mind. What happens, he speculated, if the Dauphin did not escape whilst in the care of Simon but spent those six months in absolute seclusion? Perhaps Simon, that revolutionary cobbler, became disillusioned with Robespierre and his party. Perhaps he returned to the Catholic faith and attended Mass to seek forgiveness for his sins? Did his masters discover this, remove him from the Temple and give him another post—Inspector of Carriages? Simon, however, may have formed an attachment to the young Dauphin and bought lodgings near the Temple so as to keep an eye on his former charge. Segalla sat down at his desk.

"It's possible," he whispered, "that the Dauphin was left to his own devices for six months, but what would happen then?"

Barras, he thought. Barras was bribed by Petitval. He went to the Temple by himself; now Master of Paris he could do what he liked. He removed the Prince, put in that sickly child and then sent the Dauphin to Petitval. But why the murders there? Did someone else find out? Or did Barras double-cross everyone? Did he hand the Dauphin over and then order troops or a gang of desperados into the area? Segalla breathed in deeply to control his excitement. Or was Barras a secret Templar? Did he have the Dauphin removed and then kill Petitval, his household and family, including the young Dauphin, and so seal everyone's fate? Segalla sighed. But what could he do?

For a while Segalla pondered the possibilities then decided to wait, at least for a while. He would eventually make a decision, either keep the information secret or return to England and declare his suspicions to Lord Liverpool.

"I will wait awhile," he murmured. "And, like everyone else, keep my cards close to my chest."

He spent the rest of the afternoon closeted in his chamber, going over what he and Tallien had found, listing his questions for the secret court. The day drew on, the sun began to set and, from the noise outside, Segalla guessed that preparations for the banquet were now fully under way. He went down to the kitchen, now a hive of activity, for something to eat and then returned to his chamber where he washed, shaved, and changed into his best clothes. At last Tallien arrived, his face flushed with excitement.

"You are not excited about the banquet?" Segalla asked.

Tallien winked slyly back. "We'd best go," he said.

Segalla followed him out of the gallery and down the stairs, thronged by a glittering array of courtiers and officers in full dress uniform. Candles and lanterns had been lit, carpets rolled out and, the farther they went through the great halls, the more packed the corridors became. Men in gorgeous dress, their ladies in silks of every hue. Footmen, flunkeys and servants, resplendent in blue-and-gold livery, scurried along the corridors lined with guardsmen dressed in full regimental uniform. The musicians in the different galleries played softly, the tunes almost drowned by the excited babble of conversation.

"Well?" Segalla asked. "What have you found?"

"A little about the murder at Vitry-sur-Seine," Tallien replied, without turning his head. "But, more importantly, Major Segalla, do you realise never, throughout the Dauphin's imprisonment, did his uncle, our present king, offer one sou for his freedom?"

Chapter 8

Segalla hid his surprise. "Never once?" he exclaimed hoarsely.

"Keep your voice down!" Tallien hissed as they moved into the main salon.

No one, however, in that packed, heavily-scented room, spared them a glance as everyone watched where King Louis, clothed in purple silk, sat enthroned on the great dais. He slouched on a jewel-encrusted silver throne under a huge white canopy decorated with golden fleurs-de-lys. The King was not in good humour but glowered round like some spoilt boy, his old raddled face coated with a thick white powder; his fleshy lips were painted carmine-red and black beauty spots, in the shape of hearts, had been placed high on his fat, painted cheeks. Beside him, sitting on a smaller throne, sat Marie-Thérèse, Duchess of Angoulême. She reminded Segalla of some china doll: her face was pastel white, her cheeks rouged, her head rigid, eyes staring at some point far down the hall. Around them flitted the courtiers and ministers who, in the shimmering light of the chandeliers, looked like myriads of pretty butterflies.

"The King is not amused," Tallien whispered, steering Segalla towards the buffet tables. "He wishes to put the clock back a hundred years. He cannot stand the word 'Parliament' but his ministers and generals are insisting he call one."

"And Vitry-sur-Seine?" Segalla asked, confident that the hubbub of conversation around them would deter any eavesdropper or professional spy.

"Ah, that's a mystery," Tallien replied. "As you say, the château was owned by Baron Petitval, a renowned banker and a very wealthy financier. He and his family were murdered there in the spring of 1796."

"And?" Segalla asked.

"Well, that's the mystery. Despite being an important man, no investigations into such a horrible crime were carried out, or, if they were, the reports have long disappeared."

Segalla followed Tallien into a corner of the salon.

"Smile," Tallien murmured, "as if we are gossiping about the weather. The curious thing," the archivist continued, "is that Petitval, his mother, maids and servants were all murdered. Their corpses were discovered by the local cure. The château was ransacked but nothing was stolen. What do you make of that, eh, monsieur?"

"What I think," Segalla replied, "or am beginning to suspect, is that the young Dauphin was taken out of the Temple by Barras."

"Barras!" Tallien exclaimed.

Segalla's grin widened. "Follow your own advice. Keep your voice down! Yes, I think Baron Petitval bribed Barras: the Dauphin was sent to Petitval's château at Vitry-sur-Seine and that was the reason for the attack."

"But who would carry out such a terrible murder?"

Segalla paused as a gold-coated flunkey brought across a tray of goblets. Both he and Tallien took one.

"There was civil war raging in Normandy at the time," Segalla continued. "Bands of armed men, outlaws and felons, roamed the highways plundering at their will. Perhaps one of these was paid to attack Petitval's château and kill the Dauphin?"

"But the corpse of a ten-year-old boy," Tallien broke in, "was not listed amongst the dead. The local priest, a man of integrity, would have noticed that."

"Perhaps the child was abducted and either imprisoned or murdered elsewhere. Who knows? Barras might have double-crossed the man who gave him the money to overthrow Robespierre. Perhaps he handed the child over and despatched those outlaws to get him back?"

Tallien shook his head. "I can't accept that," he murmured. "If Barras removed the Dauphin then he must have put that sickly child in the Temple. Surely people would have recognised the difference?"

"Ah, but they did. The reports after Barras' visit are of a very sickly child, a sharp contrast to the vigorous, healthy, young boy who, despite a few minor ailments, was imprisoned in the Temple under Simon's custody."

"But you've seen some of the reports and you'll question witnesses tomorrow," Tallien observed. "Time and again these witnesses maintain that the child in the Temple was the same they had seen playing in the gardens of the Tuileries a few years earlier."

Segalla found he couldn't answer that. He glimpsed Decazes and Fouché standing together at the far end of the salon, so he smiled and, whispering to Tallien to follow, walked across to greet them. Decazes was dressed in a mode Beau Brummel would have envied: medals and stars emblazoned across his silk jacket, the cross of Saint Louis hung on a silver chain round his neck. Fouché, however, looked like some bad-tempered crow: shoulders hunched, head stooped—he was, except for a high-collared white shirt, dressed in black from head to toe.

"Your researches are finished, I understand." Decazes limply shook Segalla's hand. "And tomorrow you join Monsieur Fouché and myself in our secret court." He glanced pointedly at Tallien. "Whatever is said there is a matter of state secrecy. Everyone will take a great oath."

"But I," Segalla retorted, "must make a reply to my masters in London."

Decazes waved jewelled fingers and smiled dazzlingly. "Là, man, don't be such a bore! Of course you can. And what will you be reporting to Lord Liverpool?"

Segalla shrugged. "From what I have seen, I shall report that the Dauphin, for a short period Louis XVII of France, apparently died in the Temple on 8 June 1795."

Only a flicker in Decaze's eyes betrayed his elation at Segalla's reply.

Any further conversation was impossible as the orchestra struck up. The courtiers separated like colourful waves and the King, wheezing and grunting, eased himself out of his throne to begin the dancing. Tallien drifted away and, after a while, Segalla became so bored he decided to return to his own room. He was almost out of the salon when he heard his name called and Madame Roquet, dressed in a white, high-waisted gown, swept towards him; Jacques de Coeur and the yellow-coated Canary followed behind. Roquet looked splendid in a white headdress decorated with green feathers; she wore long gloves of the same colour and busily brushed her pink cheeks with a gold fan.

"Major Segalla." Roquet's eyes sparkled and Segalla wondered how much she had drunk. "You did not seek me out?" she simpered.

"Madame, I did not know you were here. My apologies."

Segalla glanced over her shoulder at Jacques de Coeur; his hair frizzed, he was dressed in a plum-coloured frock coat, tight-fitting breeches of the same colour, silk white stockings and black pumps. His shirt collar stood so upright it touched his cheeks whilst his huge neckcloth, folded in the form of a cravat, tilted his chin and gave him a heavy-eyed, arrogant look.

"God save us!" De Coeur pouted, looking Segalla up and down from head to toe. "Major Segalla, this is a ball, not one of your English tea shops." He brushed by Roquet and tapped Segalla on the chest. "You should have come to me. I could have advised you on the correct 'ton' for such gatherings." He raised his lorgnette and peered at Segalla's jacket. "Lord save us!" he whispered. "We can't let this happen again."

Roquet playfully pushed him aside. "Jacques, behave yourself. The English are noted for their sobriety, particularly their officers. Tell me, Major," she continued breathlessly, "has your stay at the Tuileries been useful?"

"Yes, madame, it has."

"And, sir?"

Segalla pulled a face. "I cannot answer here, madame." He bowed. "Except I think Lord Liverpool was much mistaken in sending me to Paris."

Madame Roquet tapped him playfully on the cheek, though her eyes were now hard. "I don't think so," she murmured. "*Viens*." She turned to de Coeur. "*Mon lys noir*." And, kissing Segalla quickly on the mouth, swept back into the crowd.

Segalla crossed to the buffet tables and tasted the delicious pâté de foie gras and slices of smoked salmon. A rather drunken young girl with a décolletage which barely restrained her thrusting breasts, waylaid him near the doorway, teasing and flirting. Segalla courteously declined her offer to dance and mentioned a pressing engagement, regretting he could not join her out on the terraces under the moonlight. The woman pouted and flounced away. Segalla left the hall and walked up the great staircase which spiralled through the palace. He was surprised he could find no trace of his usual armed escort.

"Not the time to complain," Segalla murmured to himself.

At last he reached his own gallery, deserted and silent, washed by the moonlight pouring through a casement window at the far end. Segalla took the key out of his pocket. He was just about to unlock his door when he heard the click behind him. He moved sideways and the assailant's knife smashed against the door.

Segalla turned. All he could see in the faint light was a masked, hooded figure, a sword in one hand, a knife in the other. Segalla edged backwards. The man silently made to follow. Segalla glanced around. He was unarmed: no sword, no dagger, but then he glimpsed a brass warming-pan hanging on a hook against the wall. He grabbed this and, as he did so, his attacker moved in but Segalla was too quick. The assassin's knife hit the brass then he backed away. Segalla, feeling slightly ridiculous, held the warming-pan before him. The attacker was about to close again when there was a sound of hurrying feet and muttered oaths. The assassin turned and disappeared down the gallery. He fled up another flight of stairs, his leather-soled boots masking any sound just as the corporal and his companion made their appearance.

"Major, what's wrong?"

Segalla shook himself, he was still in a fighting stance, the warming-pan held up before him. He sighed, dabbed at the sweat which had broken out on his face, and thrust the warming-pan into the surprised soldier's hand.

"Nothing," he murmured. "Why, did you see anything?"

The soldier shook his head.

"I have drunk too much wine," Segalla muttered. "I thought someone was coming up behind me. By the way, where were you?"

"Looking for you," the corporal replied. "But then we saw your friend the archivist. He said that you had probably returned to your room, so we followed."

Segalla wished them good night. He entered his chamber, locking the door behind him. He lit the candles and lamps and stared round. Nothing had been disturbed. He pulled off his jacket, loosened his shirt collar and collapsed onto the bed.

Why had the assassin struck then? he wondered. Who had sent him? What did they hope to achieve? After all, both he and Tallien were singing the same song. They had discovered nothing to suggest that the Dauphin had escaped from the Temple. But could Tallien be trusted? Segalla recalled the archivist's face: years of living in the shadows had sharpened Segalla's wits yet, if Tallien was a traitor, then it would not be the first time he had been so disastrously wrong. And if it was not him? Someone else must know that neither he nor Tallien accepted the usual story about the Dauphin, and wished to prevent any further progress in the investigation.

Segalla smiled grimly into the darkness. He would never die, not yet. Some chance or luck always turned the dagger or jolted the aim of the would-be murderer. Oh, he had received wounds, his body was a crisscross of scars. They always healed, but he could still bleed and hurt as much as the next man. Segalla breathed slowly, calming his mind, clearing it of all distraction. Whatever Tallien said, Segalla really did believe that the murderer at the Château Vitry-sur-Seine in 1796 was linked to the fate of the Dauphin. But, even if he could prove it was, what next? His eyes grew heavy, even as he vowed that the next time he met Monsieur Decazes, he would ask him bluntly why his master Louis XVIII had not tried to ransom or free his nephew.

"Because it was impossible."

Decazes looked quizzically at Segalla as they gathered in the library the next morning. Segalla had risen early, washed, shaved and broken his fast. His escort, which had now been changed, two simple soldiers from the regiment of line, had taken him to the library where Decazes and Fouché were sitting at the table sipping their morning coffee. Fouché seemed no different, but Decazes looked pale-faced, black rings round his eyes as if he was still suffering from the effects of a long drinking bout. Segalla wished them good morning then bluntly asked the question which had bothered him the previous evening. He now glanced at Decazes, his face a mask of disbelief.

"What do you mean, Louis XVIII couldn't intervene for his nephew?"

Decazes put his cup down. "Major Segalla, for almost a quarter of a century the Comte de Provence, Louis XVIII, was in exile. He was a penniless refugee at foreign courts, despised and hated by the revolutionaries in Paris. Why should they listen to him? What could he offer them in exchange for the Prince's life?" He wagged a finger. "Monsieur Fouché would agree with that, wouldn't you?"

His companion just pulled a face, shrugging a shoulder as if it was a matter of little import.

"What did happen," Decazes continued, "is that the Bourbons of Spain, King Charles in particular, entered into negotiations with Barras and his gang to free the Dauphin. He offered lands in dispute between Spain and France, as well as his solemn oath that, if the Dauphin was released and handed over to the Spanish court, he would never be used against the government of France."

"And?" Segalla asked.

Decazes pulled a mouth. "Negotiations took too long. By the time they were completed, the Dauphin was dead."

Segalla decided to press matters further. "But when Louis XVIII returned, he ordered funeral Masses to be sung for his dead brother and Marie-Antoinette. Why not for his nephew the Dauphin?"

"Are you a Catholic?" Decazes asked abruptly.

"Well, yes." Segalla stammered. "But I . . ."

"But you don't practise!" Decazes declared. "Eh? But, if you did, Major Segalla, you would know a little more about your faith. The Dauphin, Louis Charles, was only a babe when he died, an innocent little child. What need of Masses for a soul which would go directly to God? And why should my master stir old memories and hatreds? The Dauphin is dead, God rest his soul! This court as well as your own searches will prove that."

Segalla glanced quickly at Fouché: his obsidian eyes gave away nothing but his mouth curled into a sardonic smirk which said more than all Decazes' protestations. Segalla did not know whether he was mocking Decazes or, being a once avowed atheist, Fouché was sneering at the whole idea of religion.

The tension was eased as Tallien joined them, nodding and bowing; he hardly looked at Segalla. A cure from the royal chapel followed him, a stole round his neck, preceded by two altar boys carrying candles; they were dressed in black cassocks and white surplices. The cure placed a copy of the Bible covered in red moroccan leather with gold embossings on the end of the table. Decazes, Fouché, Segalla and Tallien each took the oath dictated in a soft voice by the weak-faced cleric. When the priest left, Decazes ordered the Bible to be left where it was. He sat at the far end of the table, Fouché and Segalla on either side, Tallien down the middle.

Decazes, his eyes still bleary, pulled out a proclamation issued by "our beloved Louis, King of France, etc., instructing a Secret Court to sit: to hear, accept all evidence and question all witnesses regarding the death in the temple of his much beloved nephew Louis Charles, Duke of Normandy and, during God's brief favour, Louis XVII King of France."

Fouché lounged as if he had been forced to watch some boring scene at an opera. Tallien kept his head bowed, already writing, his pen skimming across the page of the ledger. Once Decazes had finished, he tucked the proclamation into the vest of his coat and gestured at the officer standing just inside the library.

"Captain, leave and close the doors. Allow no one in!"

The soldier obeyed and the library fell strangely silent.

"This court is being held in camera," Decazes abruptly announced. "Its proceedings are most secret. You are sworn to confidentiality except for Major Segalla, envoy of His Britannic Majesty's government. However," Decazes smiled sideways at Segalla, "His Britannic Majesty's government has given us a guarantee that whatever they learn will be kept confidential." He snapped his fingers at Tallien. "That ledger will be given to me at the end of this day's proceedings. Now," he continued briskly, "let the court begin!"

After such a dramatic declaration the first witnesses proved something of an anticlimax: old men, most of them in their mid-fifties or early sixties, some dressed shabbily, others trying pathetically to impress their betters by appearing in tawdry finery. All were frightened. Segalla studied them curiously; relics of a bygone age, these men had once been commissioners representing the forty-eight sections of revolutionary Paris. They had served on the dreaded Committee of Public Safety, the Revolutionary Tribunal or the radical, anti-royalist Paris Commune. Some of their colleagues were long dead or had gone into hiding but these had been rounded up by Decazes' secret police and were compelled to give evidence. One by one they shuffled into the room, bobbing and curtseying, their dusty, dirty faces streaked with sweat. The ritual was always the same: Tallien would read the oath out. Each, in turn, would take the oath, one hand pressed against the Bible, then the questioning would begin.

"What is your name? How old are you? What was your occupation in 1795? Did you serve as a commissioner at the Temple?"

Tallien would write down the details and then Decazes would ask more questions.

"You spent a day as a guard at the Temple when the Dauphin was imprisoned there?"

"Yes, Your Honour."

"And you saw the Prince?"

"Yes, Your Honour."

"Describe him."

The answers were usually the same. A sickly boy with a dull, dead look, shoulders hunched, chest contracted, legs and arms thin and wasted. Some of the witnesses would add how the Dauphin had tumours on his right knee and left wrist.

"Tell me." Decazes would lean forward. "You have heard the rumours? How the real Dauphin escaped from the Temple and was replaced by some sickly boy from a local hospital?"

Most of the witnesses just shook their heads. One, Galliard from the parish of St.-Sulpice, was more forthcoming.

"Impossible," he declared.

"Why is that?"

Segalla tapped the desk. Galliard narrowed his eyes.

"You are English?"

"I have already explained Major Segalla's presence here," Decazes interrupted.

"No, Your Honour," Galliard replied defensively. "I merely mention this because, before the Revolution, I served as a gardener here at the Tuileries. Many Englishmen came to pay their compliments to the King before he and his family were moved to the Temple. I thought I recognised the Major. I have an excellent memory."

"You said it was impossible," Segalla remarked abruptly.

"Because," Galliard replied, "the Revolutionary Tribunal put me in charge of the guard at the Tuileries. I often saw the King, God rest him, and his family. What I am saying, Your Honour, is that the child I guarded in 1795 and the child I saw at the Tuileries in 1792 were one and the same person."

Galliard's testimony was corroborated by other witnesses and, as the morning drew on, Segalla tried to hide his despair. Now and again he would catch Tallien's eyes: the archivist shared his mood. Segalla realised these witnesses were terrified. They had served the Revolution, they would be like putty in the hands of a man like Decazes. They were all so cooperative, providing meagre details about the last few months of the Dauphin's life, but insisting, time and again, that he truly was the son of Louis XVI.

One of the most eloquent witnesses was a shambling old man, his shabby coat covered in snuff. Bellanger had once served Louis XVI as an architect but, falling on hard times during the Revolution, he had joined the Revolutionary Guard and also served as a commissioner at the Temple.

"Oh yes." Bellanger sat, his hand cupped to his ear. "Oh yes," he bellowed. "The child I saw in the Temple in the early months of 1795 I recognised: He was sickly, paler, taller, but he was Louis XVI's son and I can prove it."

The library fell silent. Bellanger stooped down and picked up a battered leather sack, untying the cord at the top. He pulled out a small, carved marble bust of a young boy's head and neck.

"When I went home," the old archivist trumpeted, "after my duty here, I carved this true likeness of the Dauphin."

Decazes told Tallien to bring it down for further inspection.

"It's a gift," Bellanger continued to bellow, "to His most Catholic Majesty."

Decazes, Fouché and Segalla ignored him as they examined what was probably the last likeness ever made of the imprisoned Dauphin.

"It's truly him," Decazes murmured.

Segalla stared, admiring Bellanger's handiwork. He recalled Harmand's report about the Dauphin: a thin, rather angelic face, beautifully formed head, hair swept back, falling down over the ears and the nape of the neck. The carved face had the look of sadness but even the most superficial scrutiny revealed a similarity to paintings of the Dauphin and even to the dead Louis XVI and Marie-Antoinette.

"Are you sure, Monsieur Bellanger?" Decazes asked. "This sculpture was done in the spring of 1795?"

"I can swear to it," Bellanger replied. "I can produce many witnesses that, for the last twenty years, that bust has stood in a place of honour in my house."

Bellanger was thanked and dismissed; Decazes promised the King would accept the bust and send a token of his appreciation to the old architect. Once he had left, Fouché rose, stretched and pointed to the tall, elegant Swiss clock which stood in one corner of the library.

"Gentlemen, it is well past noon and I am hungry."

Segalla watched Napoléon's old fox curiously. Never once had he asked any questions but, throughout the whole proceedings, had just sat as if lost in his own reverie. You don't care, Segalla thought, you think this is a farce. But why?

Decazes, who was now apparently enjoying himself, loudly agreed with Fouché. He rubbed his stomach and glanced at Segalla.

"If an army marches on its stomach," he declared, smirking at Fouché, "then so do His Majesty's judges. A good morning's work, eh, Monsieur Segalla? We will have lunch and resume at two o'clock. Tallien will look after you."

Decazes and Fouché left. Tallien and Segalla went down to the kitchens where a chef served them lunch at one of the tables. They ate in silence: only when they walked into the park to enjoy the stiff breezes did they dare to speak.

"We are finished," Tallien said. "This is only going to end with one verdict: The Dauphin was imprisoned in the Temple where he stayed until he died. Oh, I agree, those witnesses wished to impress. They want the likes of Decazes to forget their revolutionary days. But men like Bellanger are not lying. The boy they saw in 1795 was the same they glimpsed at the Tuileries two or three years earlier."

"Isn't there anyone," Segalla asked, "who knew the Dauphin from the time of his birth, who was present when he died in the Temple?"

Tallien shook his head.

"Yet, something happened," Segalla insisted. "Fouché knows it! God rest her, Madame Josephine knew it! I also believe Decazes and his master, Louis XVIII, are party to the secret. I was attacked last night," he added quickly.

"Attacked? Where?"

"When I returned to my room during the banquet. Someone was waiting in the passageway."

"But that's impossible." Tallien scratched his cheek. "The palace is closely guarded. Your assailant must have been one of the guests. And what about your escort?" Tallien jabbed his thumb over his shoulder. "Even now you are being watched."

"In ancient Rome," Segalla replied, "when someone was assassinated the guards were always withdrawn. Last night mine apparently became lost."

"Yes, I saw them looking for you," Tallien replied. "But whom do you suspect?"

"I wondered about Decazes," Segalla replied. "Though I don't think either he or Louis XVIII would like to explain to the British prime minister why an English envoy was murdered in the royal palace of the Tuileries. I merely mention it," he continued, "because someone wishes to prevent me from continuing this investigation." He glanced quizzically at Tallien.

The archivist puffed his little chest out. "Don't think that, Major," he replied softly. "I am no spy. I, too, am under oath—to Madame Josephine."

Segalla grinned and patted him on the shoulder. "In the dark," he murmured, "it is difficult to tell friend from foe."

A bell began to chime.

"Come!" Tallien urged. "Perhaps this afternoon's session will not be so straightforward."

On their return the archivist was proved right. Decazes announced that they would now interrogate the Dauphin's last two warders, Gomin and Lasne, as well as the surgeon Pelletan, who not only tended the prince in his last days but also conducted the postmortem. Segalla realised he was now entering the eye of the storm. These were not commissioners who spent a day in the Temple, but men who had lived with the Dauphin, important nominees of the Revolutionary government. However, the first one, Jean Baptiste Gomin, did not look the part. An old man with a dried, seamed face and straggling grey locks, he shuffled into the room, chin pressed to his chest, hands hanging by his side. He took the oath in a lacklustre manner and sat down, staring fixedly at the tabletop. Decazes had to tell him twice to sit upright and speak more clearly.

"I am Jean Baptiste Gomin."

"And when were you appointed as the Dauphin's warder?"

"On 8 October 1794. I took the job reluctantly," he hastily added, wetting thin, bloodless lips. "I was to act as assistant to the Créole Laurens."

"And how did you find the Dauphin?" Decazes asked.

"Laurens took me into the Temple on 9 October," Gomin

answered slowly. "Before I met His Majesty the Dauphin," he stuttered, "Laurens asked me if I was acquainted with the Prince. I answered that I had seen him here at the Tuileries but I had never spoken to him. 'In which case,' Laurens replied, 'some time will elapse before he says a word to you.'"

"And the Dauphin's appearance?"

"He was mournful, sickly. The state of his room was terrible."

"I am sorry," Segalla leaned forward, recalling Laurens' list of expenses. "I thought Laurens cleaned his rooms up."

Gomin shrugged. "It was clean, of a sort, but the boy had suffered terrible neglect. I brought him flowers, four pots. I cleaned his chamber and arranged for him to have a light when darkness fell. I spent several hours a day with him. The Dauphin's knees and wrists were swollen. I think he was suffering from rickets."

"Did you always keep him in the room on the second floor?" Segalla asked.

"Oh no. Sometimes I took him down to the garden and, when Lasne joined me, we would carry him up to the top of the tower for fresh air."

"And you did all you could?" Segalla asked sympathetically.

"Oh, yes." Gomin's protuberant eyes brimmed with tears.

"And you talked to him?"

"Yes." This time more warily.

"You felt sorry for him?" Segalla added.

"I could do nothing, monsieur." Gomin flapped flabby, vein-streaked hands. "I did what I could."

"I merely asked"—Segalla ignored Decazes' angry look—"because here is a small boy who, as you say, is suffering a terrible imprisonment. He is ill, he is lonely, he is frightened. Yet, on the floor above is his elder sister. Didn't you ever think of bringing her down? Or allowing them to play together? Or walk in the garden or stand at the top of the Tower?"

Gomin's seamy face became pallid. He opened his mouth to

reply but no sound came out. Decazes lifted his hand to intervene.

"My question still stands," Segalla declared defiantly. "I demand that you answer it. You are on oath."

"He never mentioned them once. . . . Well," Gomin paused at the disbelief in Segalla's face, "one night in March, when I was alone with the Dauphin, he got up from his bed and went towards the door." The tears now rolled down Gomin's face. "He looked at me with such an appealing expression. 'I want to see her once more!' exclaimed the Dauphin. 'Let me see her before I die. Please!' " Gomin began to sob. "That's all."

Segalla leaned back in his chair. He felt like shouting that he didn't believe a word of it: Gomin's pathetic story was unbelievable. Segalla could not accept that the Dauphin did not know his mother had died. Decazes would have dismissed Gomin there and then.

"I haven't finished," Segalla exclaimed, ignoring Tallien's warning glance. "I asked you a question, Monsieur Gomin. Why did you not allow the Dauphin and his sister to meet?"

"We were under the strictest orders," Gomin confessed. "On pain of death, such a meeting was not to take place."

"Why?" Fouché suddenly stirred.

Gomin, now overcome, put his face in his hands. "I don't know," he wailed. "Monsieur Barras ordered that."

Chapter 9

É tienne Lasne was the next witness to be called. A grey-haired, long-faced, dour man: hard-featured, close-set eyes over a jutting nose and determined chin. He sat beside Gomin because Decazes had determined that all who had been with the Dauphin when he died should be questioned together, in case a fresh witness provoked more questions. Lasne took the oath, his words ringing throughout the chamber; he sat down, flicking up the tails of his threadbare coat.

"What is your name?"

"Étienne Lasne."

"Profession?"

"House painter."

The fellow fished into the pocket of his waistcoat and drew out a thickly folded piece of paper.

"Monsieur Decazes, I have written my own statement."

"Then, Monsieur Lasne, read it. Whilst you, sir," Decazes tapped the table and Gomin looked up, "will compose yourself."

Decazes was angry, apparently disappointed at Gomin's performance. Lasne unfolded his paper and read from the document.

"I was the last warder of Prince Louis Charles, Duc de Normandie, the son of Louis XVI, in the tower of the Temple. During my period of service the Prince died. I had seen the Prince before this when I commanded a battalion in the district of the Droits de l'Homme. Accordingly I frequently had to find the guard in the Tuileries, when I several times attended him in his walks on the Feuillantes Terrace. Besides this, during the imprisonment of the Royal Family in the Temple, I was frequently there on duty with my battalion, and so had plenty of opportunities to see the Prince, whom I was able to recognise with certainty.

"In Germinal of the year III [March–April, 1795] I was entrusted by the Committee of Public Safety of the Assembly with the charge of the Prince and the Princess his sister. I certify that I recognised him throughout as the child whom I had seen before, and after that date, either in the Tuileries or in the Temple. I also certify, on my honour, that this Prince, in spite of the care which I bestowed on him, died in the Temple after two days' illness. He breathed his last sigh on my left arm, just as I was lifting him up from the bed. I was present at the postmortem."

"Do you believe," Decazes interrupted, "that it was possible that another child could have been substituted for the Prince during your absence, or without your knowledge, and that the Prince could have been secretly taken up into the roof of the Temple tower?"

"The first is impossible," Lasne replied. "And so is the second: Because the Temple tower, in which the Prince was imprisoned, had neither roof nor attic, but was finished with a terrace. There was indeed a spire on a part of this building, but it could not be entered, and I do not even know whether there was a staircase in it. In any case it could only have been entered by the tilers and workpeople; it is quite out of the question that anybody should have been concealed there."

Segalla was surprised at Decazes' question. Such a thought had never occurred to him—that the Prince might have been hidden in the Temple whilst another boy took his place. Was that why Napoléon had the prison pulled down? Was he looking for something?

"Monsieur Lasne." Fouché, who had been sitting sideways, now turned to face the witness. "Your colleague here, Monsieur

Gomin, has informed the court that you were given strict orders that the Dauphin was never to meet or talk to his sister. Is that true?"

"Yes, sir, it is."

"And you never asked why?" Fouché persisted.

"I was a soldier," Lasne replied. "I carried out orders. Moreover, I do not think it would have been an act of compassion to allow his sister, the Archduchess, may God bless her, see into what a sorry state her brother had fallen."

"Do you think it's possible," Segalla asked, "that if the Dauphin wasn't hidden away in the Temple, he could have been smuggled out whilst you guarded some boy from a local hospital?"

"I have heard such rumours," Lasne said. "But, as I have said, I served in the guard at the Tuileries. I knew the Dauphin quite well."

"Why?" Segalla asked abruptly, hoping to shatter this man's self-confidence.

"Why what?" Lasne asked stonily.

"Why were you appointed?"

"Monsieur Barras arranged it."

"So," Segalla continued. "You were friends with Monsieur Barras?"

"Oh yes," Lasne replied quickly. "If Robespierre had not fallen, both Monsieur Gomin and myself would have gone to the guillotine."

Segalla sighed. He had made his point: The two witnesses had been creatures of Barras's.

The next person to be called caused a stir. Pelletan, lecturer and physician, was dressed elegantly in a dark blue suit and white lace shirt. He had the raddled face of an old roué and came into the room on high-heeled shoes, swinging his silver-topped cane. He had a twisted, sneering face; Segalla took an immediate dislike to him. Pelletan took the oath in a languid, offhand manner and tried to sit well away from Lasne and Gomin, whose greetings he barely acknowledged. Pelletan gave his name and occupation, smiling ingratiatingly up at Decazes and Fouché as if they were old friends.

"Monsieur Pelletan," Decazes began. "You are well known at court, where your services are deeply appreciated."

"I never yet met a doctor who could save a life," Fouché suddenly barked, then turned sideways in his chair, as if once more bored by the whole proceedings.

Pelletan, however, refused to rise to the insult. Instead he turned his liverish, cadaver-like face towards Decazes.

"I will answer," he announced, "any question this court shall ask me."

"You signed the death certificate?" Segalla asked.

"Well, yes, of course."

"And you conducted the postmortem?"

Pelletan nodded.

"And you were present when the Dauphin died?"

Again the nod.

"And what would you say was the cause of death?"

"Neglect, rickets, scrofula. The poor prince had lost the will to live."

Segalla smiled falsely. "But you did what you could?"

Pelletan drew a roll of notes out of his pocket. He laid these on the table, smoothing them out carefully.

"I prescribed a diet: breakfast at ten o'clock; chocolate, bread and currant jam. A meal in the afternoon and a supper of grilled meat and vegetables." Pelletan cleared his throat. "And, of course, there was the medicine. A weak concoction of hops and, every morning, three tablespoonfuls of antimony syrup."

"Yet your patient died?" Segalla asked.

"Yes, yes, he did, monsieur," Pelletan sneered. "I am a physician, not a miracle worker and, of course, I was not brought into the Temple until 3 June, five days before his death."

"Five days!" Segalla exclaimed. "Such a famous doctor as yourself was called so late?"

Fouché turned in his chair as if he sensed the hunt had begun.

"Well?" Segalla asked, not daring to glance at Tallien, who now had his head down, scribbling away furiously.

"Ah, er . . ." Pelletan stammered. "I had been called before, but I had not been the physician in charge."

"Yes, that's right," Segalla replied. "According to the receipts I studied, Pierre Joseph Desault, Principal Officer of Health, looked after the Dauphin. However, he visited the Dauphin on 29 May and never returned. Why is that?"

His words created a pool of silence. None of the three witnesses dared meet Segalla's enquiring glance. Decazes shuffled the papers noisily on the desk in front of him.

"What happened to Desault? Was he incompetent?"

"He died," Fouché interrupted. "Monsieur Desault died on 1 June."

"Of what?" Segalla asked.

"Apoplexy, a stroke . . . God knows!" Pelletan snapped.

Segalla sensed he'd touched a raw nerve.

"Monsieur Desault's death," Decazes intervened, "has nothing to do with this matter. It is the Dauphin's death that we are concerned with."

"I was assisted," Pelletan spoke us as if desperate to break the silence, "by others."

"Yes, yes," Decazes intervened angrily. "But, Monsieur Pelletan, keep yourself to the facts of the case."

The physician, now shaken, went back to his notes.

"I paid a second visit," he continued, "on 7 June. I recommended that the Dauphin be fed white bread made with pure wheat and a broth of beef and chicken. The following day we came back in the morning. We found the young Dauphin had grown much worse: He had a weak pulse, his abdomen was distended and painful. He had suffered vomiting and diarrhea. We left just before one o'clock in the afternoon." He shook his head. "I never saw the Dauphin alive again."

"Then what happened?" Segalla asked.

"About two o'clock in the afternoon," Lasne spoke up, "the boy's condition deteriorated so I asked Gomin to go and ask the authorities for help. I gave the Dauphin some more medicine but his health grew even worse. He broke out into a cold sweat and I could hear this strange rattling in his throat." Only then did Lasne's composure break. "I sent an urgent message for Pelletan but it was too late. The boy said he wanted to relieve himself. I went to assist. He put his arms round my neck. The boy went rigid, he gave a sigh." Lasne wiped his eyes on the back of his hand. "It was finished," he whispered.

Even Tallien stopped writing. Fouché studied a painting on the wall. Decazes played with the quill pen but his hand trembled whilst Segalla felt a deep revulsion at the absolute hopelessness of that young boy's death. Only Pelletan remained unmoved, shuffling his notes as if violent death was an everyday occurrence and the Dauphin's demise, pathetic though it may be, was nothing out of the ordinary.

"What happened then?" Segalla asked. "Do continue, Monsier Pelletan."

"I came back to the Temple," the doctor replied, "but there was nothing I could do except draw up the death certificate. The government in Paris decided to keep the Dauphin's death a secret for as long as possible. It was not until the next day that the Committee of General Security issued a statement. Until then, Lasne, Gomin, myself and the guards were ordered to remain in the Temple under strict security, even pretending the Dauphin was still alive."

"Continue," Decazes murmured.

"On 9 June, after the news was published, I and three other doctors conducted a rigorous postmortem."

"Why?"

"To identify the cause of death. It was what we suspected: scrofula—an infection which attacks the intestines. After we had finished, the corpse was bandaged and laid out on the bed." He shrugged. "My duties were over. I left the Temple."

"On the tenth," Lasne intervened. "We were instructed to carry out the burial. I ordered a coffin of white wood, four and a half feet long. For a while the body lay exposed. It was not until nine o'clock the same night, that the coffin was nailed up, covered with a pall and carried on a stretcher to the cemetery of Ste.-Marguerite. This lies almost half a league from the Temple."

"And where was it buried?" Segalla asked.

"In the common grave." Lasne shrugged. "I regretted it but those were my orders."

"Tell me." Segalla rose, stretched the cramp out of the small of his back, then sat down again. "You say the Dauphin's corpse was viewed by the officers and guards at the Temple?"

Both Lasne and Gomin nodded.

"Did it not occur to you," Segalla asked, "to ask his sister down, if not to identify the corpse, then at least so she could bid a last farewell to the remains of her brother?"

Lasne pressed his hands against the table, swaying slightly in his chair. "Why should we do that, monsieur? The Dauphin's sister was only a young girl and our orders were quite explicit."

The same song, Segalla thought; and he turned away as if he had heard enough. Decazes then thanked Pelletan, Lasne and Gomin. They withdrew and Decazes, pushing back his chair, rose and went down to the library and stared out in the gathering dusk. After a while he walked back.

"Our business is finished, Major Segalla. You have talked to witnesses. You have seen the documents. What recommendation will you make?"

"The Dauphin died," Fouché intervened throatily. "He is dead and buried in a cemetery, God rest his soul! Napoléon is defeated and His Majesty Louis XVIII has come into his own." He glanced quickly at his companions. "Let the dead bury their dead. France must go on."

Segalla rose to his feet and watched how Decazes went round the table to collect the ledger from Tallien.

"I only have one question and I have asked it," Segalla declared. "I am puzzled, very puzzled, why they kept the Dauphin so strictly hidden from his sister?"

"Study the history of those creatures," Decazes replied, "who governed France under the Terror. They kept the Dauphin's father away from his family and incarcerated Marie-Antoinette in the Conciergerie. Why should they show compassion to the royal children?"

Segalla nodded as if he accepted such an explanation.

"And now," he asked, "am I free to leave the Tuileries?"

"Of course." Decazes smiled back. "You are now finished here, Major. Though, before you leave Paris, I must insist that you share your conclusions with me." He sighed. "As for my part, I shall seek an audience with His Majesty and declare that the Dauphin Louis Charles, Duke of Normandy, died at about three o'clock on 8 June 1795 in the Temple prison."

Segalla picked up his own notes and placed them in the leather valise he always carried.

"You need not leave now, monsieur," Decazes added jokingly. "The hour is growing late."

Segalla thanked him, sketched a bow at Fouché and, without a backward glance, left the library and returned to his own chamber.

For a while Segalla paced up and down. Everything he had learnt in that library seemed to point to the Dauphin dying in the Temple. Only one real doubt existed. Why had the revolutionary authorities been so insistent that the Dauphin could not meet or even see his sister? He paused, listened and, going to the door, opened it.

The gallery was silent and deserted. Apparently Decazes had now withdrawn the guard, leaving Segalla to decide whether he came or stayed. He shut the door, took off his jacket and cravat, loosened his collar and sat on the stool staring at his notes.

"Pelletan," he murmured. The physician was a sinister, secretive man. What had his role been in those last days of the Dauphin? Segalla got up and continued his pacing. The Dauphin had been ill but, as soon as Pelletan appeared on the scene, the boy's condition had become grave. And what had happened to the first doctor, Desault? Was his sudden death a coincidence or something more sinister? Outside, the floorboards creaked. Segalla watched as a small note was pushed beneath his door. He picked it up and recognised Tallien's handwriting: the archivist promised to keep in touch. Segalla pushed this into his waistcoat pocket. He glanced out of the window; darkness had fallen and he had no inclination to go wandering round the palace. Feeling ill at ease and lacking any appetite, Segalla decided to retire to bed, still wondering whether he should pursue the investigation or return to England and tell Lord Liverpool he could go no further. He slowly undressed and for a while lay listening to the sounds of the palace. Somewhere an orchestra was playing and, in the courtyard below, a girl began to sing, which abruptly ended in muffled laughter.

"What am I to do?" Segalla spoke into the darkness. The war with Napoléon was now over. Soon the English government would dispense with his services, and where to then? Across the Atlantic to his friends in Williamsburg, Virginia? Or should he go south to Italy? Offer his services to the Vatican? Segalla tossed restlessly. What did it matter, he wondered, if the truth about the Dauphin remained a mystery?

"It matters," Segalla whispered. "It matters."

He recalled Marie-Antoinette's sweet face, her courage as she walked up the scaffold steps whilst all around her the Paris mob bayed for her blood. How bravely she had walked to the guillotine. Segalla smiled. Had she deliberately stepped on the executioner's foot? Was it her last act of defiance? Segalla closed his eyes. He had made his decision; he would pursue this matter to the bitter end.

The next morning Segalla woke and allowed the usual train of servants to shave him, lay out fresh linen and bring him hot chocolate and freshly baked bread. After that he packed his belongings and walked down into one of the main halls of the Tuileries. A chamberlain informed him that Monsieur Decazes had left for Versailles; however, the minister would be in touch with Major Segalla and asked him not to leave Paris until he had done so.

"A carriage has been ordered for you, sir," the chamberlain continued pompously. "It will leave here at ten o'clock and take you directly back to your lodgings."

Segalla had no choice but to wait and, for a while, kicked his heels, admiring the paintings, statues or watching the workmen continue their efforts to obliterate every sign of Napoléon's stay in the Tuileries. The carriage, a black cabriolet, arrived a little early: its driver was dressed completely in black, his face half-hidden by a muffler. He silently got down and stowed Segalla's baggage on the back. Segalla opened the door then hid his surprise at the pale pink features of Fouché staring out from the darkness.

"Close the door, Major Segalla. And do not speak until we have left the Tuileries."

Segalla obeyed, sitting back against the leather upholstery and listening to the rattle of the wheels and clip-clop of the horses' hooves as they rolled across the pebble-strewn paths towards the main gates of the palace. The carriage was hot, dark and stuffy, the blinds pulled fully down. At last, it stopped. Segalla heard the cries of the sentries, the gates being opened, and then the carriage continued on its way.

The morning was bright and clear but Fouché was dressed as if it were the depths of winter. A dark greatcoat, its collar pulled up, the top hat tilted so it almost concealed the master spy's obsidian eyes.

"The driver will go the long way round." Fouché took his hat off, wiping the sweat from his brow. He smiled at Segalla. "You enjoyed your stay at the Tuileries, Major?"

"It was memorable."

"Like your previous visits?"

Segalla glanced away.

"I have always wondered about you," Fouché continued. "For almost fifteen years, Major, I ran a spy network second to none. Time and again your name comes up. You are in St. Petersburg or Vienna, Berlin and, for the last few years, in London. You have no visible means of support yet you dress and dine well. You move in the shadows of the great ones, yet you never grow old."

"I come from a large family," Segalla replied drily. "Who I am, Joseph Fouché, where I am going and where I come from, are my business!"

"Aye, as the proverb says, 'Woe to us who live in interesting times.'" Fouché unbuttoned his coat. "You met Napoléon," he added curtly, "before the *Bellerephon* sailed?"

Segalla nodded.

"And how was my old master? Did he send me his regards?"

"He mentioned you, but love and affection did not figure prominently."

Fouché chuckled. "I have survived so many rulers," he remarked. "Others go but old Fouché remains. Do you know why, Major Segalla? Because I remember so much. Oh, Decazes and his fat master would love to dismiss me. They would clap their hands and sing if I was knocked down by a carriage in some Paris street. But they know what treasures I've hidden away in some bank vault or lawyer's office. And that's why I am here this morning, Major. Louis XVIII and his ministers are enjoying their honeymoon. France is tired of war but, as you know, honeymoons soon pass and the fighting will begin. Joseph Fouché does not want to find himself in prison or put under house arrest in some cold, draughty château in the forests of Alsace-Lorraine. So, I want insurance and you will provide it."

"Me?" Segalla asked innocently. "What protection can I offer the great Fouché?"

"Lord Liverpool in London can. He can make it known to those in Paris how His Britannic Majesty's government has a high esteem and regard for me."

"Such insurance is expensive."

Fouché laughed and his thin, sallow face was transformed. Segalla recalled how this cold, sinister master spy had a reputation as a loving husband and the most doting father of his large brood of children.

"Nothing in life is free." Fouché undid the rest of his buttons. "For myself I am not frightened, but my family . . ." He didn't finish the sentence but, as if distracted by the noise from the city, pulled back the blinds and stared out. "Paris is busy," he murmured. "Always has been and I love it. I do not want to spend my days in exile like Monsieur Barras. So." He let the blind fall and sat forward on the edge of his seat. "Let me buy the protection of Lord Liverpool and his cabinet. First, the Empress Josephine was poisoned. God knows by whom! But my whisperers inform me she knew the true fate of the Dauphin." He shrugged. "Or at least some of the truth."

"And what is this truth?" Segalla asked.

"Pilate asked the same question: he didn't even wait for an answer."

"I am waiting," Segalla remarked. "But, there again, I could travel to Brussels and make enquiries of Monsieur Barras."

Fouché shook his head. "Barras lives in an alcoholic haze. He has no papers, he has no proof. He lives in constant fear for his life. He would never talk to you."

"I could persuade him to return to England."

"Pshaw!" Fouché lay back on the seat. "I do not think Lord Liverpool would give refuge to such a scoundrel and so alienate his new friends in Paris."

"Then, what did Madame Josephine know?" Segalla asked.

"The Dauphin escaped."

Fouché paused as the carriage entered a noisy, busy square. The driver began to shout and crack his whip to force a passage through the stall-holders and people thronging there. Once they were across Fouché continued.

"Come, come, Major Segalla. You know the Dauphin escaped."

"But when?" Segalla asked. "Who arranged it? What happened to him?"

"Ah." Fouché's eyebrows rose. "That's the great mystery. Barras was party to it, and those dreadful murders at the Château Vitry-sur-Seine are connected with it. But, so far, all I have are pieces in the puzzle. I cannot put them together." He took off his gloves and slapped them against his lap. "Tell me what you think, Major Segalla."

"That Barras took the Prince out, put a sickly boy with a passing resemblance to him in the Temple and sent the real Dauphin to the banker, Baron Petitval."

"And?"

"Petitval's château at Vitry-sur-Seine was then attacked. The baron and his family were massacred but only God knows what happened to the Dauphin."

"Very good," Fouché remarked briskly. "But what proof do you have of that?"

"None whatsoever."

Fouché laced his bony fingers together. "Yet, that's exactly my theory: It's what I told Napoléon."

"Who attacked the château?" Segalla asked.

Fouché spread his hands. "As God is my witness, I don't know."

"You have heard of the secret Templars?" Segalla asked. "And their leader Monsieur de Paris. Is it possible that the scoundrel Barras double-crossed Petitval, released the Dauphin and then sent Monsieur de Paris and his gang to Vitry-sur-Seine?"

"But why should he do that?" Fouché replied. "Barras belonged to many secret societies. He had so many fingers in so many pies he reminds me of myself. He was a swindler, a black-

141

mailer, a cunning man, but bloody murder?" Fouché shook his head. "No, that was not Barras." Fouché pulled back the blinds of the carriage. "Walk round Paris, Major Segalla," he continued. "Drink its wines, taste its cakes, sit in the cafés. You can talk about anything, at least for a while, but mention Monsieur de Paris and the mood will change. For years my agents tried to trap him. All we learnt is that he is male, a consummate actor and a master of disguise. More importantly, he has a black fleur-de-lys tattooed high on his left shoulder."

"What else do you know?" Segalla asked. "And what about the secret court we have just sat through? You heard the witnesses. You saw the bust Bellanger carved."

Fouché gently tapped the blind of the carriage window.

"Eight years ago when the pretender Hergevault appeared, Napoléon ordered an investigation into the Dauphin's fate. I had access to many manuscripts, though perhaps not as many as you and your colleague Tallien saw. We tried to search the common grave where the Dauphin was buried but little remained. There was a suspicion . . ." Fouché paused, finger to his lips. "Yes, a suspicion that Betrancourt had moved the coffin, but that old rogue stuck to his story; now he has been murdered and perhaps I should have pursued the matter further. Anyway, my searches discovered something. First, Pelletan is a snake incarnate." He grinned boyishly at Segalla. "And that's damnation coming from a man like me. He was the most furious of revolutionaries and acted as a spy in the Conciergerie prison where he tended some of the inmates. He is also skilled at poisoning. I merely mention this because of poor Desault. Now, I spoke to Desault's sister and she told me a wondrous story; how Desault and his assistants were apparently invited to dinner by members of the Revolutionary Convention. After this dinner, Desault and both of his assistants, I believe one of them was called Chopet, became suddenly ill and died. Bouille, a friend of Desault's, was so terrified about what had happened, he fled to England, but not before confessing that Desault and his two companions had been murdered to keep their mouths shut."

"You mean Desault realised the boy he was treating was not the true son of Louis XVI?"

Fouché shook his head. "Far from it. Desault believed that the patient he was treating in the Temple was going to die."

Segalla looked perplexedly at him.

"To put it bluntly, Major, Desault and his two assistants were instructed to poison the boy. They refused, like the good men they were, and so had to be silenced."

"And you think Pelletan agreed to the task?"

"Yes I do."

"But Gomin and Lasne were there?"

"Now listen to this." Fouché leaned forward. "I have met Messieurs Lasne and Gomin before: Lasne is a thick-headed soldier. He did his duty and that was the end of it. But, ten years ago Gomin confessed that it was due to the influence of a certain marquis that he was appointed as the Dauphin's warder." Fouché smiled at the surprise in Segalla's face. "Yes, I too thought of that. How on earth could a nobleman have so much power when the Revolution was at its height? I put that to Gomin—he just shrugged then denied it."

"You did not believe him?" Segalla asked.

"No I didn't. My view is that Gomin, a skilled actor, was secretly a royalist, as were Barras and others. They were trying to stand on either side of the campfire. Barras ended up by getting his balls burnt: others just disappeared into the darkness."

"What about witnesses like Bellanger?"

"They saw what they expected to see. It would not be hard even now, to go into the streets of Paris and find a ten-year-old boy with more than a passing resemblance to the bust Bellanger produced."

Segalla leaned back, so intent had he been on what Fouché had been saying to him, he had almost forgotten he was travelling in a carriage rattling through the busy, noisy streets of Paris.

"But why should Pelletan poison the boy?"

"Because it was 1795," Fouché remarked. "King Charles of Spain, not to mention the Catholic generals in the west, were increasing the pressure on the government in Paris to free the Dauphin. What would happen, Major Segalla, if they released the boy, only for Spain and the rest of Europe to find out it was not the Dauphin?" Fouché coughed and cleared his throat. "What I have told you, Major Segalla, is in confidence. There is little you can do about it. Gomin, Lasne and Pelletan are well protected. I doubt if they would change their stories even under torture."

Segalla sighed. "True, true," he exclaimed in exasperation. "And what proof can I produce that Pelletan poisoned the prisoner? Even if we exhumed the body, it would be a mammoth task just finding it. Which explains," he added bitterly, "why Betrancourt was murdered. We would need a team of doctors to establish first, that the corpse belonged to the boy buried there in June 1795. Secondly, if the boy wasn't the Dauphin, then what is the use?" He paused as the carriage began to clatter across the Pont Neuf.

"Ah well," Fouché commented. "There is very little more I can tell you, Major." He leaned across and grasped Segalla's hand. "You will make known to Lord Liverpool what a friend England has in Joseph Fouché?"

Segalla nodded.

"I have your promise?"

"You have my promise," Segalla declared.

"Good!" Fouché leaned back and drew from the voluminous folds of his great, black coat a buff envelope and handed it to Segalla. "That is the last assistance I'll give you."

Segalla turned the envelope over in his hands. "What is it?"

Fouché laughed. "It's the address of one witness they didn't call." His grin widened. "You remember the cobbler Simon? Well, he may have gone to the guillotine but his wife is still alive!"

Chapter 10

Segalla sat at his table in his chamber in the Lion d'Or and began to list the questions remaining. Fouché had been useful but had provided nothing he didn't already suspect himself, except for Madame Simon's address which Segalla intended to visit the next morning. He finished his notes, took one further sip from his goblet of red wine and began to list his conclusions.

Primo—*The Dauphin was separated from his family in October 1793. He never saw them again.*
Secundo—*In January 1794 the cobbler Simon and his wife were removed from their posts as the Dauphin's guardians or warders.*
Tertio—*For six months, January to June 1794, the Dauphin was kept incarcerated.*
Quarto—*In the summer of 1794 Barras visits the Temple. The boy imprisoned there has more than a passing resemblance to the Dauphin but there are dramatic physical and psychological changes: the boy is stooped, taller, depressed and withdrawn.*
Quinto—*He has three new warders: Laurens, Gomin and Lasne. There is no indication that any of them believe that their prisoner was any other than the Dauphin Louis Charles.*
Sexto—*The boy is then well looked after but he is kept away from his sister.*
Septimo—*In June 1795 his condition rapidly deteriorates. He dies but his death is kept secret for twenty-four hours, followed by a swift burial at night in the cemetery of Ste.-Marguerite.*

Segalla chewed the tip of the pen. The boy who was discovered by Barras and inspected by Harmand of Meuse is supposed to have had light auburn hair but his picture of the Dauphin shows him to have dark hair. Moreover, the boy Gomin and Lasne looked after was apparently taller, thinner, of poorer physique than the rather boisterous young boy whom Simon cared for. Were these changes caused by ill treatment? Or, because the Dauphin escaped and someone else was put in the Temple? If this was so, when did the escape occur?

Segalla threw his pen down and stared at the ceiling.

"It must be Barras," he exclaimed. "Barras removed the Dauphin, handed him over to Petitval but then what happened? Petitval's château was attacked but the records do not mention the corpse of a boy being found amongst the dead. So, what on earth happened to him? Who organised that attack?"

Segalla started at the rap on the door. It was pushed open and a grey-haired, dusty-faced servant entered, carrying a tray with two cups of steaming coffee and some pastry cakes on a linen-covered plate. Segalla rose, pulled open the drawer of his desk and felt where his pistol lay.

"I did not order that."

The servant put the tray down on the table and stretched, shaking the grey dust from his hair.

"Isn't it marvellous, Major Segalla," Tallien declared, taking off his dirty apron, "how, if you dress in a certain way, no one ever notices."

Segalla clapped his hands slowly. "But why the subterfuge?"

"Too dangerous," Tallien said, pushing across a chair. "I suspect, Major Segalla, that both you and I will be under close surveillance from Decazes' spies until you leave Paris."

"If they find out," Segalla commented, "that we are meeting secretly"—he leaned over and grasped the archivist's shoulder—"you'd bleed as easily as any man and your corpse just another dragged from the Seine. And, before you ask," Segalla rose and bolted the door. "I have drawn my conclusions."

He told Tallien exactly what Fouché had said. The archivist could hardly keep still with excitement.

"Madame Simon's alive!" he breathed.

"You know where the Hospital of the Incurables is?"

"In the Rue de Sèvres," Tallien replied.

Segalla pulled out his fob watch. "I shall leave now. Go back to the Tuileries. Search amongst the papers. Pretend you have lost something and wish to refresh your memory. Forget about the poor boy imprisoned in the Temple from June 1794 onwards. Search the manuscripts for the period October 1793 to January 1794, even earlier. See what you can find: I'll visit Madame Simon."

Tallien agreed and left. Segalla drank the coffee. He donned his sword-belt and put a pistol in the deep pocket of his greatcoat, then sent a tap boy to hire a carriage.

Half an hour later, the blinds of the carriage pulled firmly down, Segalla was taken across the Pont Neuf, his driver having assured him that he knew the Hospital of the Incurables in the Rue de Sèvres. Once they were across the Pont Neuf, heading into a dingier part of Paris, Segalla pulled the blinds up to look at the sights, a comfortable distraction from his constant introspection. As the streets became narrower, winding between the rotting, shabby houses on either side, progress became slower. Tradesmen thronged about shouting, "Pears and Pippins!" "Brooms for sale!"

They passed a series of half-burnt-out buildings now occupied by the sellers of secondhand clothes. These came rushing out, seeking Segalla's custom, but the driver cracked his whip and drove them off. They crossed a small square where shabby, evil-looking men stood by barrows piled high with nuts, ginger bread, oranges and oysters. Old crones in straw hats or flat caps offered shoes, needles and plum puddings for sale. Here, the poor of Paris flocked to buy anything from a pair of whalebone stays or a toothbrush to a patch box or a squirrel's cage. Trinkets, toys, gloves and bottles of cheap perfume were stacked high on tawdry stalls, available for a few sous. Trade was brisk. Segalla even glimpsed English soldiers in their red jackets and white facings looking for bargains. At last they entered a broad, tree-lined avenue before turning into the Rue de Sèvres, a quiet street which led down to the main gate of the Hospital of the Incurables.

At the porter's lodge Segalla paid off the carriage but told him to wait, and entered the hospital gardens. After the dirt and filth he had witnessed, this proved to be an oasis of calmness. Sisters of the Order of St. Vincent de Paul, dressed in their habits—dark blue dresses with white, starched cuffs and ornate billowing, white headdresses—sat or walked with patients. The majority of these wore the same uniform consisting of a skirt and bodice of grey wool, a linen fichu and a black cap over a band of white batiste. As he approached the main stairs, one of the sisters came up, fingering the great, black rosary beads which hung from a cord around her waist.

"Monsieur, can I help?"

Segalla doffed his cap and bowed elegantly.

"Madame." He paused. "Sister." He smiled apologetically at his lack of etiquette. "I am looking for a woman, in her mid-fifties or early sixties, Madame Simon. Her husband was a cobbler, a former Jacobin."

The smile faded from the nun's face. "Such men did terrible damage," she whispered, "to our order—not a priest, not a nun nor any religious was safe in Paris. I doubt if such a woman is here. But, come, follow me."

She led Segalla into the hospital. A lofty, sombre place with vaulted corridors and flaking walls though everything looked clean and polished, smelling of soap and disinfectant. The sister looked anxiously over her shoulder.

"I must apologise, monsieur. We are poor and depend upon charity." She stopped, her eyes rounding, as Segalla grasped her hand and pressed two gold coins firmly into it.

"Monsieur," she exclaimed. "Are you sure?"

"For the information I want," Segalla replied, "I'll pay twice as much when I leave."

The young nun needed no further encouragement. Segalla was hurried up to the Mother Superior's office. A tall, forbidding lady dressed in the same garb as his escort, Mother Superior sat like a queen behind the broad oaken desk. The nun went across and whispered in her ear, placing Segalla's gold coins on the table. Mother Superior nodded, her eyes never leaving Segalla's.

"You may leave us, Sister Angela," she declared softly. "I will look after Major Segalla."

As the nun left, Mother Superior rose and came forward to clasp Segalla's hand.

"You are not French?"

"It is best, Mother Superior," Segalla replied, "if you do not know who I am."

The nun's black-button eyes studied her visitor curiously.

"So," she whispered. "It begins."

"What does, sister?"

"Madame Simon," the Mother Superior replied. "Usually keeps quiet about her past, though, now and again, she has been heard to cry, 'Ah, if my children were only here, they would not leave me without assistance.'" She stepped closer. "Now," she continued in a whisper, "when one of our sisters asked her which children, Madame Simon replied, 'My little Bourbons whom I loved with all my heart. I was their governess.'"

"But the Dauphin died," Segalla commented.

The Mother Superior looked at him archly. "Oh, yes, that's what we told her. But Madame Simon just shook her head and cried, 'No, no, he's not dead!' Anyway." She plucked at his sleeve. "You'd best follow me."

The nun led Segalla out of her room and along a maze of corridors. Here and there, lay sisters, buckets slopping-full with soapy water, scrubbed the stone floors. Others carried trays of food or medicine whilst, now and again, an old man or woman,

149

lost in their dreams about the past, staggered around, eyes staring, mouths gaping, chattering incomprensibly to themselves. As they rounded one corner, an old crone suddenly grasped Segalla's arm.

"You have come back!" she cried.

Segalla smiled placatingly and tried to extricate her surprisingly strong fingers.

"Madame, you are mistaken."

"No, I am not." The milky-blue eyes stared up; the gumless mouth parted in a grin; a drool of saliva dripped out of the corner of her mouth.

Segalla stared at this ancient face, lined and seamed; tufts of hair appearing on her chin and corner of her mouth. The woman flicked her iron-grey hair.

"It used to be beautiful." She rubbed a wispy curl between her fingers. "Like spun gold. When I danced at the Duke of Orléans's ball at Versailles. Don't you remember? Fairylights in the trees? The orchestras on the lawn? Wine flowed in the fountains."

"My dear, go back to your bed."

Mother Superior tried to come between her and Segalla but the old woman clung on more tightly, her eyes shining with excitement.

"You danced with me," she exclaimed. "Your name's Segalla. You danced with me on a moonlit night, sixty years ago. You held me close and whispered in my ear."

Segalla stared unbelievingly down at this woman whose eyes looked as if she was a thousand years old.

"It's your face," the old woman whispered. "I never forget a face. We talked about Villon's poetry."

Now the Mother Superior was looking strangely at Segalla.

"My father," he explained. "He was in Paris at that time; an envoy of the English court."

The old woman let her grip drop and looked away, her fingers flying to her mouth. She looked guiltily at Mother Superior, who waved Segalla on.

"Monsieur Segalla! Monsieur Segalla!"

He stopped and turned: the old crone was leaning drunkenly against the wall.

"It was you!" she cried. "I know it was you!"

He just bowed and followed his guide down the passageway, through a door, its paint all flaking, and into a small room. The woman sitting on a stool beside the bed was busy praying, her lips moving soundlessly as she tried to read from a battered prayer book. She rose as they entered, bobbing and curtseying, then looked quickly at Segalla.

"Madame Simon, you have a visitor."

The woman's face broke into a smile. "A visitor? For poor, old Mère Simon? Here, here, sit down, sit down."

She waved Segalla to the edge of the narrow pallet bed. The Mother Superior said she would wait outside and left, closing the door quietly behind her.

"And what do you want with me?"

Mother Simon's smile had now faded and her thin, white face was full of suspicion. Segalla calculated she was well past her sixtieth year, a sickly woman with a racking cough and a nervous tic high in her left cheek; an unprepossessing woman with strong features, a slightly hooked nose, bloodless lips and calculating eyes.

Segalla stared round the tiny but neat room. He absentmindedly stroked the eiderdown, a red quilt strewn all over with blue and white flowers.

"I brought that from the Temple," Madame Simon declared. "Sometimes I would wrap it around my little boy."

"You mean the Dauphin, Louis Charles?"

"Of course." She laughed. "Who else?"

"You and your husband guarded the Dauphin?"

"Aye." Madame Simon's eyes became watchful. "But we

never hurt him. It's all lies. Lies, do you understand?"

"I believe you, Madame," Segalla replied softly. "I have been through the archives. The boy had birds, toys, sweets."

"Oh, yes, a lovely child." Madame Simon glanced away. "Lovely," she whispered. "Auburn-haired, he was."

"Not dark?" Segalla asked.

"Oh no, not dark. Bright, golden locks."

"And you bathed him?" Segalla asked.

"Oh, yes, many a time. He had a hip-bath, warm, soapy water, some herbs to ease the cramps."

"A healthy boy?"

"Of course. Full of life. Why do you ask?" Madame Simon pushed her face closer. "Who are you?" Her voice became fearful. "What are you doing here? Why are you asking me these questions and going through the archives? You are from the police, aren't you? You are here to arrest me, accuse me of being a regicide!" She started to cry. "I never hurt that child. Doesn't the world know we freed him?"

Segalla grasped the old woman's vein-streaked hand.

"Madame Simon, I am not from the police nor am I here to punish you. My name is Major Nicholas Segalla. I am the special envoy of His Majesty's government. All I want to do is discover the truth."

The old woman dried her eyes on the back of her hand.

"You promise that?"

Segalla pressed two silver coins into her hand. "You have my word. Ask Mother Superior, she'll tell you the same. All I want to hear, Madame Simon, is your story."

The old lady straightened in the chair; now and again she wet her lips and scratched the lobe of her ear, blinking as if trying to recollect every detail.

"My husband," she began, "was a cobbler, one of the best in the faubourg St.-Antoine. We had a house opposite Danton— you know, the lawyer who became Robespierre's most hated enemy?" She paused. "Well, the Revolution broke out and the world was turned on its head." Her eyes became bright. "We were at the Bastille the day it fell. My husband was brave, fighting the Swiss guard whilst I attended the wounded. And that's when it all began." She tapped her sabot against Segalla's leather boot. "No more shoemaking for us. We became important people."

"And it was Robespierre who appointed you as guardians of the Dauphin?"

"Oh, yes. We became like kings and queens. And, whatever people say, we are good people, Englishman. We cared for the Dauphin as if he was our own child."

"So, why were you removed?"

Madame Simon pouted and shook her head. "We weren't removed. A new law was passed. No elected representative could hold office."

"But your husband became Inspector of Carriages?"

Madame Simon rubbed her brow. "Major, I become muddled." She put the coins into a pocket of her dress just in case Segalla changed his mind. "I keep forgetting. Anyway," she stammered, "in the last months of 1793, my husband became very strange. He'd go away at night—so he later told me—to meet shadowy, cloaked figures in an auberge just outside the Temple. The authorities became suspicious. You may not have found this amongst the archives, monsieur, but they began to restrict our movements. We became as much prisoners of the Temple as the Dauphin was." She paused and drew a deep breath. "On Christmas Day 1793, my husband told me that he was sickened by the bloodshed and fearful of the growing extremity of Robespierre and the rest. We went to Mass, secretly, at a house in the Rue Coligny and met some royalist agents. They talked strangely, keeping their faces hidden."

"What do you mean? They talked strangely? Were they French? English?"

"Oh, they were French, but Bretons and Normans: They told my husband to resign his post and take new quarters in the old

Franciscan convent in the Rue de Marat." She shrugged her bony shoulders. "I was surprised, astonished, at my husband but, when we returned home, he told me the reason why. If the Dauphin remained in the Temple, he declared, he would die. After that Simon would say no more but announced we were to leave the Temple on 19 January late in the evening. A new child, a sickly boy from one of the hospitals would be smuggled into the Temple in a pasteboard horse which was meant as a new toy for the Dauphin." Madame Simon's eyes filled with tears. "I don't know who the poor child was. He was given a potion, some drugged wine to render him insensible. The cart was taken into the Temple by a royalist agent."

"What was his name?"

Madame Simon chuckled. "Who said it was a man? It was a woman. Françoise Desprey. She and my husband carried the pasteboard horse up the stairs to the second floor of the Temple."

"But where were the guards?"

"Oh, Major, don't be stupid! The guards were roughnecks. Show them a bottle of wine and they'd sell their own mothers. I entertained them. Meanwhile, my husband took the hospital boy and put him down on the bed. The Dauphin was then rolled into some bedclothes and linen and carried downstairs to the waiting cart."

"And no one stopped you?"

"Monsieur, don't forget, it was January, dark and cold, the weather was freezing. The guards were happy, guzzling their wine." She shrugged and, leaning across, picked up some battered rosary beads from the bedside table. She began to finger these anxiously. "The Dauphin was removed. We loaded the rest of our possessions into the cart and that was it."

Segalla got to his feet and walked down to the other side of the bed and stared down at this old woman.

"Madame, I mean no offence, but you must be lying."

"I'm not!" Madame Simon jumped to her feet, red spots of

anger high in her cheeks. She stamped her foot, her wooden clogs smashing against the paved floor. "I am not lying!"

"Madame, I can accept that the Dauphin was smuggled out of the Temple, but surely the next morning the guards would have realised they had been duped."

Madame Simon smirked. "Ah, monsieur! Go back to your archives; you will find the discharge paper whereby my husband and I were solemnly assured that we had given up our office in good order and that the Dauphin had been left in their charge."

Segalla sat down on the bed, his back to the old woman.

"Yes, Madame Simon." He glanced over his shoulder. "I have seen such a paper." He turned round and walked back to her side of the bed.

"Don't you understand?" Madame Simon continued excitedly. "What could the guards do? Before whom could their complaints be laid? On what grounds? Our discharge had been honourable and signed by them."

"But surely someone in the government would know of this? Recognise they had been deceived?"

Madame Simon tapped the side of her nose. "Some of the government knew." She laughed. "Didn't I tell you, monsieur? We were appointed to our post through the influence of Monsieur Danton, Robespierre's most ardent enemy. The Revolution was beginning to fail. There were revolts in Brittany and Normandy. Allied armies were massing on the frontier, taking one fortress after the other." She closed her eyes and smiled.

"Madame Simon?" Segalla asked. "What happened then?"

"Well, back at the Temple, they had no choice but to wall the prisoner up in his room without either fire or light. The door was fastened with nails and screws and the poor boy beyond was only visible through a small gate. It was all done within two days of us leaving the tower. The guards dared not complain. The truth was concealed." She rubbed her eyes and began to thread the rosary beads through her fingers. "You'll find that they all disappeared or died rather mysteriously and were replaced with others." She chewed the corner of her lip. "Robespierre, that arrogant pup, only found out when it was too late. He was so busy fighting Danton he never checked. Then he went to the Temple to see the child, only to realise what had happened."

"But the boy survived?" Segalla asked. "Why didn't he talk? Why didn't he declare the truth to the men who looked after him? People like Lasne and Gomin."

"Why should he?" Madame Simon pulled at the strands of grey hair falling over her face.

Segalla narrowed his eyes. "What do you mean?"

"The boy replaced in the Temple was a mute," Madame Simon whispered.

"Nonsense!" Segalla declared. "I have talked to men who spoke to him: Gomin, Lasne, Pelletan the doctor."

Madame Simon just sneered. "Oh, I am sure you have. They will tell you the Dauphin said this or the Dauphin said that. But what proof do you have?" she mocked. "They will tell you anything you wanted to know. After all, they were Barras' creatures. Now they are terrified."

Segalla looked down at one of his hands and tried to hide his despair. Of course, he reflected. If he was the . . .

"If he was the Dauphin?" Madame Simon broke into his reverie. "If he was the real Prince of France why didn't they let his sister see him? Poor Marie-Thérèse." She plucked at the cuff of Segalla's coat and shook her bony finger under his nose. "Whatever you have been told, Major Segalla, about that boy being able to speak is a lie. He was a mute, dumb from the day he was born, and he was frightened. More importantly, the men who guarded him knew he was not the Dauphin, so why should they reveal it?"

"And the real Dauphin?" Segalla asked.

Madame Simon sucked through her gums, baring her mouth like a dog.

"I don't know, Major. My husband—well, we had two dwellings: one near the Temple stables and the other in the Rue

156

de Marat. We took the boy there. A day later he was collected. I don't know by whom—men masked and hooded. They left some gold, disappeared and that was that." She blew her cheeks out. "For a while we were fearful. My husband often used to go back to sleep in his lodgings near the Temple to keep an eye on what was happening. But you must remember, Major, in the first six months of 1795 Paris was a terrible place. The Terror was reaching its climax. Danton was fighting Robespierre, Barras was plotting against both. Who cared about the little boy imprisoned in the Temple?" She spread her hands. "And then it was over. Danton went to the guillotine, Robespierre followed, and my husband with him. No one ever tried to save him."

"Then Barras went to the Temple?" Segalla interrupted. "He must have taken one look at that prisoner and realised it was not the Dauphin."

"Yes, yes." Madame Simon chattered on. "Of course he did. But what could he do, Major? Tell the world he had been duped? He was as much a partner to the game as I was. So he had to play it along. I kept my ears open. I heard about the new warders but they were all Barras' men. They could do no other."

"One thing, madame," Segalla asked.

"Oh, you can ask what you like," the old woman cackled. "What does it matter now, Major?"

"Those who went into the Temple after your husband had been executed, claim that the boy they saw was the same child they had seen years earlier at the Tuileries." He paused at the knock on the door and Mother Superior came back into the room.

"Major Segalla," she asked, such a look of concern on her face he wondered whether she had been eavesdropping. "Major Segalla, will you be much longer?"

"Oh, let him stay, Mother Superior!" Madame Simon cried. "He keeps an old woman company!"

"In which case . . ." Mother Superior smiled and backed out of the room, closing the door gently behind her.

"As for these men," Madame Simon resumed, "how could they know? It had almost been three or four years since the Dauphin had been at the Tuileries. Moreover, the mute was sickly, ill, with more than a passing resemblance to the Dauphin." She plucked at her lips. "And, of course, people see what they expect to see, don't they?" She grinned slyly. "And now Louis XVIII has returned, who dares say any different?"

"How long were you with the Dauphin?"

"Four, five months."

"And you said you bathed him?"

"Yes."

"Did you ever see a mole on his left breast, so large it looked like a second teat? A mark on one of his feet or an inoculation scar high on his right shoulder?"

"Oh, Lord save us, no!"

Segalla tried to hide his confusion. "I am sorry, Madame Simon, perhaps the passing of years has dimmed your memory?"

"My memory is not dimmed!" she snapped. "Nor are my wits dull. I cannot bear children, Major Segalla. The Dauphin was my son and that boy's body was white, smooth and soft as a piece of silk, not one blemish on it. Why, monsieur, you look confused."

Segalla forced a smile. "And you do not know what later happened to the Dauphin?"

"No, sir, I do not."

Segalla got to his feet. "And there is nothing else you can tell me?"

"The Dauphin is still alive." She smiled back.

Segalla adjusted his coat. "Madame, I do not think so."

"Well, he was ten years ago." She grinned as Segalla's jaw dropped.

"What do you mean?"

"He visited me here in the hospital. He and a young Negro passed by my bed. Check the visitors' register. Oh no, Englishman, the Dauphin is still alive!"

158

Chapter 11

Segalla came back and sat down, his confusion so apparent Madame Simon chuckled, which ended in a fit of asthmatic coughing. She clutched her chest.

"Oh, yes." She swallowed hard. "Towards the end of June 1805 some ten years ago at the height of summer, the Dauphin came here. It was very hot: Paris was rejoicing at the Emperor's victories. I wasn't here, I was in the general ward when a young man with a beard and moustache, he looked about nineteen, came and stood by my bed and stared down at me." Madame Simon wetted her lips. "Beside him was a tall Negro, dressed in the most garish costume, a tattered, silk jacket, shirt and pantaloons. I smiled up at my visitor; he took his hat off, his hair was cropped. He turned down the quilt which I had pulled up over my face because I was shy. It was the Dauphin." She fell silent.

"And what happened then?"

"He put his hand to his heart and bowed slightly. He then said: 'Madame Simon, I am pleased you are alive. I can see that they have not deceived me.' "

For a while Segalla sat in silence.

"Madame, you are sure of what you say? Eleven years have passed since you had seen him."

"Can a mother forget her child? He had the eyes, cheeks and chin. And, above all, the same cheeky smile. It was the Dauphin Louis Charles!"

"And he never came back?"

"Never!"

"Is there anything else, madame?"

"Nothing, monsieur, except why do you ask all these questions?"

"I am trying to find the Dauphin."

Segalla got to his feet and looked pityingly down at this frail old woman, a relic of France's violent past. He bent down, raised her cold hands to his lips and kissed them softly. He then gently pressed some coins between her fingers. The old woman's eyes filled with tears.

"If you find him, monsieur, will you bring him to me?" She grasped Segalla's hand. "Believe me," she whispered. "The Dauphin escaped. Seek out Françoise Desprey at 14 Rue de St.-Pierre, she'll tell you!"

Something in her face and her voice convinced Segalla, whatever other people might say about her wandering wits or dimming memory, Madame Simon really believed the Dauphin had escaped from the Temple.

Outside the room Mother Superior was sitting on a bench, fingering her rosary.

"You are finished, Major Segalla?"

He nodded. "Except for one thing, mother. Do you have a visitors' book?"

"Yes. Why?"

"Is it possible for me to look at the entries for the summer of 1805?"

The nun agreed and took Segalla back to her office. She handed over a calf-skinned ledger, inviting Segalla to sit down whilst she served him a delicious-tasting glass of lemonade.

"Who are you looking for, Major?" she asked as Segalla, cursing under his breath, leafed through the pages.

"At the end of June 1805, a young man accompanied by a Negro, visited Madame Simon."

The Mother Superior fairly snatched the ledger from Segalla's hands.

"I am sorry, monsieur," she chattered. "The young man I

cannot help you with; so many people pass through our doors. But I remember the Negro: tall, majestic-looking, he walked with a certain swagger and was dressed in the most tattered finery." She thumbed over the pages and jabbed one finger, its nail bitten to the quick, at an entry in faded purple ink. "The Negro's name was Lécure and, see, his companion's."

"Mathurin Bruneau," Segalla read.

The Mother Superior smiled. "And, before you ask, Major, we do not know the reason why anyone visits here. During the Revolution France was in turmoil, particularly here in Paris. Families were torn apart. Many people lost contact with mothers, fathers, brothers and sisters. Even today we have young men and women looking for this aunt or lost cousin." She took the ledger from Segalla's lap. "Yet the name Bruneau"—she tapped the side of her head—"awakes memories but, unfortunately, Major, I cannot tell you what."

Segalla sucked at his upper lip and, whilst the Mother Superior chattered about the work at the hospital, he finished his lemonade, half listening as he too tried to recall the name Bruneau. He was sure he had heard it, not in France but during one of the interminable briefings delivered in London by Lord Liverpool's secretary. At last he got to his feet and, brushing aside Mother Superior's objections, insisted on making a donation towards her good work, and left the hospital.

The carriage was not in the grounds. A porter told him that the driver had moved it outside the gates. For a while Segalla stood in the portico watching a faint drizzle fall as he wondered what to do next. Then, swinging his cane, he walked down towards the gate, determined that, before the day was out, he would corroborate Madame Simon's story by visiting Françoise Desprey.

The afternoon was drawing on. Segalla was so absorbed in his thoughts, he'd dropped his usual caution. Four men, hats pulled down well over their eyes, came racing out of an alleyway. At first Segalla thought it was some street fight but, as the men fanned out, he realised they were heading straight for him. The leader struck first. Segalla lashed out with his boot, knocking the man's legs from beneath him. He then drew his sword from his walking-cane and, with his back to the metal railings of the hospital, began a most desperate fight.

Segalla had been attacked before but the sheer speed of these assailants and the ferocity of their attack took him by surprise. For a while he just blindly lashed out, his sword cutting like a scythe as the men jabbed, parried and thrust with an array of rusty cutlasses and wicked stabbing-knives. Perhaps they had expected an easier victim and, for a few seconds they drew away, frightened by the fury of Segalla's counterattack. He stood, sword half-lowered, chest heaving. The man he had kicked tried to get up. Segalla lashed out once more with his boot, its metal toe catching the man full in the face. He rolled away screaming, blood streaming from his broken mouth. The others closed once more but Segalla recognised their strategy: the one in the centre was the most dangerous. The two on either side were more cautious. Again they paused and Segalla drew the musket from his pocket. The men backed away.

Segalla, musket held out, cocked the hammer even as he desperately wondered whether it was fully loaded and primed. His attackers talked to each other, muttering in some guttural patois. The one in the centre pointed to Segalla and screamed, "*Attaquez! Attaquez!*" The other two shook their heads. Segalla stepped forward and, losing their nerve, his assailants collected their wounded companion and disappeared back up the alleyway. Segalla waited for a few minutes, eased back the hammer of the musket, resheathed his sword and hurried along to his waiting carriage.

"Why didn't you wait in the hospital?" Segalla glared up at the driver.

"But, monsieur, you sent a message. I was in the hospital. A porter told me to wait farther down the street for you, so I obeyed." He saw the sheen of sweat on Segalla's face. "Why, monsieur, did I do wrong?"

Segalla shook his head. "No," he muttered. "You did nothing wrong. But you know the Rue de St.-Pierre? Take me to number 14, the house of Françoise Desprey."

The man nodded. Segalla climbed into the carriage, slamming the door behind him. He took off his coat, loosened his collar and sprawled back on the seat. For a while he just concentrated on controlling his breathing and steadying his mind. He knew the recent attack had been planned. A clever ambush, but who had organised it? Decazes? Segalla dismissed that possibility. Why should he? It would only cause the most dreadful row with Lord Liverpool, as well as alert the suspicions of the British Government. Or Monsieur de Paris?

Segalla straightened in the seat: Monsieur de Paris, with the black fleur-de-lys tattooed on his left shoulder. Why should he want him dead? Segalla reflected on what he had learnt since his arrival in Paris. Why had this monsieur assassinated Betrancourt and Harmand of Meuse? For a while Segalla closed his eyes: Harmand was murdered, he concluded, because of his report. Further questioning might have established that the boy he saw was not the Dauphin. Segalla played with the top of his swordstick. And Betrancourt? He must have been killed for the same reason. If the grave-digger could be used to find out where the supposed Dauphin had been buried there might be an exhumation and an autopsy, this would only reveal the corpse buried there was not the Dauphin's.

Segalla smiled to himself. He would have to draw a line: Anything which happened after 19 January 1794, if Madame Simon was correct, was irrelevant to his investigation. In a sense the murders of Harmand and Betrancourt had been unnecessary. His own suspicions, not to mention Madame Simon's testimony, clearly established that the child who had been imprisoned in the Temple after January 1794 had been an impostor.

Segalla concentrated on following the line of argument through. But why should Monsieur de Paris and his secret Templars be so keen to hide that? What was it to them? To be sure, Louis XVIII and his ministers would be seriously alarmed if they thought that the true heir of Louis XVI was still alive. Did Louis XVIII's government, Segalla wondered, control the Templars? Did they know the Dauphin had escaped but just wished to suppress the facts and peddle the accepted story that the Dauphin died some twenty years ago? Segalla wiped the sweat from the back of his neck. Madame Simon had spoken the truth, he was sure of that. However, why hadn't she glimpsed such a prominent birth mark on the real Dauphin's chest? And why didn't the revolutionary government know of these birth marks? And who was that young man who had visited Madame Simon some eleven years later? Where had he been for the previous ten years? Abroad? In America or the West Indies? That would explain the presence of the Negro. Segalla closed his eyes and dozed for a while. He woke with a start; the carriage had stopped and the driver was staring curiously at him through the open door.

"Monsieur, we are here."

Segalla rubbed his eyes and stepped out of the carriage. The drizzle had now turned to a steady downpour. The carriage had stopped before a tall, dilapidated house; the paintwork on its shutters was shabby and tattered. Segalla knocked on the door, telling the driver to wait for a while. There was no reply, so he knocked again. This time he heard the slap of sandalled feet and the door swung open.

"Who are you?" the woman asked, "the angel Gabriel?" She stared fiercely at Segalla.

"I am looking for Françoise Desprey."

"Well, you have found her." The woman ran her hand through her close-cropped, steel-grey hair. She had a tanned, open face, watchful, light green eyes with a pleasant mouth, but she spoke and dressed like a man; her accent was guttural. She was dressed in trousers and a rather tattered shirt, unbuttoned to reveal a thick, muscular neck.

"Well," she said. "What do you want?"

She looked over Segalla's shoulder and saw the grinning driver.

"Don't you laugh at me, man! I may be sixty years of age but I've cut the throats of better fellows than you. Oh, for the love of God!"

She grasped Segalla by the arm, pulled her bemused visitor through the door and slammed it behind him. The passageway inside was gloomy but the flagstones were scrubbed, the walls freshly painted, and candles in smart black holders gave off a fragrant smell.

"You are Françoise Desprey?" Segalla repeated.

"I was when I answered the door!" the woman snapped. "But you looked so confused, I am beginning to wonder myself!"

Segalla smiled and bowed. "Madame, I am sorry. I just expected someone else."

"Well, go on, say it!" Desprey urged. "I look like a man and I speak like one. I can't help it. That's the way God made me."

Segalla stretched out his hand and introduced himself. Desprey grasped his hand and smiled.

"An English officer. You are welcome. Your French is very good, monsieur." She stared more intently. "You look troubled." She stepped back, looked down at Segalla's mud-spattered boots, then tapped the top of his walking-stick. "You have been in a fight, haven't you? Well, come on upstairs, Françoise Desprey will soon put you right."

Off she strode, arms swinging by her side. Segalla followed her up into a small cosy parlour, though everything was now packed, stacked into cases and bundles.

"I am moving soon," Desprey declared, "to the Hôtel Trois Maillets in the Rue Montorgeuil." She pushed Segalla into a chair before the weakly burning fire and pulled up a stool opposite him, then, muttering under her breath, rose and came back with two goblets. "That's the best claret you'll find in Paris, Major. It will put warmth in your belly and fire in your loins."

She sat down, legs apart, toasted Segalla and noisily smacked her lips.

"I was a Chouanne, a royalist," she began abruptly. She rolled back the sleeve of her shirt and showed Segalla the silver fleur-de-lys tattooed on her brown, muscular arm. "I am sixty years of age," she continued defiantly.

"Madame, I would never have guessed it."

"Spoken like a gentleman." Desprey leaned forward and, from a bucket, tossed some more coal on the fire. "Spoken like a gentleman," she repeated. "During the Revolution I worked for the royalists in the west, bringing messages in and out of Paris. No one ever suspected someone like myself. Now the King has returned, I have a pension and new lodgings in a comfortable hotel." She stared round. "I'm finished here. Well, Major Segalla, what does an English officer want with an old Chouanne?"

"I have just spoken to Madame Simon," he replied, believing that bluntness was the best policy. "She told me an incredible story, how the Dauphin was smuggled out of the Temple in January 1795 and entrusted to you."

Desprey hardly flinched. She flexed her sunburnt, scarred arm. Segalla watched the silver fleur-de-lys tattooed there move under her rippling muscle. She caught his eye.

"We all wore these," she explained. "Towards the end of the civil war it was difficult to establish who was working for whom. Ah," she whispered, "*ma petite lys blanche!*"

Segalla tensed: Where had he heard a phrase like that before?

"Well?" she asked. "So you met Madame Simon? Soon all Paris will know about her story!" She shrugged. "It's the truth. Don't look so surprised, Major Segalla. I am not out of my wits. Two months ago I sent a similar letter to the King, describing my exploits on behalf of his family."

"And you received a reply?"

"Yes. A pension and comfortable lodgings in a hotel. The letter was brought by a royal equerry, one of those perfumed flunkeys. I could tell by his eyes and the cast of his mouth that they thought poor old Françoise was mad."

Segalla stared at the blackened mantelpiece. "Why didn't they tell me?" he murmured.

"Nobody believes me!" She laughed. "In the early spring of 1795," she continued, "I acted as an agent between royalist sympathisers in Normandy and Britanny, and those in Paris opposed to the Terror under Robespierre and his gang." She sipped from her wine cup. "In the main, I worked for Baron Petitval from his château at Vitry-sur-Seine. Now, you may or may not know the story: Petitval was a dyed-in-the-wool royalist. The old king, Louis XVI, had appointed him as his principal attorney. Petitval had powerful resources at a time when the revolutionary paper money, the Assignat, wasn't worth blowing your nose on. Petitval possessed good silver. He realised that any restoration of the Bourbons could only be brought about by the total annihilation of Robespierre, Danton, St. Just and the other terrorists. He therefore chose his client very carefully."

"Barras?"

"Yes, Barras. He was bribed to undermine Robespierre. Barras used Petitval's silver to win over the other deputies as well as leaders of the Commune and officers in the Revolutionary Guard. I played a part in this."

"And the Dauphin?" Segalla intervened.

"Well, Simon was a secret royalist. Oh, not out of conviction. He had been bought as well. By the beginning of 1794, Paris was rife with rumours about a plot to free the Dauphin. Even leading members of the state, like Danton, were involved." She shook her iron-grey curls and fingered a small earring in the lobe of her left ear. "I paid little attention to these. My task and that of others was to undermine the revolutionary government, set them at each others' throats, and that wasn't hard. Danton fell and went to the guillotine. A few months later Robespierre travelled in the same tumbril to have his neck shaved. And then, in June 1795, I received instructions to be waiting at the corner of a street just near the Pont Neuf. A carriage would collect me."

"Who told you this?"

"Messages just came and went. Anyway, I was collected by the carriage and we drove down to the designated place. The driver stopped, the door was flung open and a girl was pushed into the carriage." She smiled. "I could tell by the voice, hair and face that it was a boy dressed as a girl. I suspected it was the Dauphin though I had little time to make enquiries because the carriage rattled out of Paris and the child, whom I believe was drugged, slept throughout. Oh, now and again, he would wake up, be given a bite to eat and something to drink. He'd smile and chatter but, like any child in a drugged sleep, what he said didn't make sense."

"Who accompanied you?"

"Nobody. At least, once we left Paris. We travelled to Fontenay. I handed the child over to Charette, one of the Royalist generals. I believe he took him to the Baron Petitval at Vitry-sur-Seine."

"You are sure it was the Dauphin?"

"Well, I was never told as such, but the care and precautions taken, the rather flamboyant disguise, as well as the reception given to the child by Charette, convinced me that it was Louis Charles, Duke of Normandy."

"But, according to Madame Simon," Segalla pointed out, "the Dauphin was freed from the Temple in the January of 1794, which means that, for almost eighteen months, he must have been kept hidden in Paris."

"I don't know anything about that," Desprey laughed. "But surely, Major, such a move would be sensible? In the countryside, on the roads, it is easy to search for a young, well-spoken child, a stranger in the neighbourhood, but in Paris?" She shrugged one shoulder. "You could spend an eternity searching for someone down its narrow alleyways and runnels. What I suspect, Major, is that the Dauphin was kept hidden away and, once Robespierre fell, he was sent into Normandy."

"And what happened then?" Segalla asked.

Desprey cradled the wine cup in her hands. "Of the Dauphin, I don't know. I never saw nor heard of him again. But, the following year, Baron Petitval's château was attacked. The financier and all his family were killed, though I understand that the corpse of a male child was never found."

"Who would authorise . . ." Segalla pushed the stool away from the heat of the fire. He repeated, "Who would authorise such an attack?"

Desprey got to her feet and refilled her cup. She offered the jug to Segalla but he shook his head.

"Only God knows," she replied, sitting down. "Normandy, in 1796, was engulfed in a savage civil war: bands of armed men roamed the countryside. But the attack on Petitval's château remains a mystery. No plunder was taken, the inhabitants were killed, and the raiders left as quietly and as quickly as they arrived. One thing I do know," she added slowly, "is that before Petitval died, he was in a terrible temper with Barras, threatening to unmask him as a trickster. Now this was just gossip, chatter."

"Do you think it's possible," Segalla queried, "that Barras double-crossed Petitval? Sent him a child who was not the Dauphin?"

Desprey raised her eyebrows and laughed deep in her throat. "You mean the real Dauphin had either died or been spirited away elsewhere and Petitval was duped? I never thought of that," she replied. "But, the little I know of Barras, it's possible." She caught her tongue between her lips and gazed fixedly at Segalla. "It's possible. Indeed, very possible. But, if that's the case, then Barras must have been behind the attack at the Château Vitry-sur-Seine." She shook her head. "I can't help you there, Major."

"But you knew most of the royalist officers?"

Desprey nodded her head vigorously.

"Did you hear any rumours or gossip about the attack?"

"No, definitely not."

Segalla pointed to the tattoo on her arm. "Madame Françoise, I apologise for taking your time. Did you ever see, or meet an officer with a black fleur-de-lys tattooed on his shoulder?"

She smiled and shook her head. "No, I did not."

"And does the name Madame Roquet mean anything to you?"

Françoise grinned. "Everyone knows about Madame Roquet and her famous house. It's wonderful what you men will chatter about when you are dancing between the sheets. She was one of our best spies in Paris. The English also used her. Most of her work was done after Robespierre's fall from power but she was not involved in the Dauphin's escape."

"And her two helpers?" Segalla insisted. "A fop called Jacques de Coeur and a small man, always dressed in yellow, nicknamed the Canary?"

"I have heard of them," Desprey replied. "Madame Roquet's creatures, but they mean nothing to me."

Segalla put his hand beneath his cloak and fingered the locket.

"The child you took out of Paris, the one who might have been the Dauphin. Describe him."

"A round, babyish face, quite pretty for a boy. Plump cheeks, generous lips, he looked well fed and cared for."

"And the colour of his hair?"

"Remember, Major, he was wearing a bonnet well over his head and a scarf or muffler round his neck. We travelled by night and, during the day, the carriage blinds were kept firmly closed." Desprey gnawed at her lips as she tried to remember. "Auburn," she said. "Yes, he was an auburn-haired child."

Segalla's heart sank. "Are you sure, madame?"

"As sure as I am of sitting on my arse and talking to you!" She tapped the side of her head. "They say I am a little mad, Major, but my memory is good. Whether you like it or not, I'll never forget your face!"

"And does the name Mathurin Bruneau mean anything to you?"

The old Chouanne shook her head. "No, I have never heard of it."

Segalla was about to rise and take his leave when Desprey gripped his knee.

"Mathurin Bruneau?" she suddenly asked.

"Yes."

"Ah! Stay there, monsieur."

Desprey went across to one of the packing-cases, cursing and muttering under her breath as she began to move things out: old ledgers, folios, scraps of newspapers, all the possessions collected over her sixty years, or so she apologised to Segalla. He sat there patiently. Only once did he rise to stare out of the window, but the carriage was waiting patiently in the street below, the driver taking refuge inside against the rain.

"Doesn't anyone ever visit you here, madame?"

"No, no," Desprey replied gruffly. "Most of my friends are dead and no one wants to hear my stories." She lifted her red face and grinned. "Except my friends from England." She stood up, gripping the side of the large chest. "What do you think, Major Segalla? Will we ever discover the true fate of this poor boy?"

Segalla shook his head. Desprey went back to her searching which ended with a shout of triumph.

"Here it is, monsieur! Here it is!" The old woman hurried across with a yellowing piece of newspaper in her hand and thrust it at Segalla. "A copy of the *Moniteur* from the winter of 1795." Desprey jabbed her finger at a headline entitled, A Curious Incident at the Château Angrie.

Segalla read it curiously. It began with the story of a farmer who had called at the headquarters of the royalist army in the west in December 1795; according to this, a boy claiming to be the son of a lord had mysteriously arrived at his farm. The rest of the story described how the boy had been taken into the care of a local noblewoman, the Viscomtesse de Turpin. How she had housed and clothed him, accepting his claim to be a member of the Devesci family. Apparently, however, a member of that same family had turned up at the Château Angrie; on being told there was a young kinsman present, he went in and inspected him, only to find that the child was not a member of his kin. After a great deal of interrogation, the young boy had confessed that he was an impostor and that his real name was Mathurin Bruneau. Segalla finished reading and handed the dusty, yellowing paper back to Desprey.

"The boy was quite famous," she declared. "Quite a scandal was caused, but he took everyone in with his airs and graces."

"Is it possible," Segalla said, "just for the sake of argument, madame, that the child you spirited out of Paris and this impostor Mathurin Bruneau are one and the same? That Barras used him to deceive Petitval who realised he had been duped and turned the child out of doors?"

"It's possible," the old Chouanne replied. "And then he decided to be the scion of some noble family. But, Major, why attack Petitval's château if the child was already gone?"

Segalla shook his head and made to leave.

"And one further thing, Major. If Bruneau was used in the place of the Dauphin, where did he come from and who taught him such courtly manners he was able to deceive grown adults?"

Segalla shook her hand. "Madame, you have given me much food for thought." He pointed to the newspaper. "You solved one riddle: When I was briefed in London, they told me of the royalists and mentioned the case of Mathurin Bruneau; I'd forgotten about it."

"But the truth about the Dauphin?" Desprey asked.

Segalla shrugged. "I am beginning to doubt, madame, if we will ever discover that."

172

Chapter 12

On his return to the Lion d'Or, Segalla struggled against the wave of depression flooding through him. He opened the locket Marie-Antoinette had given him and stared at her face, then that of the dark-haired, chubby-faced Dauphin.

"I am sorry," he murmured.

He heard a knock on the door and, easing his hand under the pillow, felt the butt of the pistol.

"Come in!" he shouted.

Tallien slipped through. He was dressed theatrically in a heavy greatcoat, a beaver hat pulled down over his eyes; in any other circumstances Segalla would have burst out laughing. Tallien tossed the hat on the table and took his greatcoat off, shaking the raindrops from it.

"It will soon be winter," he moaned, "and Paris will be as bleak as ever."

Segalla watched him intently. So far he had trusted this little man, but he wondered how far this trust could develop.

"Are you happy, Tallien? I mean, in Paris?"

His guest sat on a chair, crossing his legs.

"Happy? I suppose I am." He shook his head. "As happy as a man could be." Then he smiled weakly. "In the circumstances."

Segalla rose and, apologising for his lack of manners, poured himself and Tallien cups of wine. He thrust one into the archivist's hands and stood over him.

"I have lived a long and curious life, Monsieur Tallien. I live and work in the shadows of the night. A world of spies, plot and double-plot, plot and counter-plot. You came to the Lion d'Or disguised but, eventually, your masters will find out."

"Find out what?"

. "That you and I know that the Dauphin is not buried in the cemetery of Ste.-Marguerite, but might still be alive."

"What are you saying, monsieur?"

Segalla succinctly described his visit to Madame Simon, the attack outside the Hospital of the Incurables and his conversations with Françoise Desprey. As he talked, he saw the fear in Tallien's eyes.

"I trust you, Tallien," Segalla concluded, "but here we have a riddle. Let us draw a line, as I have said, through our investigations. I believe that the boy who died in the Temple was not the Dauphin: that's why Harmand was murdered and his report suppressed. The corpse buried at Ste.-Marguerite is not that of the Dauphin: that's why the grave-digger, Betrancourt, had his head blown off, just in case he remembered where the coffin might be. Men like Bellanger the sculptor were tricked. Others like Gomin, Lasne and Pelletan were creatures of Barras' and now belong to the government which has a vested interest in maintaining that the Dauphin is dead. But we know different.

"However, as one door closes another opens. We have entered a maze of mystery. As we go round one corner, another problem confronts us. Was it the real Dauphin who was sent to Petitval? If not, what did happen to Louis XVI's heir? If he was sent there, was he abducted? If so, by whom? Who was behind that dreadful massacre? Above all, where is the real Louis Charles now?"

Tallien rubbed his face in his hands.

"Or did the Dauphin just die?" the archivist intervened. "And Barras send some dupe to trick Petitval, then, when the banker objected, arrange for the massacre at Vitry-sur-Seine to prevent any blackmail or counterthreats?"

Segalla scratched his head. "Interesting, but now we turn another corner in the maze. This boy Mathurin Bruneau, if he was a peasant, he duped quite a number of intelligent noblemen and women with his courtly graces."

"Are you saying Mathurin Bruneau was the child sent by Barras?"

"It's possible: Petitval realised he was duped and turned the boy out to fend for himself. This pseudo Dauphin was then quite experienced in deception; he turned up at that farmer's house and assumed another role."

"And the real Dauphin, the one under Madame Simon's care?"

"Ah," Segalla sighed. "There's the real mystery!"

"Which is?"

"Madame Simon may be old and garrulous"—Segalla tapped his waistcoat pocket—"but I have a picture of the young Dauphin when he was two years old. He had black hair as well as a mole above his left teat and a deep inoculation mark high on his right shoulder. According to Madame Simon the boy she tended did not have these marks and his hair was auburn."

"What are you saying?"

Segalla leaned his elbows on the arm of the chair, clasping his hands before his mouth. "I now wonder why Robespierre and his agents weren't aware of these physical characteristics, but Petitval was. And there's more."

"Such as?"

"Petitval took the boy from Desprey but then turned him out, let's say in December 1795, yet his château was not attacked till the following April." He gripped Tallien's wrist. "I want to follow one last path."

"Yes?"

Segalla ran the rim of his thumbnail round his lips. "I want you to return to your masters in the Tuileries. Tell them that we would like to go back through the records from before the Dauphin's removal from his family."

"Why?" Tallien stammered. "What reason can we give?"

"Say that our report needs further background. Make up some excuse. How can they object?"

Tallien put his hand inside his coat. "If it is a time for truth, Major Segalla—" He lifted his face and Segalla saw the fear there. "If it's a time of danger then you, sir, are an English envoy. Within ten minutes you could be in the English embassy or sheltering behind those troops still camped outside Paris. But what would happen to poor Tallien, eh? An accident as I walked through the Tuileries gardens? Or would I be attacked by footpads one night in winter, my body found bobbing alongside the icy, reef-filled banks of the Seine?" Tallien gulped from the wine cup. "Or even worse," he continued, "bundled into a carriage and taken to some château to be interrogated until I tell them what I know."

"What do you want?" Segalla asked.

"Your friendship," Tallien replied.

"You have that."

"Protection and guarantees," Tallien added hurriedly. "When you leave for England," he smiled, "I want to go with you."

Segalla recalled his conversation with Lord Liverpool. *"Promise what you have to,"* the Prime Minister had urged. *"Give whatever guarantees are needed."* Segalla recalled the great libraries being built in London. "Agreed." He pushed back his chair. "Who knows? You may even meet another Priscilla Johnson!"

"I doubt it," Tallien retorted. "Though even a faint shadow of her would be welcome enough." He put his hand inside his coat and drew out the prayerbook Madame Josephine had given him. Only this time the back was torn away and, between the binding, was a yellowing, greasy, flimsy manuscript. "I am committed already," Tallien remarked. "When I returned to the Tuileries I sat and thought about everything I knew about this mystery. I kept remembering how my mistress Madame Josephine was poisoned. I picked up her prayerbook. I realised this was more than a gift, so I removed the leather backing." He plucked out the yellowing page and handed it to Segalla who unfolded it and studied the small, cramped writing.

"It's written in cipher," Tallien explained. "I could decode it but I was too frightened to write it out. It's a report of a meeting with Barras and his fellow directors on 28 April 1796."

Segalla looked up, startled.

"It proves what you say."

"Why didn't you hand it to me immediately?" Segalla asked.

"I was too frightened," Tallien confessed. "Before I came here I knew I had reached a crossroads. I could turn one way and be Tallien the little mild-mannered archivist, safe and secure, patronised by the great and mighty as if I were some pet mouse. But if I did that, I'd dishonour the truth, my dead mistress, the Dauphin and finally, you, Major Segalla. So I am going to go the other way, into the darkness. You have told me the truth. Your conclusions are corroborated by that piece of paper. More importantly, you have shown me, a stranger, friendship and trust."

"You are sure?" Segalla asked. "Remember, no man who puts his hand to the plough can look backwards."

"I am committed," Tallien replied. "By yourself you could never have deciphered that document. It's written by Barras himself. He used the same cipher in his love letters to Madame Josephine. Apparently he met with his fellow directors late at night on 28 April 1796. They talked about Petitval and his contribution to the overthrow of Robespierre. Barras had agreed that, because of this help, the child would be sent to the Château Vitry-sur-Seine: Petitval would hold him there because they could not set the son of Louis XVI at complete liberty."

"They talked about it so openly?"

"Yes," Tallien replied. "The Dauphin's despatch had been approved by the other four Directors. This is a résumé of their conversation: The Dauphin had been sent, then they go on to talk about the attack on the château seven days earlier. Barras described the massacre: Madame de Chambeau, Petitval's mother-in-law, was found lying in bed, her throat slashed. Two of madame's lady friends, as well as their maids, had also been killed, the head of one of them being separated from the body. Petitval's corpse, his throat slashed, was found in the garden. Other servants' bodies were found strewed about, either in the château or in the gardens outside."

Segalla stared down at the piece of paper, his hands trembling. "Did everyone die?"

"No, certain servants got away."

"And the Dauphin?" Segalla exclaimed.

"We don't know. The document," Tallien continued hurriedly in a whisper, "goes on—I thought this strange—to claim that the massacre had been organised in order to . . ." Tallien closed his eyes to remember. "That's it, to avoid the payment of debts due to Petitval, but also to seize documents Petitval possessed and so prevent certain revelations. Barras and his colleagues concluded that, and I quote directly, 'powerful men had decided on the banker's death.' "

Segalla sat back in the chair, startled by the archivist's declaration.

"And did the survivors recognise any of their attackers?"

Tallien shook his head. "No, the assault was brutal and quick: it was carried out just before dawn. Nobody could remember a thing. Two of Barras' special agents were sent to Vitry-sur-Seine to investigate. According to them, the outlaws had been masked and cowled: They never spoke but moved quickly and ruthlessly, slaughtering all they found in their path." Tallien leaned forward. "What is important," he whispered hoarsely, "are four things. First, Barras did not know about the murder. Secondly, the attack was not motivated by desire for plunder. Thirdly, the child who was there had already gone." Tallien closed his eyes again. "All Barras says about him, and I quote the words directly, is 'the lady's maid who had looked after that child, had her head cut off.' " He opened his eyes. "Yes, that's it."

"And fourthly?"

"One of the survivors claimed that the leader of the band was short in stature."

"Why didn't Barras pursue matters any further?"

"It doesn't say," Tallien replied. "They just decided to let justice follow its course."

Segalla stared down at the piece of paper. "Why would Barras write this?" he said.

"Possibly to safeguard himself," Tallien replied. "A memorandum to prove his loyalty to the royalist cause: that he sent the Dauphin to safety and that the massacre at Vitry-sur-Seine was not of his doing. He must have given it to Josephine to hold. This was the document which led her to confide in other people and brought about her death. She must have put it in the back of that prayerbook and handed it to me, confident that one day I would let the truth be known."

Segalla pushed back his chair and got up. He opened the door but the passageway outside was deserted.

"So," he declared, locking the door behind him. "We have Barras' words that the Dauphin was released from the Temple and sent to Vitry-sur-Seine. He stayed there for a while. Later the château was attacked, Petitval and his family were massacred. We also know the attack was not organised by Barras, but other, very powerful men, were behind it. What is more interesting," he continued, "is Barras's reaction: He organised no search for the Dauphin and seems frightened of those behind the massacre." Segalla walked over and clapped Tallien on the shoulder. "Tomorrow morning," he said, "I shall join you at the Tuileries. Go back there, make up whatever lies you can. Let us continue our search."

Tallien got to his feet. "One question, Major Segalla. I am now involved because of Madame Josephine. . . ." His voice trailed off.

"And why am I?" Segalla interjected, "you mean, above and beyond the call of duty?"

"Yes," Tallien replied. "You are not just an English spy, are you? but something else. I have heard rumours about a man like you at the French court, long before the Revolution ever broke out."

"Court tittle-tattle," Segalla replied. He took the locket out of his pocket, opened it and handed it to Tallien. "The child on the left is the Dauphin. The woman, of course, is Marie-Antoinette, Queen of France. I can't tell you the reason why, Monsieur Tallien, but I am as much at the beck and call of that dead woman as you are yours."

"What was she like?" Tallien asked.

"Very beautiful in a strange sort of way. Haughty, vain, empty-headed, but she had a great capacity to love. She made mistakes and thought others would forgive her if she forgave them: A terrible mistake—they were out to destroy her from the very start." Segalla took the locket back and stared down at the smiling faces. "Somehow, Tallien, Marie-Antoinette—not Robespierre, Simon, Danton and the rest—controlled this game. Louis Charles was her second son." Segalla clasped the locket shut. "The eldest boy, Louis Joseph, was born on 22 October 1781, but then, in the summer of 1787, he fell ill and died. He was laid out in his coffin with his crown and gold spurs. This left our Dauphin, his younger brother, born in 1785—Louis Charles. Marie-Antoinette was very protective of him. She not only feared an outbreak of violence in France but the possibility of the King's own brothers, the Comte de Provence and the Comte d'Artois, not to mention the Duke of Orléans, who later joined Robespierre's Jacobins." Segalla shook himself free of his reverie. "Tallien," he murmured, "take a carriage back to the Tuileries. I shall be there about ten o'clock tomorrow morning. Do what you have to."

Tallien shook Segalla's hand, unlocked the door and disappeared down the passageway.

For a while Segalla sat staring down at the locket.

"What is it?" he kept murmuring at the face staring up at him. He ran his forefinger carefully over the picture then looked at the sweet, smiling boy on the other side. Marie-Antoinette had given him this in 1787, when the child was two years old. There was no mistaking the likeness between him and his mother except for that hair: dark, almost jet-black. Segalla clasped the locket shut and put it away.

Then, on the spur of the moment, he decided to go for a walk. He donned his greatcoat, slipping two pistols into the deep pockets and, swinging his walking-cane, he went out into the streets. On the corner of the street he turned quickly round but no one was watching or following him. The steady drizzle had kept everyone at home. There was only the occasional beggar whining for alms, or the ladies of the night, bright in their colours, slipping in and out of the taverns, lifting the hems of their red skirts as they grasped the helping hand of some beau, into his carriage. Nevertheless, Segalla felt his unease deepen as he remembered the attack earlier in the day. He hailed a cabriolet and, giving the driver instructions, settled back in the warm, fusty darkness, letting the clip-clop of the hooves across the cobbles soothe his mind. He had almost fallen asleep when the driver stopped and tapped the top of the carriage.

"Monsieur, we have arrived."

Segalla got out. He went across the street, stood under the shade of a dripping lime tree and stared across the great, deserted common where the huge Temple had once stood. Napoléon Bonaparte's destruction had been thorough: not one stone had been left upon another. Segalla heard the carriage behind him creak and groan as the driver tried to keep the horses steady.

"There's nothing here, monsieur!" the fellow called out.

"Oh yes there is," Segalla replied softly. "A veritable horde of ghosts."

"What is that?" the driver asked.

Segalla turned. "Nothing! Nothing at all. You know the church of Ste.-Marguerite?"

The driver nodded and, once Segalla was inside, the carriage swung out of the Rue de Temple down the Rue Bassroy to the crumbling church of Ste.-Marguerite. Segalla told the driver to wait and went inside and along the narrow nave. An old lady, praying before the statue of the Virgin, showed him the corpse-door into the cemetery. Segalla pushed this open. The graveyard was a small enclosure bound on one side by the church and, on the other three sides, by tall, crumbling walls. The cemetery was overgrown with thick grass and shrouded by oak trees. In one corner was the death-house: a tumbledown old place with a slate roof and dusty windows protected by iron bars. Segalla walked across, past the decaying headstones and weather-soaked wooden crosses. In the centre lay the common grave. A long, broad strip of open ground: a veritable trench which would be opened up to receive a corpse; once this was thrown in, it would be covered up again. Segalla gazed up at the thick clouds beginning to break. He took out the locket, opened it and stared at the faces pictured there.

"It did not end here," he whispered quietly. "All this is a sham. Nevertheless, I swear before God," his eyes held those in the painting of Marie-Antoinette, "that I shall do all in my power to establish the truth."

He walked back into the church, lit three candles and, for a while, knelt beside a granite pillar and stared up at the cross hanging above the high altar. He repeated his solemn oath, asked for guidance, then left. Outside, the driver was trying to fend off a group of urchins who insisted on climbing on the back of the carriage and scrambling under the wheels, making the horses skittish. Segalla drew some coins out of his pocket.

"*Garçons!*"

The boys turned. When they saw the coins fall, they leapt down from the carriage and began to scrabble furiously amongst themselves at this unexpected windfall.

A woman, hair tousled, her black dress covered by a white, soiled apron, came bustling out of the house. She grabbed one of the boys by the ear and pulled him away from the rest. She must have hurt him, for the boy suddenly began to cry. This evidently brought about a change of heart, the woman clasping him to her ample bosom.

"*Mon chéri! Mon chéri!*" She cried. "*Mon petit fleur! Mon petit lys!*"

Segalla was back in the carriage, the driver had already cracked his whip, when the echo of the woman's voice made him start, lurching forward so he gripped the rim of the door.

" '*Mon petit lys!*' " he whispered.

He'd heard that phrase once before; leaning back he recalled what Desprey had said to him. Segalla, fingering the locket, stared out of the window at the gathering night and began to weave the possibilities together.

When he arrived at the entrance hall to the Tuileries the following morning, Tallien was waiting for him, neat and spruce, not a hair out of place.

"No problems whatsoever," Tallien whispered as they climbed the great staircase. "Decazes accepted my explanation without a murmur."

They stopped in a small antechamber where footmen were clearing up the remains of a buffet breakfast, and broke their fast on milk, bread and steaming cups of black coffee before adjourning to the library. No one bothered them. The library remained empty and they worked steadily in the secret room without any interruption. They hardly talked, only now and again would they scribble messages on scraps of paper.

What are we looking for? Tallien wrote.

You will know when you find it, Segalla replied.

As they began to search through coffer after coffer packed with papers, memoranda, rolls of parchment, ledgers, the tittle-tattle of a bygone age, Segalla decided they would concentrate only on evidence which preceded January 1784 and the Dauphin's solitary imprisonment in the Temple. He whispered to Tallien, not to waste time on household accounts, but to concentrate on the letters of the King, those of his wife as well as the speeches and reports of their enemies in the Convention.

As the day wore on, Segalla became immersed in the red fury of the Terror which had gripped Paris twenty-two years before. One document brought tears to his eyes: Written in Marie-Antoinette's hand, it was the Queen's last letter finished, according to a pathetic entry at the bottom, *at half past four in the morning,* the date she died. Segalla reread the postscript:

Oh my God, have pity on me. My eyes have not tears to weep for you, my poor children. Good-bye. Good-bye.

Segalla read the letter carefully, fighting back the tears. This letter, written to her fellow prisoner, Madame Élisabeth the King's sister, showed Marie-Antoinette at her best: courageous, determined, more worried about those she was leaving behind than her own impending fate on the guillotine.

"What's the matter, Major?" Tallien murmured.

Segalla brushed his eyes with the back of his hand. "The Queen's last letter to Madame Élisabeth."

"It was never delivered," Tallien replied. "Robespierre kept it. When he fell from power and was taken to the guillotine with his jaw half shot away, they found it under his mattress."

Segalla nodded and returned to the letter. He had always fought to keep his emotions and imagination in hand but, reading those last pathetic paragraphs, he felt as if the dead queen was standing behind him, whispering the words in his ears. His eyes stopped at one phrase.

I hope my son never forgets his father's last words which I now repeat: "He must never try to avenge our deaths."

His heart lurched as the Queen turned to deal with the terrible allegations the revolutionaries had put in the child's mouth, claiming he had been sexually corrupted by his own mother and aunt. He put the letter down on the table, cupping his chin in his hand.

"What's the matter?" Tallien asked.

Segalla rose and walked back into the library, indicating his colleague to join him. At one end of the library were bay windows. Segalla opened these: He went out onto the balcony and stared out across the courtyards and jumble of buildings of the Tuileries.

"I have just read the last letter of Marie-Antoinette," Segalla whispered, "written a few hours before her execution. Now, Marie-Antoinette may have been a poor queen but, as a mother, she was a tigress. Now and again in the letter she refers to her son, but sometimes she changes, especially when dealing with the allegations laid against her. She calls him 'this boy,' 'this child.' Would a mother call her only son that in the last letter she was ever going to write? In the last words she'd ever use to or about him? 'This child'!" Segalla repeated. He turned and stared at Tallien. "Put yourself in her place, man. You are in a condemned cell, writing to someone you love about your most precious, only son whom you love dearly."

"That's exactly the same phrase," Tallien murmured, "which Barras used in the memorandum I showed you last night: 'that child'."

Segalla squeezed him on the wrist. They went back to the secret room, closing the door behind them. Tallien had apparently grasped Segalla's line of thought because, an hour later, he jumped up, almost running round the table, to lay a yellowing piece of paper before Segalla. It was a Jacobin's speech, delivered in January 1792 at the Demophile Society. Tallien jabbed his finger at one line, the Jacobin's surprising statement:

> . . . that the King (Louis XVI) exhibited daily a child who bore a passing, striking resemblance to Monsieur le Dauphin.

Segalla passed it back. "And no one took it up?" he asked.

Tallien shook his head. Segalla went back to his searches, though, time and again, he found repetition of the same allegations by different speakers. Segalla worked on. At last he unearthed a small bundle of papers entitled *Correspondence Sécrète*.

"What are these?" he asked.

Tallien took the bundle and studied them carefully.

"When the King was imprisoned in the Temple, the revolutionary leaders made sure the King and his family were spied upon. Each spy sent in a daily report."

Segalla took the bundle back and read these reports carefully. The spies, ever watchful, with mean and narrow souls, reported on the King's every movement: whom he spoke to, where he walked, what books he read, even what he ate and drank at supper. But then, time and again, the spies also reported another phenomenon as one did on 18 June 1792:

> *The King, the spy wrote, is often subject to absence of mind. Recently he could not even recognise his young son the Dauphin and, on seeing him advance towards him, asked who he was.*

Segalla kept his excitement hidden. He put the papers together again, retied the cord and tossed them at Tallien.

"I think we are finished," he declared loudly. "There's nothing here. You and I, Monsieur Tallien, have fought the good fight, we have run the race, we have kept faith." He nodded his head imperceptibly and, grasping a pen, wrote hurriedly on a piece of paper as if making his final notes. He casually tossed this across the table.

> *Tomorrow, Segalla wrote, take whatever possessions you have. Leave Paris by the southern gate. Travel two or three kilometres. There's a Tavern L'Oriele, frequented by English officers. You are to stay there. Agreed?*

Tallien studied it and, whilst the archivist began to put the papers away, Segalla sat, arms crossed, probing in his mind the next step to take. He then took up the pen, wrote one final note. He handed it to Tallien and made to leave.

"You can find that?" Segalla asked.

Tallien looked at him expectantly. "Yes, but must you leave so abruptly?"

Segalla studied his fob watch. "If I am to leave Paris," he commented drily, "then I must bid farewell to Madame Roquet. Last night I sent her a note. She has kindly invited me to supper this evening."

Chapter 13

Supper at Madame Roquet's proved to be a splendid affair. Segalla's hostess looked resplendent in a simple white, woollen dress fringed at the neck and cuffs, all trimmed with gold lace. Her hair was piled high on her head and held in place with a silver comb. She looked much younger, more serene, in the flattering candlelight. The meal was served in Madame Roquet's private dining room. Jacques de Coeur was there, looking splendid in a salmon-coloured silk jacket and matching breeches. The Canary, however, looked as miserable as ever in his yellow soiled coat. All the courtesies were observed, Madame Roquet, Segalla and Jacques de Coeur chattering about the weather and the doings of the court.

The room had been specially prepared: Under the great hooded mantelpiece flames greedily licked the scented logs and, in the centre of the room, the table had been laid out and covered by a creamy silk cloth which, in the faint light from the fire and the candles, shimmered like a sea of glass. Six three-branched candelabra made of wrought silver had been placed down the centre of the table. Next to each of these were vases of flowers, golden cruets and tall, thin Venetian glassware.

Segalla and Madame Roquet sat at either end of the table with de Coeur and the Canary sitting opposite each other in the centre. Segalla revelled in the good food cooked specially by Roquet's chefs who, she declared, eyes dancing, came from Paris's most famous cookhouse.

"You are leaving, Monsieur Segalla." She pouted. "And the

least we can do is send you off with the best Paris can afford."

Segalla caught the note of mischief in her voice and smiled back. Madame Roquet's companions were not so gracious. The Canary played sullenly with his wineglass whilst Jacques de Coeur lounged sideways, one arm over the back of his chair, much the worse for drink.

The servants brought in the food: ham stuffed with cloves and seasoned with cinnamon; fillet of venison and truffles; partridge; beef, flavoured with marjoram and surrounded with slices of freshly cooked pheasant and golden capon, specially cooked with herbs and stuffed with fresh oysters. Segalla ate carefully; he hardly touched the rich claret. Now and again Madame Roquet would indicate with her fingers for Segalla's glass to be filled. He always waved the servant away.

"I leave for England tomorrow, madame," he declared.

For a few seconds Madame Roquet's fixed smile slipped. "So soon!" she exclaimed. "Will you not take your leave of the court?"

"Madame, my masters are in London. I have written a letter to Monsieur Decazes. It might take me days, nay even weeks, to receive an audience with His Majesty."

Madame Roquet, raising one alabaster shoulder in a diffident shrug, returned to teasing Jacques de Coeur about the exquisite but quite preposterous high-heeled shoes he had so recently bought. De Coeur answered, then turned and gazed heavy-eyed down at Segalla.

"And what will you say to your masters in London, Major Segalla?"

"I shall say," Segalla replied, setting his trap, "that the Dauphin escaped, that he was sent to the Château Vitry-sur-Seine in Normandy. The château was later attacked, probably by a band of ruffians under the command of Monsieur de Paris, Master of the Secret Templars. This man," Segalla continued, "either killed the Dauphin along with the household of that château or abducted him. God knows what happened to him then!"

Segalla glanced up. Madame Roquet sat, mouth slack, one hand fingering the string of pearls round her neck.

"You jest, monsieur."

"I do not jest," Segalla retorted. He put his knife and fork down and leaned back in his chair.

"You have proof of this?" Madame Roquet stammered.

"I have proof," Segalla replied, "of a sort, but it's only speculation. I suppose His Majesty's government and Lord Liverpool will accept the conventional story about the Dauphin's death in the Temple and leave matters at that."

Segalla went back to his meal, eating as if his statement had been no more than mere gossip. The course finished, the plates were cleared away and Segalla quietly prayed that Roquet would rise to the bait.

As the Canary went to a large buffet table at the side of the room to serve cognac, a glass of which he slammed down in front of Segalla, Madame Roquet rose. She went to the door to ensure there were no eavesdroppers outside.

"This attack," she asked, retaking her seat, "you know who led it?"

Segalla sipped at the brandy. "Oh yes, madame, as I said—Monsieur de Paris, a sinister, shadowy rogue. No one knows anything about him, except that he has a black fleur-de-lys high on his left shoulder."

He watched Roquet carefully. She grasped the brandy glass and almost pushed it between her lips, her face white as a sheet, drinking it so quickly she choked and put the glass down.

"Are you sure, Major?"

"As sure as I am here. Now," Segalla pushed back his chair and rose. "Madame, I really must thank you for your hospitality but my bags have to be packed. I must leave Paris early tomorrow morning."

Segalla walked to the door, turned and bowed to the guests. Madame Roquet followed him out of the hallway. One of the servants brought his greatcoat. Segalla surreptitiously felt the pockets and touched the small pistol hidden there. He then collected his walking-cane and turned to make his farewell. Madame Roquet, however, was like a sleepwalker, someone heavily drugged, her carmine lips seeming even redder against the smooth, ivory skin of her face.

"You are sure?" she repeated.

Segalla looked into her eyes and saw how small her pupils had contracted. He grasped her hand, cold as ice, and raised it to his lips.

"Madame knows I am." He kissed her hand and walked into the darkness.

A carriage came by and stopped. Segalla waved him on. For a while he walked through the dirty streets, tapping his cane on the cobbles, a sure protection against the beggars who slipped in and out of the shadows, whining and begging for alms. At the Pont Neuf he stopped. He went across to the wall of the bridge and looked over the parapet at the black, swollen waters of the Seine. Then he walked on. He was almost across when he heard footsteps behind him. He quickened his pace. Rounding a corner, he could almost see the lights of the Lion d'Or when he heard the rush of footsteps.

Segalla turned; dropping to one knee and pulling the musket from his pocket, he shot blindly at the two figures hurtling towards him. He heard a cry, a scream; one figure crumpled to the ground. In the flickering light of a lantern-horn hung high on the wall, Segalla glimpsed the yellow, soiled coat of the Canary as he lay writhing on the ground, the musket-ball in his throat. The second figure, taller, loosed his musket but the ball flew above Segalla's head. Then his assailant was on him. Segalla glimpsed the glint of the sword swinging back in a sabrelike cut towards his head. He moved sideways and, by the time Jacques de Coeur regained his poise, Segalla was standing, his sword drawn from the walking-cane.

De Coeur was no longer the fop. He was still dressed in his salmon-coloured jacket, his shirt collar loose, but even in the dim light of the lantern, his face and eyes showed no sign of his supposed heavy drinking. De Coeur was breathing easily, hardly sweating; he did not even spare a second glance as his companion coughed and spluttered his lifeblood out onto the rain-soaked cobbles.

Segalla loosened the buttons of his coat, slipping the pistol back into the pocket; he and de Coeur edged around each other, turning slightly sideways, looking for the advantage.

"You had to come, hadn't you?" Segalla taunted. "You attacked me that night in the Tuileries and organised those footpads to waylay me outside the hospital. So it was either tonight or never. Tomorrow I'll be amongst English soldiers."

De Coeur just watched him.

"Madame Roquet knows," Segalla continued. "She has seen the black fleur-de-lys high on your shoulder, Jacques de Coeur, or whatever you call yourself—leader of the secret Templars—but you're really nothing more than an assassin."

De Coeur moved in quickly, the point of his sword seeking Segalla's face then dropping suddenly, aiming towards his chest. Segalla beat him off. De Coeur edged back.

"Who gave you orders?" Segalla taunted. "Madame Roquet?"

De Coeur's eyes never even blinked.

"Barras?" Segalla edged backwards. "No, not Barras. I think I know."

Again de Coeur closed, his sword twisting and turning in false parries and feints as he tried to make his opponent panic. Segalla now had his back to the wall. He glanced quickly at the Canary but he now lay still, an ever-widening puddle of blood seeping out from underneath him. De Coeur attacked again. This time a different feint, and Segalla beat him off even as he wildly wondered how this sword-fight would end. What happened if he was pierced? Would his long life end here? Their swords clashed; this time Segalla went on the offensive, his sword jabbing and cutting, trying to break through de Coeur's defences. His opponent backed off, standing in the mouth of the street, a dark shadow.

Segalla lifted his sword. "A fight to the death," he murmured. "You'll get no help from anyone. Paris is so full of violence, as you know."

Segalla just wished he could provoke his opponent into either a temper or into some admission. De Coeur edged forward, adopting the stance and poise of a classical duellist: sword up, then down, twisting towards Segalla's chest. Segalla blocked it just in time. De Coeur gave a grunt of pleasure as he recognised a weakness in his opponent. He stood back; he was raising his sword again when the musket cracked. Segalla didn't know where it came from. One minute de Coeur was there, poised like a steel spring, then he staggered forward in a crouch, shoulders slumped, hands falling, the sword slipping out of his hand. De Coeur took one, two steps; his face and mouth twisted, eyes rolling. He half turned, his hand going up his back, then he sighed and fell at Segalla's feet. Segalla flattened himself against the wall as the woman, caped and hooded, came out of the shadows. He lifted his sword.

"You can put that down, Major Segalla!" Madame Roquet declared, walking towards him, the smoking musket still in her right hand, the other pulling back the cowl of her cloak. She came up close, almost pressing her body against him, her eyes large and dark in her pallid face.

"You knew," she whispered hoarsely.

"I was told," Segalla replied, "that Monsieur de Paris had a black fleur-de-lys tattooed high on his shoulder. I remembered you calling de Coeur 'mon lys noir,'—my black lily."

"He very rarely revealed it," Madame Roquet replied conversationally. "Only once did I see it." She stood over the fallen assassin, bent down and pressed her fingers against the side of his neck. "I took him in," she whispered. "He came with letters of accreditation from a royalist general in the west. I never suspected." She straightened up. "Now he's dead." She tossed the musket onto the cobbles.

"He was your lover?" Segalla asked.

"I have no lovers, Englishman. I have a husband whose spirit never leaves me. The rest are men who pass through my life like ships in the night. De Coeur was one of these."

"Did he talk much about his life?"

"Never once. He acted the fop, the dandy, the dilettante." Madame Roquet drew in a deep breath. "But, like all men, he was one thing on the outside and another within." She stared up at the great walls on either side of the alleyway. "He even chose this place to ambush you. No houses, no one to hear any scream or cry for help."

"So why did you come?" Segalla asked.

"After you left," she replied, "I sat on a chair in the hallway. When I went back in the room de Coeur and his creature had gone." She looked up at the clear night sky. "As I must." She shivered and pulled her cloak close around her. "The war is over, Major Segalla. England and France are allies, the Bourbons have returned to the throne and the Dauphin probably sleeps with his ancestors. You will leave for England?"

"I have a little business to finish," Segalla replied, "but, yes, madame." He clasped her hand. "I doubt whether we will ever meet again."

"Then, Major, tell me what happened before you go. What really did happen to the Dauphin?"

Segalla took her arm and led her back towards the entrance of the bridge. He heard a scuffling behind him. He whirled round and saw shadowy figures creeping along the wall. Roquet glanced over her shoulder.

"The beggar men," she whispered. "When you walk back, de Coeur and his creature will have disappeared. It will be weeks before the Seine gives up their naked corpses."

Segalla watched the beggars, an eerie, ghastly sight. They

seemed to gather like spectres around the two fallen men. The corpses were picked up and the macabre group took their grisly burdens and disappeared up the shadowy alleyway. Madame Roquet caught him by the arm.

"You knew they'd come after you, didn't you?"

"Yes," Segalla replied. "De Coeur was Monsieur de Paris. He sent the Canary to the château at Vitry-sur-Seine. One of the survivors described the leading assailant as short of stature. Neither could let me live knowing what I did. In the daylight they could not attack me. At the Lion d'Or I was protected and, tomorrow—well, by the time they could organise their band of cutthroats I would be protected by English troops. There are enough bivouacking in the fields outside Paris."

"Were you so confident?" she asked.

Segalla stopped and grasped her by the shoulders.

"I don't think I am, madame. But there are times when you have to tempt fate. De Coeur deserved to die. I could not let him walk away, knowing what I did."

"And the rest?" she asked. "Those who hired de Coeur?"

Segalla pulled a face. "The Templars, like other secret societies, permeate every level of the community. Now, such mysterious organisations enjoy strange bedfellows. Perhaps Barras was a member and, when the Dauphin was released, told his masters what had happened."

"And one of these was de Coeur?"

"Apparently. What I wonder about," Segalla added, "is how deeply involved other people were. Men like Decazes; even the Dauphin's uncle, your fat king, Louis XVIII." Segalla dug a hand deep into his pocket. "God be my witness, madame, but we don't even know if de Coeur was a secret Templar, whether that organisation really exists, or whether it was pretence for those who wished to wage a secret war against the royal family. Whatever, in the end they were successful: Louis XVI and his wife went to the guillotine. Their daughter now lives on the edge of madness and only the good Lord knows what happened to the Dauphin. Now, madame, I must go." And, kissing her on each cheek, Segalla strode off into the darkness.

Segalla left the Lion d'Or early the following morning, long before the bank of mist which came swirling in along the Seine lifted to reveal a weak, dim sun. Paris was still sleeping as he made his way by carriage along the boulevards, through the gates of the city and into the countryside. He felt refreshed, a little heavy-headed but with no regrets. De Coeur and his creature the Canary had lived by the sword, so they'd died by it. Segalla was more concerned about Tallien: This only deepened when he reached L'Oriele. A large, spacious tavern, standing in a great cobbled yard, L'Oriele was packed full of English officers, members of those regiments left by Wellington outside Paris to ensure the Bourbon restoration proceeded peacefully. A burly sergeant dressed in the dark green of the Durham Light Infantry, guarded the main tavern door, his white, heavy whiskers yellow with tobacco from the pipe he held between blackened teeth. He looked Segalla up and down from head to toe.

"You'd best piss off, monsieur, this place is for English officers."

"Which is exactly what I am!" Segalla retorted.

The man's pipe fell from his mouth and he snapped to attention. Segalla brushed by him into the sweet-smelling passageway, shouting for the landlord. The fellow was in the kitchen, cursing and yelling at a motley gang of sweating scullions and cooks.

"No room here!" he yelled at Segalla.

Segalla placed a silver coin into his outstretched hand; the fellow's sweaty face creased into a smile.

"On second thought, monsieur, there's a sweet little garret at the top of the house which looks out over the fields. You'll have a good view of the road, not to mention the troops bivouacked there."

"Has a Frenchman arrived here?" Segalla asked, plucking at the man's sleeve and drawing him away from the rest. "Small, mousy-haired, a civilian—Monsieur Tallien?"

The tavern keeper shook his balding head dolefully.

"No, monsieur, no Frenchman. But I'll take you to your room."

Segalla's "sweet little garret" was nothing more than a yellowing hole just beneath the roof, with peeling walls and a narrow, cracked window pitted with dead flies. The bed was ramshackle, lurching dangerously as Segalla put his bags down on it. It boasted a chair, a battered table, some hooks on the wall and a large, weather-beaten trunk with its locks removed. Segalla gave the man a second coin.

"When Monsieur Tallien arrives," he warned, "you must report to me immediately."

The fellow mumbled his thanks and shuffled out. Segalla went across, opened the window and stared out at the curling smoke from the morning campfires of the troops who had camped in the fields beyond. The air was thick with the smell of burning chicken; trumpets sounded amidst the shouts of officers and sergeants. Segalla closed the window and lay carefully down on the bed. He wished he had waited for Tallien but, there again, that might have provoked suspicion. After a while he went down to the taproom, struggling through the throng, to order some onion soup, dark rye bread and a cup of watered wine. The din in the taproom was deafening: officers shouting at each other, sergeants and corporals coming in to deliver orders and messages, the crash of boots, the clatter of plates, whilst the tobacco smoke rolled about like clouds.

Segalla hurriedly finished his meal and went out into the clean fresh air. He spent most of that day walking in the country lanes, returning to the tavern late in the afternoon for something to eat. Now and again he was drawn into conversation, or half-heartedly playing cards with some of the officers. Tallien, however, did not arrive.

On the following day, late in the afternoon, just as Segalla was thinking of returning to Paris, Tallien arrived, splattered in mud from head to toe. The archivist strode into the taproom, cases and bundles clasped under his arms.

"Thank God!" Tallien dropped his cases and eagerly grasped Segalla's hand.

"What kept you so long?" Segalla asked, then turned to shout at the landlord. "This man will share my room! You will put a truckle bed up?"

The innkeeper nodded. Tallien's bags and cases were seized by a gaggle of urchins who disappeared up the stairs.

"I had to pack," Tallien murmured. "It was hard to decide what I should take and what I could leave. Monsieur, the task you gave me proved more difficult than I thought." He sighed. "I then took a carriage but the wheel came off. So I had to beg a lift off a farmer." He gestured at his mud-soaked boots. "I felt every jolt and jar on the road from Paris."

Segalla laughed and took him to a window seat, ordering the best wines and food. He let the tired little archivist take off his coat and satisfy his hunger. Afterwards Tallien leaned back, pushing his chest out and rubbing his stomach.

"Do you know what you are doing?" Segalla asked.

Tallien pressed his lips together. "No," he answered sharply. "But, there again, that's half the excitement of life, isn't it, Major Segalla? Not knowing what might be round the corner?" He leaned over and gently gripped Segalla's hand. "I have every faith in you." He eased himself in the seat then pulled up his shirt to reveal a heavy money-belt strapped round his waist. "I shall not starve."

"Did you have any difficulties?" Segalla asked.

"No, no. Decazes and his master now believe the issue is settled. The Dauphin is twenty years dead and who really cares?"

"And what did you discover?"

"Mrs. Mary Anne Meves-Crowley," Tallien replied. "She was educated at the Convent of St.-Omer. She returned to London and became the favourite pupil of the celebrated maestro Signor Sacchini. Her father then took her back to Paris to continue her education. In 1781 Mr. Crowley died and Mary Anne returned to England where she stayed with the Dowager Countess, Caroline of Harrington. In 1783 she married Mr. Meves but, the following year, returned to Paris. There, because of her friendship with Sacchini, she secured an appointment in the private service of Queen Marie-Antoinette at the Petit Trianon near Versailles." Tallien paused.

"And did you discover anything else?" Segalla asked.

"Yes, yes I did," Tallien replied. "Apparently Mary Anne became pregnant." He shook his head. "No one knows who the father was."

"Definitely illegitimate?" Segalla asked.

"Oh yes. Her husband never came to France whilst, during that same period, Mary Anne never returned to England."

"But she eventually did?"

"Yes, she and her baby returned to London when the Revolution broke out. That's all I know. Or, at least, that's all I could discover in the household books of the royal family."

Segalla got to his feet. "Then, believe me, sir, it's time we shook off the soil of France and got out of this flea-pit."

They returned to Segalla's room. The prospect of leaving France seemed to depress Tallien. He sat morosely on the small truckle bed the landlord had set up, answering Segalla's attempts at jollification with monosyllabic replies.

"Is it worth it?" he asked abruptly. "Is it really worth it?"

Segalla pulled up a chair.

"Do you believe in God and Le Bon Seigneur, Monsieur Tallien?"

"Sometimes, though my problem is, do they believe in Monsieur Tallien?"

"In the Gospels," Segalla replied, "the only question ever asked of Christ, which is never answered, is Pilate's 'What is truth?'"

Segalla got up and walked to the window, slipped the locket out of his pocket and opened it.

"To the powerful ones in Paris the truth doesn't really matter. To them Louis XVI, Marie-Antoinette, their children as well as those who fought and died for them, belong to a different era and another century. But to God and to the souls of the dead people the truth does matter. It matters so much that men killed because of it. Josephine died because of it. Yesterday evening, in a stinking alleyway near the Pont Neuf, I killed a man because of it. So, yes, it does matter." He looked over his shoulder at Tallien. "Jacques de Coeur, Madame Roquet's valet, gigolo, whatever, was Monsieur de Paris. Don't look so shocked. He organised the massacre at Vitry-sur-Seine. He wiped out Petit-val's family and he would have cut your throat, Monsieur Tallien, spluttering your life out like a candle-wick."

"If you find this truth," Tallien asked, "will you tell the English government?" He grinned. "Or even me?"

Segalla crossed his arms and leaned against the wall.

"Only you," he whispered. "But bear with me; no more questions until I discover that truth myself."

Segalla and Tallien left the tavern early the following morning. Segalla used his letters from Lord Liverpool to secure a military escort for the three-day journey to Dieppe: a pounding, bone-wrenching ride through the wet, cold Normandy countryside. The soldiers, under their young, baby-faced lieutenant, hardly ever bothered them. They were used to the strange comings and goings of special envoys from England.

At Dieppe, Segalla secured passage on an English man-of-war, HMS Centaur. After a two-day Channel crossing which left them soaked to the skin, their stomachs churning and their appetites dulled by the brackish wine and weevil-filled biscuits, they landed at Dover. Tallien was too exhausted to continue so they spent two days in a tavern quietly cursing the sea and everything in it. Another three days elapsed before they left in a mail coach for London. Tallien soon recovered, greedily watching the sights, exclaiming at the greenness of the countryside, the elegant houses painted white or pink. He grew nostalgic, telling Segalla about his romantic courtship and betrothal to Priscilla Johnson. Segalla listened to his chatter. He had sworn Tallien to silence about their quest before they left Dover.

"England may be more peaceful than France," he had warned, "but government men are as thick as flies upon a cowpat. Someone will have noted our arrival. I do not wish to be summoned to the Foreign Office until this business is finished."

When they reached London, Tallien's mood changed: He became rather subdued at the noisy bustle, the clatter of the traffic and the heavy fog which swirled amongst the buildings, muffling the cries of the hucksters and stall-men.

"What will I do?" he wailed as their carriage rattled across London Bridge.

"I have friends," Segalla assured him. "There's many a noble lord or rich merchant who requires the services you offer."

They dismounted at the Exchange and Segalla led Tallien through a maze of winding streets to a house in a small alleyway just off Lothbury.

"I have rooms here," he explained, "and the landlady does not ask questions."

They entered by a side entrance and went upstairs to a pleasantly furnished suite of rooms. The archivist stared round curiously.

"What's the matter?" Segalla asked.

Tallien pointed to the heavy oaken furniture, cupboard and four-poster bed.

"It's like going back in time," he murmured. "I have seen rooms like this. Oh, don't get me wrong, it's very welcome but," he glanced at Segalla, "I have heard the gossip. . . ." His voice faltered.

"You are my guest, Tallien," Segalla declared, "and my

friend." He waved round the room. "I have chambers like this in several cities in England and Europe. I ask you one favour. Never pry."

The arrival of Mrs. Dalrymple the housekeeper, a rubicund-faced Scottish widow, provided light relief. A pretty slip of a thing, and the perfect hostess. Mrs. Dalrymple never questioned Segalla where he had been, but seemed as attracted as a bee to honey for Monsieur Tallien. She fussed and clucked over him like a mothering hen: How tired he looked. How far had he travelled? Was this his first time in England? The questions came out in a rush and Segalla admired the clever way Mrs. Dalrymple soon elicited a great deal of information about the Frenchman, including the fact that he was a widower. When she left, promising to return with a tray of food, Tallien slumped into a high-backed chair, mopping his face, pretending to be overcome, though clearly flattered by Mrs. Dalrymple's attentions.

"I'll have to be careful of you, Monsieur Tallien," Segalla teased. "Not a week in England and already setting the ladies' hearts all aflutter." He picked up his coat, removing the pistols from the pockets. "The kingdom is full of Mrs. Dalrymples," he continued. "Napoléon Bonaparte has the blood of millions of men on his hands. But we," he sat opposite Tallien, "we have to find Mrs. Mary Anne Meves-Crowley." He grinned. "Yet I can't have you trotting round London. I know where to go and whom to ask. There'll be electoral rolls in the Guildhall, not to mention the many music circles which meet in the city's assembly rooms." He patted Tallien's shoulder. "I'm nearly finished."

Tallien was too exhausted to object. Segalla made him feel at home, and the following morning began his own searches, though in the end it proved not to be so difficult.

Four days after their arrival in London, he managed an invitation to the Old Argyle Rooms in Regent Street where Steibert's concerto, *The Storm*, was being played. Segalla arrived promptly and, after discreet enquiries, a gentleman pointed out Mrs. Mary Anne Meves-Crowley sitting in one of the boxes. Segalla borrowed a pair of glasses and studied the woman curiously: grey hair neatly piled up on her head; a plump, pretty face, like that of a porcelain doll. She sat like a statue listening to the music. Segalla turned his attention to the young man accompanying her, a little farther back in the box, hidden in the shadows. Segalla found his hand trembling. If only there was more light!

"Sir?" The man he had borrowed the glasses from was looking at him curiously. "Sir, of your courtesy, may I have my glasses back?"

Segalla apologised and handed them over. He would have stayed, but the woman, as if aware someone had been studying her, now looked fixedly in his direction. Segalla withdrew and, going downstairs, waited in a carriage until the concerto was finished.

Mrs. Meves-Crowley was one of the first to leave. Segalla followed her carriage along Regent Street to a well-furnished three-storied house in an adjoining road. He returned to his own chambers where Tallien was holding court, much to the round-eyed admiration of Mrs. Dalrymple. Once the housekeeper had left, Segalla told the archivist what he had found. He then filled two brandy glasses and handed one to Tallien.

"Tomorrow morning"—he raised his glass in a silent toast—"we shall solve this mystery and allow Marie-Antoinette's ghost to rest in peace!" He smiled at Tallien. "Now, Monsieur Archivist, let me tell you the truth; and it all centres around our Mrs. Mary Anne Meves-Crowley. . . ."

Chapter 14

W hen Segalla and Tallien, dressed in their sober best, called at the house the next morning, they were ushered into the parlour.

"Wait here," the maid said. "Madame will soon be down. Your names, sir, again?"

"Major Segalla and Monsieur Tallien," Segalla replied. "Tell your mistress not to be alarmed."

The maid bobbed a curtsey whilst Segalla and Tallien sat down in the thickly quilted chairs placed at either side of the fireplace. The room itself was clean and tidy but certainly not luxurious. The furniture was tasteful: dark-coloured, it looked like the parlour of any country vicar. A few paintings hung on the walls but these were bland country scenes, whilst the ornaments on the mantelpiece were porcelain figurines, nothing remarkable. In fact, so ordinary was the room that Segalla received the distinct impression that this was intentional, as if Mrs. Meves-Crowley just wished to blend in with the background and provoke little interest in her or her family.

"Good morning, sirs."

Segalla turned. The woman he had seen at the musical evening stood in the doorway. She was dressed in a dark blue muslin gown, fringed at the collar, with simple white lace. Her greying hair was gathered up into a bun on her head and held in place by a simple comb. The creamy skin of her face had no makeup; neither on her red, full lips nor under those grey, watchful eyes. She moved soundlessly towards him. Segalla remembered his manners and sprang to his feet. He grasped her hand, kissed it and, as Tallien did the same, made the introductions.

"What on earth, sirs, do you want? Major Segalla, I have no business with you, though my husband may."

Segalla raised one eyebrow. "Your husband, madame?"

"Well, we are separated. I live here alone with my son. . . ."

Segalla gave a slight bow. "Madame, it is your son we have come to discuss."

Mrs. Meves-Crowley's fingers flew to her lips. She blinked and gulped, fighting hard to control her breathing. Segalla, so alarmed by the change in her, took a step closer and grasped her elbow gently.

"Madame, I apologise, perhaps you had best sit down."

Tallien pulled up a chair and the woman allowed herself to be gently lowered into it. She smiled wanly at Segalla.

"It's early but, in the cupboard over there——" She pointed to a corner. "Please join me in a little brandy," Mrs. Meves-Crowley whispered.

Segalla poured some brandy into three glasses. He gave one to the woman, one to Tallien, then sat back in the chair, his eyes never leaving Mrs. Meves-Crowley. She had used the respite to calm herself and, when she lifted the brandy glass to her lips, her hands never trembled. She sipped it carefully then cradled the glass in her lap.

"You are from France, Major?" she asked abruptly.

"Monsieur Tallien is. I am the envoy of the Prime Minister."

"And what would such a person want with someone like me?"

"That I shall tell you, madame. A few months ago, Napoléon Bonaparte was defeated at Waterloo. The Bourbons, Louis XVIII and his brother the Comte d'Artois, have been restored to power. Now, in the eyes of the world, Louis XVIII is the legitimate successor of his brother who died on the guillotine in 1793. For the murdered king left no heirs; his own son, the Dauphin, Louis Charles, Duke of Normandy, supposedly died in the Temple prison on 8 June 1795—he now lies buried in the derelict cemetery of Ste.-Marguerite in north Paris." Segalla paused and sipped at his brandy.

Mrs. Meves-Crowley never flinched but watched him closely.

"Now, the Prime Minister," Segalla continued, "wished to establish that the Dauphin did indeed die. I was commissioned to go to Paris, where I met Monsieur Tallien. We examined all the evidence and the French government gave what cooperation they could."

The woman smiled faintly as she caught the sarcasm in Segalla's voice.

"The story is a well-known one," Segalla continued. "Louis XVI, his wife, son and daughter were imprisoned in the Temple. Louis later went to the guillotine. Later in the same year the Dauphin was removed from his mother's custody and placed in the care of a cobbler Simon: that lasted until 19 January 1794. Simon left the prison and the Dauphin was incarcerated in a cell, kept in virtual isolation until the fall of Robespierre in the summer of 1794. The new government in Paris, shocked by the change in the Dauphin's health, appointed a succession of warders but the prince never recovered. He died in June 1795."

"And?" Mrs. Meves-Crowley raised her head. "How does that concern me or my son?"

"Let me finish, madame. We believe that the child actually escaped from the Temple prison, in January 1794, with the help of the cobbler Simon, who was a secret royalist, or bribed to act as one by certain people in Paris. A sickly child from one of the local hospitals, probably some orphan, a mute who had more than a passing resemblance to the Dauphin, was smuggled into the Temple to take his place."

"And the real Dauphin?" Mrs. Meves-Crowley asked quietly.

"Well, we once believed he was kept hidden in Paris for at least a year before being smuggled out to a powerful banker called Petitval at his château at Vitry-sur-Seine. Later, the château was mysteriously attacked. Petitval was killed and the child disappeared, though, later on, a boy called Mathurin Bruneau appeared in the same area, claiming to be of noble birth."

"But what happened to the real Dauphin?" Mrs. Meves-Crowley sipped from her brandy.

"Ah, that's where the real mystery begins, madame. You see, I have on my person a small locket. In it there is a picture of Mare-Antoinette and that of her young son Louis Charles. He has very dark hair but the Dauphin who died in the Temple in 1795 had very light auburn hair. He also did not have the Dauphin's birthmarks: a mole on his left breast and a rather deep inoculation scar high on his right shoulder. Now, Monsieur Tallien and I reached the conclusion that the real reason for the change in appearance was because of the Dauphin's removal in January 1794."

Segalla paused and stared into the brandy glass. "However, madame, you can imagine our consternation when, on further research, we found that the child imprisoned in the Temple before January 1794 also had light auburn hair and did not carry the Dauphin's birthmarks. At first I thought a mistake had been made, but I have actually talked to Madame Simon and she has confirmed that. We then looked at other evidence and noticed there were rumours that the Dauphin may have escaped from the Temple, even before his father's execution in January 1793. There are occasions when Louis himself did not recognise his son. Whilst, in her last letter, his mother Marie-Antoinette calls her beloved son Louis Charles, 'this child,' and so I began to wonder."

Mrs. Meves-Crowley sat still as a statue. She started only when, from the floor above, a piano began to play, the tinkling notes sounding rather eerie through the tomblike silence of the house.

"I wondered," Segalla continued, "if the Dauphin had ever been imprisoned in the Temple—I mean the real Dauphin. Did the Simons guard a replacement? Is this what Baron Petitval found out? And, being disgusted and angry, sent the boy away, giving him to some local peasant farmer to raise?" Segalla sipped from his brandy. "I think he did. He may have even taxed Barras, who arranged the child's departure from Paris, but Barras was a scoundrel. He had been paid his money to deliver a child and he had. What else could he do? The child he sent was later called Mathurin Bruneau, but how could Barras know that? He, too, had been duped and what was the point of raising speculation and ordering a thorough search to be carried out?"

Mrs. Meves-Crowley pulled down the cuff of her sleeve, balancing the brandy glass in her lap.

"And the assassins of Baron Petitval?" she asked.

Segalla shrugged. "They were definitely despatched to the château, sent by a man calling himself Monsieur de Paris—the head of a secret underground organisation dedicated to the overthrow of the Bourbons. Louis XVI and Marie-Antoinette had been sent to the guillotine. Somehow or other Monsieur de Paris knew, or thought he did, that Louis's son was sheltering in the Château Vitry-sur-Seine. They killed Petitval, silenced him, but were too late to catch the child."

"Madame," Tallien interrupted, pulling his chair forward, his face alight with excitement. "We believe the real Dauphin was never imprisoned in the Temple but spirited out of France years earlier! I studied the household books of Queen Marie-Antoinette. Amongst her ladies-in-waiting at the Trianon we found your name, Mrs. Meves-Crowley. You were educated as a Catholic, you were married to a certain Mr. Meves in 1783 and, on 16 February 1785, were delivered of a son by the Queen's own surgeon. You then returned to England. A month later, on 27 March 1785, Marie-Antoinette was delivered of a second son, the future Dauphin, Louis Charles. You returned to Paris in September 1789, two months after the Revolution had broken out: your four-year-old son accompanied you."

The woman leaned back in her chair; her face was now icy-pale, eyelids half-closed, mouth slightly open. She was breathing quickly as if Tallien's words were recalling some dreadful dream.

"You only stayed a month in France," Tallien concluded, "and returned to England in October."

"Because the Revolution had broken out," Mrs. Meves-Crowley intervened hastily.

"Nonsense, madame," Segalla broke in gently. "Paris was already in turmoil. Why did you go back?"

The woman stared at the ceiling. "She was beautiful," she murmured. "Gracious, kind."

"Who, madame?" Tallien asked softly.

"The Queen, Marie-Antoinette." Mrs. Meves-Crowley blinked, sat straighter in the chair and took a sip of the brandy. "We used to talk," she continued, "late at night. We shared a love of music. She cared for me." Mrs. Meves-Crowley's eyes filled with tears. "She looked after me after I had been violated."

"Violated!" Segalla exclaimed.

Mrs. Meves-Crowley put the glass down on the table and got slowly to her feet. She walked across and stood over Segalla.

"Look at me, sir."

Segalla stared up at this faded, pretty woman.

"You don't remember me, Major?"

Segalla shook his head.

"In the orangery at Versailles that autumn day when Marie-Antoinette caught up with you?"

Segalla smiled. "You were there?"

"I came behind the Queen and, from the shadows, saw her give you the locket." She ran one finger down Segalla's face. "The Queen said you were strange, eerie but not sinister. She said if you were ever to return, I should trust you. I now know what she meant. The Queen is gone, the Trianon is derelict. The ladies who danced and played there have been eaten up by the Terror, swallowed in death, but you, Major Segalla, are the same as that autumn day." She glanced over her shoulder at Tallien. "Can he be trusted?"

"As myself," Segalla replied.

The woman sighed. "Then I shall tell you the truth. I was born Mary Anne Crowley, the second daughter of my parents, baptised in the church of St. Peter and Paul on 11 April 1754." She went back to her seat and sat down, closing her eyes as if reciting some lesson. "I was educated in France and brought up as a Catholic. In 1784 I married my husband, now estranged, Mr. Meves. The marriage was not a happy one. I found—" She paused and opened her eyes and smiled at Segalla. "I have always found England a difficult place to live. My husband made matters worse so, early in 1784, I travelled to France. I became lady-in-waiting to Marie-Antoinette, but 'service' is not the proper word. We fast became firm friends. Now, I have heard what they say about the Queen, but to me, she was kind, gracious, high-spirited and impetuous—a lovely bird trapped in a golden cage. She loved her husband." Mrs. Meves-Crowley opened her eyes. "But Louis XVI was . . . well, he was dull: unexciting, faithful, well-meaning." She stopped as if collecting her thoughts and half turned in the chair, her eyes now hard, lips curling. "The King's brothers, however, the Comte de Provence who now styles himself Louis XVIII, and that other imp of Satan, the Comte d'Artois, were wicked men. They hated Marie-Antoinette. I believe both lusted after her and, when she spurned them, they began a campaign of vilification against her. You have heard all this, surely?"

"Aye, madame, I have. The Comte de Provence, the Comte d'Artois and the Duke of Orléans were an unholy trinity."

" 'By their fruits ye shall know them.' " Mrs. Meves-Crowley replied, quoting from the Gospels. "When the Revolution broke out, Orléans joined the Terror, becoming a friend of Robespierre, Marat and others, whilst the King's brothers scuttled like rabbits to the nearest frontier." She turned back in her chair. "I run ahead of myself. The Comte de Provence was a rake; he tried to seduce the Queen and, when frustrated, forced his attentions on me. One day, not long after my arrival in Paris, he inveigled me into his chambers." The woman's breathing grew quicker. "I will spare you the details. Two men held me down whilst de Provence raped me. I fled to the Queen. She was furious but realised there was little she could do. Anyway, when my monthly courses stopped I found I was pregnant."

She rubbed her hand across her stomach. "God forgive me! I prayed the child growing within me would die. The Queen, however, would hold my hand, a strange look in her eyes, and tell me to be patient, that the child was a gift from God and could be of good service to France." Mrs. Meves-Crowley picked up her brandy glass. "I didn't know what she meant, but in the February of 1785 I went into early labour. I was delivered by the Queen's own surgeon." Mrs. Meves-Crowley rolled the brandy glass between her hands. "The Queen insisted, even swore me to silence about the child's father." Mrs. Meves-Crowley shrugged. "At the time I was distressed. I knew my husband would demand a divorce, if not separation. But the Queen insisted that I take the child to England and register it as a British citizen as soon as possible. I did. The boy, born prematurely, was baptised on 25 March 1785, in St. James's Church, Piccadilly."

"And your husband's reaction?" Segalla asked.

"At first he was furious. I swore an oath on the Bible that the child was a result not of any illicit liaison, but of violent rape." Her glance fell away and she blinked to hide the tears. "Our marriage had always been one of convenience but the birth of the boy ended any real love between us. My husband declared he had been cuckolded. He could do nothing but accept what had happened."

"What name did you give the child?" Tallien asked.

"Augustus Antoine. At first I hated the very sight of him, but he was a beautiful child. After his baptism I returned immediately to France."

"By the time you returned," Segalla asked, "Marie-Antoinette had been delivered of a second son?"

"Yes, yes. And that's when the mystery really deepened. You

see, there was a strong likeness between my child and Louis Charles. Louis Charles had darker hair; Augustus' was fairer, but the Queen, now and again in the royal nurseries, used to insist that we exchange the children. At first it was a joke between the two of us but then the period of duplicity became longer and longer. Eventually, the exchange became permanent."

Segalla looked up in surprise. "Madame, I can understand your lack of attachment to a child who was the result of a brutal rape, but Marie-Antoinette was the most loving of mothers. Why would she consent to that?"

"She told me herself," Mrs. Meves-Crowley replied. "In the spring of 1787, she, Madame Élisabeth and her other confidante, the Princess de Lamballe, who was so barbarously murdered by the revolutionaries, invited me to a secret meeting at the Trianon. Only the four of us were present. Marie-Antoinette knew a storm was about to break over France which would rock, even topple, the throne. She was very concerned about her two sons—not that they might perish in any revolution, but that in the chaos her enemies, the King's brothers, would strike. Marie-Antoinette was terrified. She declared she had a mission from God to keep her children alive. I agreed and, in the summer of 1787, I returned to England in the retinue of the Princess de Lamballe."

"And Louis Charles came with you?"

"Yes, he did. The Princess de Lamballe ensured that Louis Charles, now masquerading as my son, was as such registered as a British citizen."

"And no one noticed, not even Louis XVI?" Tallien intervened.

Mrs. Meves-Crowley shook her head. "I am not too sure. Marie-Antoinette was skilled in dealing with her husband; he certainly had no illusions about his brothers. He may have been party to the secret, though by 1784, his mind was very confused."

"But what did they intend?" Segalla asked.

"Survival," she replied. "King Louis knew a terrible and bloody revolution was imminent. He wished to protect his sons: a better life in a calm, serene background, rather than a bloody death in some prison. Go back over your history, monsieur; it wouldn't be the first time that French kings hid their sons. You have heard of the Man in the Iron Mask? That may well have been an attempt by Anne of Austria, Louis XIII's wife, to hide an illegitimate child in England. Perhaps that incident gave Marie-Antoinette the idea in the first place. Whatever—whilst I was in England, I received a secret pension from France. Now and again I would return with the Dauphin to meet the Queen but then disaster struck. On 4 June 1789, Louis Charles's elder brother, Louis Joseph, died suddenly. The doctors said it was a malady of the spine, Marie-Antoinette always believed the child had been poisoned. A month later the Bastille was stormed and the Revolution had begun."

"But madame," Tallien intervened, "I can accept that one baby looks like another." He smiled. "Cases of switching children at birth are common. But, as the children grew older, surely other people would have noticed."

"No, Monsieur Tallien." Mrs. Meves-Crowley shook her head. "First, until 1789, Louis Charles was only the second son. His elder brother was the centre of attention: Marie-Antoinette could do little to protect him. Secondly, Louis Charles was only two when the permanent exchange was made. He was only four when the Revolution broke out. People would not really pay much attention to a small child, especially when he had no claims to the throne and France was entering a period of such great turbulence. Thirdly, the child had his own household, hidden away: Even his sister Marie-Thérèse saw very little of him. It wasn't until the Revolution entered its most violent phase in 1791 that the royal family were confined together. And, finally, don't forget Marie-Antoinette and her two closest confidantes, Madame Élisabeth and the Princess de Lamballe did all within their power to maintain this deception. There are few paintings of Louis Charles: If you study them carefully, apart from the picture in Major Segalla's locket, the boy could be any handsome child."

Tallien scratched his chin and nodded. "I agree, madame. And, of course, your son was of the same stock. He would have Bourbon features."

"Is that why you returned to France so suddenly in September 1789?" Segalla asked.

"Yes." Mrs. Meves-Crowley put the brandy glass down and brushed the tears from her eyes. "Marie-Antoinette begged to see her son for one last time. For a while she was even tempted to take him back. But, you may recall, in that month the Paris mob attacked Versailles. The Queen had to flee her own apartments. She was convinced she would not survive." The woman sighed, her body slumping in the chair. "A month later I returned to England. Both I and Louis Charles now live here." She stopped and lifted one hand. "You heard the piano music? To everyone else that is Augustus Antoine Meves, but to me, messieurs, he is Louis Charles, Duke of Normandy, the rightful son of Louis XVI and Marie-Antoinette: the real King of France." She glanced at Segalla. "Do you believe me, Major?"

"Yes, madame, I do. What you say does not conflict with any of the evidence we have studied. Witnesses maintain that the child imprisoned in the Temple under the care of Simon the cobbler was the same child they had seen playing at the Tuileries, and, of course, it was your illegitimate son unwittingly playing his part. It resolves the mystery of the prisoner's auburn hair and lack of birthmarks. It explains why Louis XVI sometimes made confusing remarks about his own son. It explains the rumours, even before the royal family were imprisoned in the Temple, that the Dauphin may have escaped. It explains the King's desire that his son never wreak vengeance for what had happened." Segalla paused. "He was, of course, referring to his own son in exile."

"But Baron Petitval," Tallien asked. "He was the King's confidant. Surely he should have been informed?"

Mrs. Meves-Crowley rose, walked over to the mantelpiece and rested against it.

"Marie-Antoinette felt guilty," she declared. "I will be honest with you, sirs. God forgive me, I felt little attachment to my son, the result of a brutal rape. However, the Queen was insistent that an innocent child should not suffer. Petitval believed he was negotiating over the real Dauphin, but that was the Queen's way of ensuring an innocent child was released." She sighed and turned round. "Of course, it all went terribly wrong. Though, thank God, my son is probably still alive." She sighed. "Though God have mercy on the poor child who died."

"Why," Tallien asked, "were the physical characteristics of the true Dauphin so little known?"

"It was part of the secret," she replied. "Very few people actually saw Louis Charles: Babies grow and, of course, the exchange obscured matters further. We were all sworn to secrecy regarding his birthmarks and, when the Revolution broke out, all the royal physicians fled. Nevertheless, rumours did circulate, as you discovered."

"But Petitval knew?" Segalla asked.

"Probably," she replied. "I met the banker at Versailles; he was a tenacious, wealthy man. He may well have bought such information. So many people at Versailles," she sighed, "but all gone into the darkness." She bowed her head. "I know some of what happened. I made a few discreet enquiries about the Simons and the others who acted as gaolers at the Temple: Gomin, Lasne and the physician Pelletan."

"And you knew about Petitval's death?"

"Oh yes. During the Revolution I read the papers very closely, both English and French." Mrs. Meves-Crowley raised her head, tears brimming in her eyes. "Sir, I beg you, what really did happen?"

"Madame," Segalla leaned forward. "You have been truthful with us and I must return the courtesy." He drew his breath in. "Now, before the Revolution broke out, you and Marie-Antoinette exchanged children. King Louis XVI tacitly agreed with this, though when he was a prisoner in the Temple, he was confused, rather dazed and occasionally made a slip which was picked up by those who were spying on him. Nevertheless, this was dismissed as rumour. The Dauphin was in the Temple. He was the same boy whom others had seen at the Tuileries. He acted like the Dauphin, he called Louis XVI his father and Marie-Antoinette his mother." Segalla pulled a face. "There again, the boy himself knew no different. When the Revolution broke out and he became a prisoner, he was only a child of five; barely eight when he was removed from his mother. Now Louis and Marie-Antoinette went to the guillotine and Robespierre ruled the roost in Paris. Petitval began his secret negotiations." Segalla held his hand up. "The banker had two specific aims: First, the destruction of Robespierre and his gang. Secondly, the release of the Dauphin from the Temple. Both were interlinked; both depended on the one man Petitval had chosen as the object of his bribes."

"Barras!" Mrs. Meves-Crowley exclaimed.

"Barras it was," Segalla replied. "Corrupt, mercenary, Barras was drawn into Petitval's dangerous game. Petitval financed the removal of the child from the Temple in January 1794. Those agents, with whom Simon the cobbler worked, were Petitval's: They bribed him and achieved considerable success." Segalla paused to collect his thoughts. "Now," he continued, "the child was out of the Temple and the mute who looked like him had been plucked from some orphanage and taken his place. Robespierre and his gang must have known about this. There is some evidence that Robespierre actually visited the Temple after January 1794."

"Then why didn't he raise the alarm?" Mrs. Meves-Crowley asked.

"He was trapped," Segalla replied. "If Robespierre had announced the Dauphin had escaped and another child had taken his place, a number of possibilities might have occurred: First, Robespierre was locked in a life-and-death struggle with members of his own gang, led by Danton. They could have accused him of abducting the child or even murdering him and putting the substitute in his place. Secondly, remember Louis and Marie-Antoinette were dead, but Robespierre was still fighting the royalists in the west. If the latter learnt that their young King was now free, it would only have intensified the struggle. Oh no," Segalla shook his head, "that was the beauty of Petitval's plot. Madame Simon was correct. Robespierre was forced to become part of a conspiracy of silence."

"But the child, my son?"

"Probably hidden in Paris," Tallien intervened. "Think of that sprawling city, madame, with its maze of alleyways, secret passageways and all those citizens who mourned the dead King and hated Robespierre."

"He was probably hidden there," Segalla continued, "because it was too dangerous to move him. Robespierre's agents would watch the roads, and Petitval's château at Vitry-sur-Seine would be kept under close scrutiny."

"And after Robespierre's fall?"

"The child still remained in Paris," Segalla explained. "Barras must have known where he was but there were complex negotiations to be completed: a price to be haggled, money to be delivered and there was still that poor child in the Temple." Segalla sipped from the brandy. "In June 1795, the prisoner in the Temple died. Now, I have never thought that Barras was an assassin, but those who worked for him, such as Pelletan, certainly were. Moreover, the child was sickly; Barras must have viewed his death as a mercy, an act of compassion."

"God forgive him!" Mrs. Meves-Crowley interjected. "That poor, poor child."

"Yes," Segalla breathed. "But now Barras was able to act, and Petitval was ready to receive the boy hidden in Paris. No one would suspect he was the Dauphin. No one would be looking for him. After all, according to public report, the real Dauphin had died in the Temple on 8 June." Segalla paused and listened to the faint piano playing somewhere in a room above him. "In June 1795," he continued, "one of Petitval's agents, Françoise Desprey, collected the child disguised as a girl and took him into the west where, sometime around the middle of August, he arrived at the Château Vitry-sur-Seine." Segalla put the brandy glass down. "That, madame, is where the tragedy began. At first Petitval must have been delighted: The boy would act, talk, behave like the Dauphin. Petitval, however, knew about those birthmarks, and his doubts began. He'd hoped to proclaim the Dauphin as King, with all the necessary proof, at a suitable time; now he found that the boy he was sheltering was a fraud. Petitval, furious, sent him away to a peasant family called Bruneau, who gave him the name Mathurin. However, that child had been raised as a prince and his appetite for luxury could not be so easily quenched. After staying with the Bruneaus, he began his wanderings, not as the Dauphin, but as the reputed scion of a local noble family."

"And then Petitval was killed?" Mrs. Meves–Crowley asked.

"Yes, Petitval must have told people that he was sheltering the Dauphin. The Comte de Provence must have known, and certainly the Templars. We must remember how that secret organisation included people of every political hue: royalist and revolutionary. It would take some time for them to organise a band of ruffians to launch their attack on Vitry-sur-Seine."

"But by then the boy had gone?" Mrs. Meves–Crowley asked.

"Oh, they didn't really care about that," Segalla replied. "If Petitval had dismissed the child as an impostor then, of course, others would. No, that attack was to silence Petitval's efforts to find the true Dauphin once and for all. The château was not pillaged, but a document I have seen," Segalla glanced at Tallien, "indicates that some of Petitval's papers were taken. The Templars, too, must have been curious about the whole affair."

"So," Mrs. Meves-Crowley concluded, "Petitval is dead. The boy, my son, stolen from the Temple in January 1794, is now cast off as an impostor. The mute in the Temple is dead and buried whilst no one knows anything about the whereabouts of the true Dauphin."

"Precisely," Segalla replied. "What is more important is that men like Barras, Gomin and the rest were cleverly ensnared in a trap of their own making."

"And afterwards?" Mrs. Meves-Crowley asked.

"Well, when the Comte de Provence returned to France as Louis XVIII, the true Dauphin had not been seen for almost a quarter of a century. Suffice to say, both Louis XVIII and the secret Templars were only too willing to strengthen the trap around the likes of Gomin, Lasne and Pelletan. How could they now publicly doubt that the prisoner who had died in their care was not the Dauphin? People would only regard them as either fools or red-handed assassins."

"But Lasne and Gomin knew that their prisoner was not the Dauphin?" Mrs. Meves-Crowley asked.

"Undoubtedly," Tallien replied. "That's why Marie-Thérèse was never allowed to see the boy. She would have realised the trickery being played. Others," he continued, "such as Bellanger only saw, for a very brief period of time, what they expected to see: a boy who looked like the Dauphin."

"And the Templars?" she asked.

"Well," Segalla replied, "they wished to keep Petitval's murder a secret and they also had a vested interest in claiming the Dauphin had died in the Temple. They killed Betrancourt, the grave digger at Ste.-Marguerite, just in case the coffin was ever discovered and an autopsy performed. Harmand was murdered not because, as I first thought, he claimed the prisoner had auburn hair, but because his report, drawn up in 1813, confirms Madame Simon's assertion that the prisoner he visited was a mute."

"Does anyone else know?" Mrs. Meves-Crowley asked.

"Fouché has his suspicions but wisely keeps them to himself. The rest, Gomin, Lasne and Pelletan, will carry the secret to their graves." Segalla forced a laugh. "No wonder they're all terrified and Barras hides behind an alcoholic haze in Brussels."

"But," Tallien asked, "Louis XVIII must still wonder where the real Dauphin is."

"Does he?" Segalla replied. "Louis fled France in 1789 and the real Dauphin hasn't been seen in twenty-six years, so why should he bother now?"

"All that lump of decay," Mrs. Meves-Crowley declared fiercely, "cares about is keeping Marie-Antoinette's great secret firmly buried." She smiled thinly. "The Queen would have laughed at the irony of it all."

"And Mathurin Bruneau?" Tallien asked.

"I suppose he would know a little," Segalla replied. "He probably thought he was the Dauphin until his interview with Petitval. He was sent away but then decided to assume another role."

"And now?" Mrs. Meves-Crowley asked.

"I think Bruneau went abroad, probably across the Atlantic, but returned in 1805 to visit Madame Simon. After that, God knows, but, I wager, he will emerge again."

"God forgive me!" Mrs. Meves-Crowley murmured. "That boy cost me my marriage." She turned, her eyes brimming with tears. "But, in the end, the Queen did save her son."

"I find it difficult—" Tallien got to his feet, easing the cramp in the small of his back. "I find it difficult, madame, to accept that the King and Queen of France were prepared to sacrifice their only son's chances, even rights, to inherit the Crown."

"You don't understand," she retorted. "Study the life of Louis XVI. He was more interested in his clocks, books and dogs than governing France. And, as for Marie-Antoinette, why do you think she built her palace at Trianon? It was an escape, her dream of living in the country—cut off, worlds away from the seething intrigue of Versailles or the turbulent howling of the Paris mob. Above all, both Louis and Marie-Antoinette could see the storm coming: Their first son had died in suspicious circumstances; Marie-Antoinette was determined that her second son should not only have life, but a good one, and now he does."

"Does he know?" Segalla asked.

She shook her head. "No." She flounced out the pleats of her dress. "He will not know until shortly before my death. And what can he do then? Sometimes, however," she continued slowly, "he has dreams. He talks to me about great palaces, flower-filled gardens and wide, sweeping staircases. What is more important"—she came and stood over Segalla—"is what you will do."

He stared across at Tallien. "Madame, I will do nothing. I will tell the Prime Minister that the Dauphin Louis Charles, Duke of Normandy, to the best of my knowledge, died in the Temple prison in June 1795." Segalla sipped from his brandy. "That," he continued softly, "was what Marie-Antoinette wanted. She continued the deception right up to her death, though unwittingly she hinted at what she had done." He smiled at Mrs. Meves-Crowley. "In her last letter she is quite equitable about the supposed Dauphin's terrible allegations against her. Yet she knew the truth about him and let this slip by the occasional reference to 'that child.' " He shrugged. "Her secret is safe with us."

The woman's body relaxed. "Thank you," she whispered, dabbing at her eyes with a kerchief pulled from the cuff of her sleeve. "You know that is best, don't you? There are those still alive who would threaten us."

"Such as?" Segalla asked.

"Oh, Major Segalla, don't play games with me. You mentioned a secret organisation called the Templars." Her face became flushed. "They are no Templars but a band of secret assassins. Marie-Antoinette knew all about them, digging up old causes, masquerading behind titles. They were managed and organised by no less a person than Louis XVI's brother, the Comte de Provence, who now squats his fat bulk on the throne of France."

"Do you realise what you are saying?" Tallien asked.

"Of course I do," Mrs. Meves-Crowley snapped. "You are correct; either Barras or Petitval told the Comte de Provence in exile that the young boy had been released from the Temple." She spread her hands. "The rest followed as day follows night. The attack on Petitval's château was ordered by the Comte de Provence, though others carried it out."

She whirled round at a knock on the door and a young man entered, holding a sheet of music in his hand. He was tall, with dark, wavy hair falling down beneath his ears. He was dressed casually, in white, pleated trousers, black shiny shoes, an open-necked shirt and a dark blue waistcoat. Segalla took one look at that face, the high cheekbones, the slightly curved nose, the full lips above a determined chin and, above all, those dark eyes. His heart skipped a beat. It was like seeing the ghost of Marie-Antoinette in the features of her son. He stared warningly at Tallien, who stood gaping, one foot drawn back ready to sink to one knee.

"This is my son Augustus." Mrs. Meves-Crowley hastened across and grasped her son by the arm.

"Maman, who are these people?" Augustus' quick eyes showed he knew there was something wrong; he put his arm protectively round Mrs. Meves-Crowley's shoulders.

"Oh, they are physicians." She forced a smile but her eyes never left those of Segalla. "They are doing research. They have come to ask . . ."

"What about, Maman?" Augustus interrupted, his hands falling away. "Are you sick?"

"No, no." She flailed her hands. "Augustus Antoine Meves, this is Dr. Tallien." She then gestured at Segalla. "And . . ."

"Surgeon Merryvale," Segalla lied.

Augustus moved forward and shook both their hands vigor-

222

ously. He was quick enough to see the sadness in Segalla's eyes.

"Sir, you look upset."

Segalla forced a smile. "No, sir, you just remind me of someone I met many, many years ago."

"You liked them?"

"Oh yes," Segalla replied softly. "I liked them very, very much."

"Then why are you here?"

"We are doing researches, as your mother said," Segalla lied. "To cut a long story short, I met your physician—um, I forget his name."

"Roynaston!" Mrs. Meves-Crowley exclaimed.

"Ah yes. He told me about the mark on the left side of your chest and an inoculation scar high on your right shoulder. We are doing research," Segalla continued hastily, "to see if birthmarks ever fade."

Augustus, who looked much younger than his thirty years, half smiled. Segalla caught that same rather haunted, suspicious look he had glimpsed in the eyes of his mother Marie-Antoinette, then the smile widened.

"There's nothing, really," he said offhandedly.

He unbuttoned his shirt then pulled it up. His body was thin, the skin white as a sheet, but there, under the left breast was the mole. Segalla took one glance at it, then Augustus turned, pulled down the loose shirt and pointed to the inoculation mark high on his right shoulder, a rather ugly white furrow in his skin. He allowed Segalla to study this, then self-consciously rearranged his shirt.

"I have always been nervous of physicians," he confessed. "Maman says the inoculation was not well done." He tapped the sheet of music against his leg. "But, as you can see, sirs, nothing has faded. I have a similar mark on my foot." He took off his right shoe, using the toe of his left to ease the slipper off. Leaning on the chair, he held up his foot and Segalla saw the white, clawlike mark on the sole. Augustus put his slipper back on. "Maman, will our guests stay for lunch?"

"No, no." Segalla grasped Mrs. Meves-Crowley's hand and brought it to his lips. "Madame," he declared, "we have taken enough of your time."

"Will we ever see you again?" Mrs. Meves-Crowley asked, her eyes watchful.

Segalla held her fingers a little longer than courtesy demanded, then squeezed them gently. "Madame, by my oath, you will see neither of us again. We have taken up enough of your time. As for your son's scars, let time heal those."

Tallien then made his farewells whilst Segalla grasped Augustus' hand and shook it warmly.

"I wish you well, sir," Segalla remarked. "I really do." He pointed to the sheet of music. "You have a fine ear. I heard you play."

Augustus blushed and shuffled his feet. Segalla let go his hand. Tallien was already at the front door as if he could no longer bear to look at the young man who had lost so much. Segalla was about to follow when Augustus caught him by the sleeve.

"Sir, that person who reminded you of me?"

"Don't take offence," Segalla replied, "but it was a woman: She had the same cast of features, the same eyes. She, too, loved music."

"Was she someone special?"

"Oh yes," Segalla replied. "More special," he whispered, "than you'll ever know."

The maid let them out; Tallien and Segalla walked quietly along the mist-covered street. At the corner Tallien stopped and looked back at the house.

"Did we do right?" Tallien asked abruptly. His face looked pale and pinched, his eyes watered—whether from the cold or tears Segalla didn't know and could not bring himself to ask.

"What can we do?" Segalla replied. "What proof do we have? How long would that young man survive, or Mrs. Meves-Crowley? We would be signing their death warrants."

"But Louis XVIII?" Tallien urged. "A traitor and a murderer now wears the Crown of France!"

"And much good it will do him," Segalla replied, linking his arm through Tallien's. "He is fat, he is corrupt, he has no heir, his sleep will be plagued by ghosts and demons and, as the years pass, these will close in. Bruneau will reappear with his claims and Madame Simon will chatter. Louis cannot murder everyone. He will peddle the story that his nephew died in the Temple, and dismiss the growing speculation about what really did happen. Louis XVIII, fat and corrupt, will bring the furies down on his house. The French are a great nation, Monsieur Tallien, they created a new order in Europe. The Bourbons, those spectres from the past, will not survive long. Louis will die, and, in that young man's lifetime, we will see the Bourbons destroyed." He looked down at his companion. "You must never interfere, never! The day you do, those two people will die. Madame Josephine would not have wanted that."

"And where are you going now?" Tallien asked anxiously.

"Where you cannot come. You have my rooms. No, they are yours." Segalla grinned. "Not to mention the lavish attention of the widow Dalrymple. You'll have a good life, Monsieur Tallien, and, if what is happening in France irks you, remember!"

They walked on.

"Remember what?" Tallien asked.

Segalla chewed the corner of his lip. "Always remember," he whispered, "that the mills of God might grind exceedingly slow, but they do grind exceedingly small!"

Conclusion

A nn Dukthas sat in the restaurant overlooking the grounds where the old Tuileries palace had once stood. Across the table Segalla was busy ordering a brandy, the best the restaurant had. Throughout the meal her enigmatic host had scarcely mentioned the manuscript she had read. Instead, he had chattered about Paris and the new buildingwork going on. Once the waiter had left, however, he turned back towards her. Ann could see the questions were about to begin.

"Do you believe what you read?" He passed her brandy over.

"How much of it is fact?" she countered.

"Everything you have read," he replied. "Oh, you won't find Madame Roquet's name amongst the archives; I have changed hers," he smiled, "to protect her descendants who still live in the city."

"Why?" she asked.

"Ann, secret organisations still exist. Remember the Italian banker, Calvi, who recently hanged himself under Blackfriars Bridge in London?"

"But did the Templars wield such influence?" she asked.

"Oh yes, and they included people of every class and political persuasion." Segalla tapped the tabletop with a beringed finger. "Louis XVI's own cousin, the Duke of Orléans, voted for the King's death on the guillotine. The King's brothers, the Comte de Provence and the Comte d'Artois, were notorious for plotting against their own flesh and blood. Respectable historians like Georges Rude do not discount the influence of the Templars and other secret organisations during the French Revolution."

"And the rest?" Ann asked.

Segalla ticked the points off on his fingers. "Napoléon did destroy the Temple in 1808. Madame Josephine's sudden death at Malmaison, because she may have known something about the true whereabouts of the Dauphin, is a matter of fact. Marie-Antoinette's last letter is published in every biography of that queen. All the statements of Gomin, Lasne and Pelletan can be found in the National Archives in Paris."

"And Harmand of Meuse?" Ann asked.

Segalla grinned. "His report is still extant. Both he and Betrancourt did die mysterious deaths. The boy who died on 8 June 1795," he continued, "was probably poisoned, as were the physician Desault and his two assistants." Segalla shrugged elegantly. "Of course, Louis XVIII and his cronies couldn't murder everyone. Madame Simon died in the Hospital of the Incurables, solemnly vowing that she had assisted the Dauphin to escape and that he had come back to visit her in 1805. The duplicity of her husband," he added, "is also a matter of record. Simon the cobbler was both a fervent revolutionary and a Catholic royalist." He grimaced. "Though much good that did him. I suspect Barras sent him to the guillotine just to keep him quiet."

"But Petitval's murder?" Ann asked. "And the massacre at Vitry-sur-Seine? Not to mention Louis XVI's own confusion about his son whilst a prisoner in the Temple."

"All a matter of record," Segalla replied. "The document Tallien found in Madame Josephine's prayerbook was eventually published in no less an academic journal than the *Révue Historique* of May–June 1918. It corroborates everything in the manuscript I gave you." He sipped from his coffee. "And as for Louis XVI's confusion, the *Correspondence Sécrète* was published by a historian called Lescure; check volume 2, page 600. Similar reports can be found in carton 190 in the National Archives here in Paris. All the people I mention," Segalla continued, "played their roles just as I described."

"And what happened to Mathurin Bruneau?" Ann asked.

"Oh, in 1816 he reappeared, claiming to be the Dauphin, as others did throughout the second half of the nineteenth century." Segalla lifted his brandy glass and silently toasted Ann. "Louis XVIII was not allowed to reign in peace. He died without an heir in 1824, succeeded by his brother the Comte d'Artois, as Charles X. He was deposed in 1830, which proves how the mills of God do grind exceedingly small."

"And Augustus Antoine Meves-Crowley?"

"His mother, or, should I say, guardian, was true to her word. She informed Augustus about his true identity just before she died. Augustus pursued his claim to the French throne." Segalla paused as the waiter returned to refill their coffee cups. "Many believed in his claims. In his memoirs, a leading French nobleman, the Marquis de Bonneval, mentions the possible exchange of babies by Marie-Antoinette and how closely Augustus Antoine resembled Louis XVI and Marie-Antoinette." Segalla poured some cream into his cup. "Of course," he sighed, "his claim was rejected. Augustus Antoine died on 15 May 1859. You can find his death certificate at Catherine House in London."

"And his grave?" Ann asked.

"In Brompton cemetery." Segalla leaned back. "You are leaving Paris tomorrow?"

"Yes," Ann replied. "Late in the afternoon."

Segalla leaned across and pressed her hand; his eyes had lost their hard, calculating look. "Tomorrow," he murmured, "please come with me. I must go to Mass in the church of Ste.-Marguerite. I want to pray for that poor mute who died, for Mathurin Bruneau, for Augustus Meves-Crowley, his guardian, and," Segalla's voice trembled a little, "I want to remind the ghost of Marie-Antoinette how I kept faith."

Author's Note

There is little I can add to what Segalla has said in the conclusion to this novel. Marie-Antoinette did actually mention him in her diaries and regretted not paying heed to his warnings. The fate of Marie-Antoinette's son is one of the great mysteries of French history but everything Segalla has said, including the references he gave in the conclusion such as the *Révue Historique* of 1918, more than corroborates his claims. Late in the nineteenth century, the graveyard of Ste.-Marguerite was thoroughly searched, and a coffin, believed to be that of the prisoner who died in the Temple on 8 June 1795, was exhumed. Apparently even in death the mystery continued. According to some medical practitioners, the skeleton could not possibly belong to a ten-year-old boy, but were the remains of someone much older. Segalla was correct: That grave did not give up its secrets.

In 1889, Imperial Vienna was the jewel of Europe, the capital of the Austro-Hungarian Empire. Lavish balls and glittering entertainments hid a world of sinister political conspiracy and sexual intrigue at the court of the Hapsburgs. It was a world that exploded with the horrifying news that the heir to the throne, handsome Archduke Rudolph had shot his eighteen-year-old aristocratic mistress, and then turned the gun on himself. Or did he? Nicholas Segalla must travel back to Gilded Age Vienna to learn the truth.

THE TIME OF MURDER AT MAYERLING

A NICHOLAS SEGALLA TIME-TRAVEL MYSTERY

ANN DUKTHAS

Coming in December 1996 in hardcover from St. Martin's Press!